The Dragon Slayer's Son

Robinne Weiss

Published by Robinne Weiss
Copyright © 2017 Robinne Weiss

ISBN: 047338857X
ISBN-13: 9780473388577

Cover illustration: Brendon Wright

Discover my other books and stories on my website:
https://robinneweiss.wordpress.com/

To my husband, who started it all.

Chapter 1
The Letter

"Have a good day at school, Nathan. I'm off to slay dragons."

That's what Dad said when he left the house for work every morning.

"Why do you say that?" I asked him once. "Dragons aren't real, and you don't slay them."

He tousled my hair. "Because it makes you smile. Besides, if you knew what I have to deal with at work…" He rolled his eyes.

I laughed. I knew Dad enjoyed his job. He was a professor of plant science at Lincoln University and talked about plants all the time. Sometimes I visited him in his office after school, and he would tell me all about his latest research. I didn't understand much of it, but it always made me feel grown-up when he talked to me as though I did.

Sometimes I wondered what it would be like to be a scientist and make amazing discoveries. I thought it might be fun, but the truth is I didn't worry much about what I was going to do when I grew up—what twelve-year-old does? I was an ordinary Kiwi kid—medium height, perpetually messy hair that most people called ginger, a few freckles. I walked to school with my friends. I suffered through maths and English at school. I skinned my knees trying new tricks on my skateboard, and I played rugby on the weekends. Even the fact my parents were divorced and I lived with Dad wasn't out of the ordinary—plenty of kids at school had divorced parents.

So the letter about my dad came as a shock.

It arrived in the post on a Saturday morning. The envelope was made of a heavy cream-coloured paper embossed with what looked like a coat of arms and sealed with a blob of red wax bearing the same mark. It was addressed to me.

I opened the envelope and pulled out a sheet of matching paper.

Dear Master Nathan McMannis,

It is with deep regret that I must inform you that your father, Sir Archibald McMannis, DSE, FRSDS, PFODSI, has not returned from his most recent quest and is presumed deceased.

As the title of Dragon Slayer is, through venerable tradition, a hereditary one, we request that you report for training immediately at the Alexandra School of Heroic Arts under Professor Drachenmorder.

Kind Regards,

Sir Magnus MacDiermont, DSE, FRSDS

PS: Your father will be sorely missed—he was a good man.

I sat down heavily in the nearest chair and reread the letter.

Dad was *Sir* Archibald McMannis? A knight?

He was a dragon slayer?

And he was…

…dead?

No.

That was ridiculous. Dragons weren't real. This was one of Dad's jokes. This letter was his silly way of telling me he was back from his week-long meeting in Auckland. He must have come in late the night before, while I was asleep.

I raced back the hallway to Dad's bedroom and burst in to jump on his bed like I always did when he got home.

But the bed was empty.

I frowned and walked slowly back to the dining room. I picked up the letter again.

Nan, who always stayed with me when Dad was away, came in while I was reading the letter for the third time. I didn't hear her behind me, but I guess she must have read the letter over my shoulder, because I heard her exclaim, "Oh!"

I turned to see my grandmother with her eyes shut tight, and her bottom lip quivering. As she opened her eyes, a tear rolled down her cheek. She sniffed and blinked furiously as she sank into a chair.

"Nan?" I asked, waving the letter.

"Oh, Nathan. I'm so sorry."

"But, Nan, what is this?"

Nan sighed. "He never did tell you, did he?"

"Who? Tell me what? Nan, has something happened to Dad?"

"Come here, child." Nan beckoned me over, and I sat on her lap like I did whenever she told me a story. "Your father was a dragon slayer, as was his father before him."

"Nan, dragons aren't real. Dad's a professor."

"Well, that too. But his primary job was dragon slayer."

"What do you mean? Why do you keep saying 'was'?"

"That letter you're holding. Your father got one of those when he was seventeen—when my David was eaten by a New Zealand green dragon." Nan sniffed and wiped

3

away a tear. "David and I had told him his father was a dragon slayer though, so he was a bit more prepared for the letter when it came."

"Wait. You're saying this is real? That Dad is…dead? Eaten by a…by a *dragon*? What, are you in on the joke too? Where is Dad? This isn't funny anymore."

"It's not a joke, love." Her watery eyes and pained smile convinced me. She was putting on a brave face, but it was the face of a woman who had just lost her only son.

I don't know how I made it through the next few days. I don't remember much about them. Dad was gone. At first, I was numb. Then I was angry. Dad was gone, but who had he been, anyway? I had always thought he was a normal dad, like the ones my friends had. A regular guy who took me hiking and kayaking. I thought he went to an ordinary job every day and worked in an ordinary office. But that wasn't him at all.

He'd lied to me my whole life.

"I wanted him to tell you," said Nan. "David and I were always up front with Archie about what his father did. We thought he needed to know, so he could be prepared for the inevitable."

"So, why didn't he tell me?"

Nan sighed. "I think he didn't want you to worry. He always fretted when your grandfather was away. I think he wanted you to have a more carefree childhood than he'd had." She shrugged. "And then, of course, there was your mother."

"What about her? I can hardly even remember her. Was I four when she left?"

Nan nodded. "Archie didn't tell her about the dragon slaying until after you were born. She didn't take it well.

4

At first, she wouldn't believe it—thought your father had gone mad. Then she couldn't handle the stress."

"So she just left?"

Nan shrugged again. "Your mother loved you, Nathan. She wanted to take you with her and prevent you from becoming a dragon slayer. But I know there is no hiding once it's your turn—the Fraternal Order of Dragon Slayers will find you wherever you are. I convinced her it was better for everyone if she let your dad raise you, so he could prepare you for your future."

"But he didn't. He didn't prepare me for anything." I wanted to scream it at her, but my breath was coming in hiccupping sobs, and I felt like a giant hand was squeezing my chest. My voice came out as a squeak.

"He did give me this." Nan pulled a thick envelope from the jumbled desk where Dad had worked in the evenings. "He wanted you to have it if...if he didn't come home."

I snatched the envelope from her hand and ran to my room, but I didn't open it. I didn't want to read anything my father had to say. He'd lied to me for twelve years. Nothing in that envelope could make any difference now. I threw it on the floor, and it skidded under the bed.

I wasn't very reasonable those few days, while Nan outfitted me for my new school and did...whatever it is you have to do when someone dies. I yelled a lot. And cried. I didn't open Dad's envelope.

Nan was right about not being able to hide. Four days after the letter had arrived, a black SUV with tinted windows pulled up outside the house. A man stepped out of the car and walked casually up the drive. He was tall and fit, but his hair was grey, and he walked with a limp.

He wore faded jeans, a slightly rumpled button-down shirt, and sunglasses.

When Nan answered the door, the man pulled off his sunglasses, revealing brown eyes crinkled with laugh lines.

"Gloria," he said, taking her right hand in his. "So good to see you again. I'm so sorry." His smile was sad, and his eyes mirrored Nan's grief.

"I suppose you're here for Nathan."

"I'm sorry. Is he ready?"

The man looked over Nan's shoulder to where I stood watching. He smiled, but I didn't smile back.

"As ready as he's going to be." Nan sighed and turned to me. "Nathan, this is Sir Magnus MacDiermont. He'll take you to your new school."

Sir Magnus stepped forward and stretched out his hand. I didn't move to take it. Truth is, I was a bit awed. This guy—this *knight*—had come here to take *me* to school?

"Shake the man's hand, Nathan," said Nan.

I reached out and took his hand. It was rough and warm and strong. Like Dad's. I blinked back tears.

"It's a lot to take in, isn't it?" said Sir Magnus. "I hate having to do it like this, but...well...it's been the tradition for five hundred years." He shrugged. "First rule of dragon slaying is to show no fear, and I'd say you're doing well, Nathan, given what you've been through. You're a strong boy."

It was a lie. I'm sure my face showed exactly how terrified and out of control I felt. But it was a lie meant to make me feel better, and I snatched at it and held on. *Show no fear.* I took a deep breath and mustered a weak smile.

"You'll have a cup of tea before you go?" Nan asked Sir Magnus, though for my grandmother, that was never a question. Nobody escaped Nan without first drinking a cup of tea. She put on the kettle and bustled around, packing up sandwiches and thick slices of cake for our lunch.

"Nathan," she said. "Go pack your things. Make sure you put in all those new clothes we bought. And don't forget your toothbrush *and* deodorant." Sir Magnus chuckled, but I didn't think it was that funny. I did as she asked, though. I stuffed my new suitcase full of everything I could fit in; not just clothes, but my rugby ball, a couple of my favourite books, and—I'm almost ashamed to say— the purple stuffed dragon Nan had made me for my sixth birthday. As I nestled the dragon beside my balled-up socks, I paused. Dragons really existed? Here in New Zealand? None of this made sense—Dad dead, dragons alive. I shut my eyes, hoping that by not looking I could force it all to go away, and the world would make sense again.

"Nathan! Magnus is waiting."

I took a deep breath and opened my eyes. It wasn't going to go away.

I zipped up my suitcase and grabbed my backpack, patting the left pocket to make sure my phone was there. I was almost through the door when I remembered Dad's envelope. I fished it out from under my bed and slipped it into the backpack. In the living room, I hugged Nan goodbye. Then I followed Sir Magnus to his waiting car, and left my old life behind.

The drive to the Alexandra School of Heroic Arts took most of the day. At first, I have to admit, I was a little worried. Here I was in a car with some guy I'd never seen before, and he was driving me to a school I'd never even heard of until four days ago. If Nan hadn't been so confident about it all, I probably would have refused to go.

It was a crisp, sunny spring morning and, as we drove out of Lincoln, we passed some of my classmates on their way to school. I couldn't help thinking I should be walking with them, talking about our latest Minecraft adventures and laughing at stupid YouTube videos. I waved as we passed, but they didn't see me through the tinted windows.

I blinked back tears as we passed the building where Dad used to work, and then wondered how often he'd actually been in his office. Was he really a professor at the university? He must have been, because I used to visit him in his office after school. But how much of what I thought I knew about him was a lie?

Sir Magnus headed west, toward State Highway 1, and I finally broke the silence to ask, "Did you know my dad?"

"Only a little. Your grandfather and I were at school together, although he was nearly ten years older than me. He married Gloria right after we graduated, and so I knew your dad when he was growing up. In fact, I was the one who drove him to school, just as I'm doing for you."

Now I understood his sadness when he had arrived at the door that morning. I was the second boy he'd taken from Nan.

I had plenty more questions, but Sir Magnus didn't let me dwell on my father. Instead, he turned the conversation to the school, dragons, and my future. Once he got going, he barely stopped talking the entire drive.

His descriptions of dragons and his stories of his own dragon slaying career—cut short by an unfortunate encounter with a southern blue dragon that had left him with a limp—were the stuff of fantasy novels. The stories, the bright blue sky, and the hum of the car's engine made me feel like we were on an adventure. I couldn't help grinning. I *was* on an adventure. A knight was chauffeuring me to a school where I would become a dragon slayer. It was like Eragon and Harry Potter put together.

"Is there magic?" I asked, thinking about Hogwarts.

Sir Magnus smiled. "No. Unlike dragons, magic isn't real."

"But aren't dragons magical?"

"In the stories they are. But their abilities are based in biology, just like yours. You'll learn all about dragon biology at the School of Heroic Arts. And their culture and history."

"They have a culture?"

"Oh, yes. Dragons are quite intelligent, and some are very social."

The six-hour drive passed in an instant. I fired questions at Sir Magnus as fast as he could answer them. I learned I would take classes in sword fighting, tactics and dragon language; and the teachers at the School of Heroic Arts were retired dragon slayers.

"Mostly blokes like me—injured in the line of duty."

"Are you a teacher?" I asked.

"No. I'm the chief financial officer. I do the books, payroll, look after the finances, that sort of thing. I also take care of admissions and counselling. It's a good job. Keeps my brain sharp." Sir Magnus turned off the main highway into the township of Alexandra, and we pulled up outside the grocery store.

"The missus'll kill me if I forget to bring home milk and butter."

Then we were off again, climbing into the hills toward Fraser Dam, through a locked gate, and along a rough farm track that seemed to wind forever up one ridge and down into the next valley. Dusk was closing in when we topped a ridge and I saw below us a cluster of buildings—sheds clad in corrugated iron, cottages, and a Swiss-style lodge.

"Welcome to the Alexandra School of Heroic Arts," said Sir Magnus.

Chapter 2
The Alexandra School of Heroic Arts

"That's it?" I had expected some huge stone castle or at least a mansion. "But it's just a sheep station."

"Yep. Two thousand merino sheep and no one gives us a second glance." Sir Magnus pointed to a large, grey shed. "Sword fighting practices are held in the shearing shed." Then he pointed to a small cottage—white painted weatherboards and a tidy little garden beside it. "That's where I live. And that," he said, finally pointing to the main house, "is where you and the other students live and study—we call it The Lodge."

It wasn't a castle but, as we drew up to the house, I couldn't help grinning. It was built like a fancy ski lodge—two stories tall with a huge central living area and giant windows looking out onto the mountains. A wide deck surrounded the house on three sides.

Sir Magnus parked on the expanse of gravel out front and carried my suitcase for me as we stepped up onto the deck. A brass plaque set above the sliding glass doors read, *Alexandra School of Heroic Arts, est. 1897. First dragon slaying school in New Zealand.* Sir Magnus ushered me through the door into the main room.

"This is the atrium."

A fire crackled in an enormous stone fireplace at the back of the hall. The room was scattered with clusters of comfortable-looking chairs and couches. A pool table

11

stood to the right of the door. Two spiral staircases, one in each rear corner of the room, rose to catwalks on either side. As I looked up, a small boy—younger than me, with dark hair—emerged from a door on the upper floor and hurtled down the stairs. He smiled as he raced by us.

"Whoa there, Oliver." Sir Magnus grabbed the boy by the arm. Oliver's feet kept moving, skidding out from under him. Sir Magnus laughed as he caught the boy and set him back on his feet.

"Sorry, Sir Magnus! It's just, I'm late for dinner again, Sir."

"I see that, but today you'll have a good excuse. Oliver, this is a new student at the school, Nathan McMannis. Nathan, this is Oliver Ng. Oliver, your job is to make sure Nathan knows how things work around here—meal times, classes, recreation, the library—and to introduce him to the other students. Do you think you can do that?"

"Yes, sir!" Oliver grinned.

"First thing is to get him to dinner. Afterwards, see that he gets settled in the dormitory. I think the empty bunk next to you would be a good place. In the morning, he's to report to Professor Drachenmorder. See that he makes it there by nine."

"Yes, sir!" said Oliver, still grinning. He tugged me into the dining hall off the atrium. "Come on! We're late. Miss Brumby makes pizza on Fridays!"

The dining hall buzzed with the conversation of twenty-five students. Oliver pulled me to the serving window, which fronted on to the kitchen.

"Sorry I'm late, Miss Brumby," he called.

A surly voice rang out from behind a rack of pots and pans. "And I'm sorry there's nothing left for kids who can't get to the dining hall in time for meals." My heart sank. Nan had packed me and Sir Magnus a good lunch,

12

but I was starving. Oliver's grin never slipped from his face.

"But, I've brought a new student! He just arrived with Sir Magnus!"

A big woman wearing a white apron over jeans and a T-shirt emerged from behind the pots, drying her hands on a tea towel. She tossed the towel onto a nearby bench as she strode toward us with a scowl. I glanced at Oliver, who continued to smile. Miss Brumby reached the window and planted herself in front of us, arms crossed over her chest.

"You know what I do to students who are late, Oliver?"

"Make us eat dessert first?"

At this, Miss Brumby's scowl cracked into a smile and she laughed so heartily, it caught the attention of the other students.

"You're such a dag. No, you don't get to eat dessert first. Here's some pizza for you. You've got to wait for dessert." She chuckled as she handed us each a plate piled with two huge slices of pizza. I turned to find the other students looking our way.

"Guys," said Oliver. "This is Nathan. He's new here. Nathan, this is…" He waved his hand around the room. "…Everyone!" The students laughed and went back to their meals. Oliver and I sat down at the nearest of the four tables.

"Hi, Nathan," said an older boy to my left. "I'm Will."

"Are you…Canadian?" I guessed at his accent.

"American, but I've lived in Rotorua for the past six years. Dad was studying North Island fire lizards in the hot pools around there."

"I'm Tui," said a girl to Will's left. Tui's long dark hair was pulled back into a ponytail, and she flashed me a friendly smile.

A big girl on the other side of the table spoke up. "I'm Ella. Tui and I are the only girls in the school."

Tui rolled her eyes. "He would have figured that out pretty quickly, Ella."

"I'm actually surprised to see any girls," I said. Tui scowled, and Ella raised her eyebrows at me, and I knew I'd said something wrong. I tried to backpedal. "I mean, you know, in all the stories, it's always men who kill dragons."

"It used to be," explained Tui, with an air of superiority. "Back when families were bigger, there were plenty of boys to inherit the job. Each dragon slayer might have three or four sons to follow in his footsteps. But as family sizes got smaller and smaller, the number of boys being trained up wasn't enough to replace those that died. So they started taking on girls, too. My mum was one of the first three girls to ever become dragon slayers." Tui laughed. "She didn't do much for the population of dragon slayers, though. Mum married another dragon slayer, and they only got me and my brother out of the deal."

"Both your parents are dead?" I blurted out, before realising it was a stupid thing to say.

Tui's smile vanished, and she blinked furiously. Without a word, she stood and walked out of the dining hall, leaving a half-eaten piece of pizza on her plate.

"I'm sorry," I said. "I just…Mum left my dad when I was little, so he's all I really had, but I know she's alive…somewhere. I can't imagine…" I sniffed back tears, sorry for myself and for Tui.

"It's okay," said Will. "Every kid here has lost a parent within the last two years. Tui's got it worse than us, and she makes it twice as hard on herself by pretending it doesn't bother her. She didn't even bring a teddy bear or anything when she came." I looked up at this boy, probably four years my senior, who thought it a shame not to have a teddy bear, and I smiled.

"Mine's actually a stuffed dragon."

Oliver grinned. "Cool! I brought Pooky my cat!"

"Pooky?" said Ella.

"Hey, I named him when I was four. What do you want? Anyway, I've heard that your teddy bear's name is—"

"Never mind what his name is."

Everyone else at the table laughed at that, and conversation came to a halt as Miss Brumby brought out trays laden with banana splits.

"Do you eat like this every day?" I asked between mouthfuls.

"Pizza and ice cream is only on Fridays," said Will.

"The rest of the week, it's pretty lame," said Ella.

"Miss Brumby makes great food," declared Oliver.

"Only if you like *vegetables*."

"What's not to like about vegetables?"

Ella shuddered. "She puts *peas* in her macaroni and cheese. Who does that?"

Will shrugged. "Well, I like the food. Could be a lot worse."

With a belly full of pizza and ice cream, I certainly had no complaints. And, if I had that to look forward to every Friday, I could put up with a lot of peas for the rest of the week. I sort of liked peas anyway and, as it turned out, the macaroni and cheese with peas in it was awesome.

After dinner, Oliver showed me to the dorm. Standing in the atrium, he explained the upstairs layout.

"There are four dormitories—two on the left and two on the right. First year students are on the left, and second-years on the right."

I followed him up the left-hand staircase, my suitcase bumping heavily behind me. At the top, he set off along the catwalk, passing the first door.

"That's the girls' room. They're lucky—a whole dorm room for only the two of them!"

He opened the second door and ushered me into a long room with big windows along one side. Eight beds stuck out from the walls, with wardrobes spaced between them. Most of the beds were singles but, at the end of the room, there were two sets of bunk beds.

"There's only supposed to be eight to a room but, because the girls take a whole room, we're a bit squished in here—ten, with you. Bathroom is down at the end. This is my bed. And this is yours," said Oliver, indicating the third bed on the left. "You even get a window!"

Oliver sat cross-legged on his bed, his stuffed cat, Pooky, in his lap. He talked while I unpacked my things. He told me about his home—he was from Queenstown and had a pet cat named, you guessed it, Pooky. He loved to ski. His dad, in addition to being a dragon slayer, had owned a used bookshop, and Oliver had spent his free time either on the ski slopes or reading in the shop. Oliver had known all about his dad's dragon slaying work. It was a point of pride for his family, and Oliver was thrilled to be following in his ancestors' footsteps.

As I unpacked, some of the other boys popped in to grab a jacket, a book, or a frisbee. Oliver introduced them as they appeared. There was Joshua Robinson, ten years old, a plump red-head from Christchurch. Then Charlie Anderson, fifteen—tall and built like a rugby player. Turns out he *was* a rugby player, and fanatic about the sport. The Mitchell twins came in, too—Thomas and Marcus. It was weeks before I could tell them apart.

Because it was Friday, we were allowed to stay up late. Oliver and I went down to the atrium where groups of students hung out playing board games, flying paper airplanes into the fireplace, or playing pool. A cheer came up from the dining hall, and I peeked in to see two boys playing a wicked game of table tennis on one of the dining tables while a small band of spectators watched.

"Those are the King brothers," said Oliver. "Noah and Jacob. They're in our room, too."

"They're not twins, though," I observed.

"No. Noah's thirteen, and Jacob's fifteen. They're from Auckland." He rolled his eyes as he said it, and I gave him a quizzical look. He lowered his voice and confided, "They're city kids—not real happy about being stuck out here on a sheep station. Dad was a lawyer, mum's a doctor, I think. They've got money and think they're better than the rest of us because of it." He shrugged and smiled. "Doesn't bother me much. They're nice enough, I suppose."

Oliver showed me where to find the classrooms and the library—on the ground floor to the right side of the atrium. The classrooms looked like the rooms at my old school, except for the diagrams of dragons, armour, and swords pinned all over the walls. The library was the same size as the classrooms—not very big, but it was full of interesting titles like *Negotiating with Dragons: Twenty-five tricks that will bring you home alive*, and *An Illustrated Guide to Fire Lizards of the Himalayas*. Apart from one boy, hunched over an open book, it was deserted.

"Leo, it's Friday night. Take a break," said Oliver as we stepped into the room.

"I want to be ready for the fire and brimstone practical on Monday," replied Leo looking up. He was a skinny kid, all elbows and knees, but I guessed he'd be taller than me when standing.

"I'm sure you'll do fine, Leo. But we won't keep you. This is Nathan. He's new here. He's bunking next to me."

Leo raised a hand in greeting and gave a weak smile, then turned back to his book.

As we left the library, Oliver explained, "Leo's finishing up his first year. He's got two weeks of exams coming up—that's why he's studying. Well, that and the fact that he's way too serious about his studies, even when he doesn't have exams coming up."

Oliver was an enthusiastic tour guide. Though he was by far the youngest boy at the school, he moved confidently among kids twice his age. His smile was infectious, and his high giggle rang out across the atrium all evening.

But I was exhausted and a bit overwhelmed. It wasn't long before I said goodnight and climbed the stairs to my new bed. I thought I would have trouble falling asleep that first night—my mind whirling with all the new things I'd learned, and missing Nan, Dad, and my own bed—but exhaustion won out, and I was asleep practically before my head hit the pillow.

Chapter 3
Professor Drachenmorder

I woke to Oliver's insistent whisper.

"Nathan! Nathan! You've got to get up. You're supposed to see Professor Drachenmorder at nine."

"What time is it?" I mumbled. Daylight suffused the room, but all I could see out the window was fog. A couple of the other boys were stirring, and there was one empty bed, but most were still asleep.

"It's already eight-thirty. Come on! Get dressed, and let's eat breakfast. It's never good to see Drachenmorder on an empty stomach." I let him drag me out of bed.

Breakfast was cold cereal and toast, wolfed down under Oliver's impatient gaze. When I had finished, he led me out the front door and into the fog. We crunched along a gravel drive, over a small hill, then past a few small chalets that loomed out of the mist. The fourth chalet was larger than the rest, and Oliver turned onto the path leading to the door. He walked up the steps onto the small porch in front and knocked.

"Ho! Well done, Oliver," exclaimed Sir Magnus when he opened the door. "Right on time."

Oliver beamed. "I told you I would have him here at nine."

"So you did. Thank you. Now run along. I'm sure Nathan can find his way back after he's finished here." Oliver wasted no time scampering back through the fog.

"See ya, mate!" he called.

Sir Magnus beckoned me into a sort of waiting room that reminded me of a dentist's office. A wooden reception desk commanded a view of the door, and an L of rich-looking leather couches and chairs positioned along the walls was anchored by a low side-table in the corner stacked with magazines. Two doors led further into the building—one marked Staff Only, and one marked Professor Drachenmorder, DSE, Head of School. Sir Magnus waved me into a chair.

"Professor Drachenmorder will be with you shortly. I need to pop out for a minute. Make yourself comfortable. Won't be long." With that, he left me alone in the silent room.

Well, it wasn't entirely silent. I could hear Professor Drachenmorder talking on the phone in his office. The wall muffled his voice, so I couldn't make out what he was saying. I plopped into a couch and rifled through the magazines on the table. *New Zealand Hunter*, *Fish and Game New Zealand*, *Rod and Rifle*, *New Zealand Pig Hunter*...every last magazine was hunting-related. One in particular caught my eye—the June 2014 issue of *Hunting Illustrated*, protected by a fancy cover. I flipped through the magazine and found a long article on hunting in New Zealand. It featured an interview with Claus Drachenmorder, 'premier provider of luxury big-game hunting safaris in New Zealand.' I wondered if Claus was related to the professor. I began to read the interview.

HI: So what makes your hunting safaris different from others?

CD: We specialise in the very high end of safari hunting—the if-you-have-to-ask-you-can't-afford-it end of the market. Our clients get VIP treatment from the moment they arrive in the country. We helicopter them in to our lodge where they are treated to the finest in accommodation and cuisine.

HI: And what can they expect to bag on one of your safaris?

20

CD: Our clients can hunt the usual New Zealand big game—tahr, deer, chamois, boar. But we also offer a premium big-game experience. We offer the opportunity to hunt some very, very big game you won't find anywhere else.

HI: And what sort of game is that?

CD: Hahaha! Well, if I told you, I'd have to kill you.

A door opened. I looked up to see Professor Drachenmorder emerge from his office. I don't know what I expected the head of a School of Heroic Arts to look like, but the Professor was not it. He was younger, for one—probably not even my dad's age. His dirty-blond hair and beard were neatly trimmed and showed no grey. They framed a smooth face with a strong jaw. He wore a tan button-down short-sleeved shirt tucked into convertible khakis. His fancy hiking boots looked almost brand new. He looked more Park Ranger than Schoolmaster.

"Nathan McMannis. Come in."

Professor Drachenmorder's office was equally at odds with my expectations. The polished mahogany desk seemed in keeping with his title of Professor but, as my eyes scanned the wall behind the desk, my jaw dropped. Photographs and hunting trophies all but obscured the surface.

The hunting trophies caught my attention first.

Dragon heads of all shapes and sizes, though none smaller than half a metre long, decorated the space. A steel-grey one with pebbly-looking scales hung next to a brown one with a huge orange fan of skin and spikes around its neck. Further along was a sky-blue one with a sleek, smooth shape. And up near the vaulted ceiling, filling much of the room, was an enormous green one, mounted to look down on the occupants of the room. It gave me the creeps.

"Ah, so you like my wall," said Professor Drachenmorder. He had a thick German accent—another surprise to me, though I suppose with a name like Drachenmorder, I should have suspected he wasn't a Kiwi.

"Most of these dragons come from right here in New Zealand, though a few, like that one"—he pointed to a medium-sized black dragon with red-tipped horns about its face—"are from Europe and other places."

"And did you kill them all?"

"Oh, no. Some of these were slain by my father and my grandfather. But the green?" he pointed to the ceiling. "She is mine."

"And the photos?" I asked.

"The school's benefactors. For a certain level of support, one can accompany a dragon slayer on a mission." He listed the names as he pointed to different photographs on the wall. It was like a who's who of the twenty-first century.

"Please sit." Professor Drachenmorder indicated a small, hard wooden chair in front of his desk. He installed himself in a commanding swivel chair behind the desk. "First, I must say I was sorry to hear of your father's death. These things happen sometimes, but it is never easy for those left behind." His words sounded rehearsed. Not quite sincere. I suspected he'd said them to so many students over the years, that they came automatically now.

"With your father's death, you inherit the position of dragon slayer. To fulfil that position, of course, you must be trained in the heroic arts. This is a two year process, as I'm sure you already know. At the end of your training, should you complete it satisfactorily, you will be inducted into the Fraternal Order of Dragon Slayers International."

I nodded. I'd learned all of this from Oliver and Sir Magnus yesterday. Professor Drachenmorder continued.

"Because dragon slaying, and the existence of dragons themselves, is best kept a secret from society at large, all students are required to take an oath of silence and secrecy before they begin their training. Only with the assurance of your complete discretion can we reveal the heroic arts of dragon slaying to you."

It was like the ultimate secret society. I'm ashamed to admit that for a moment, I was happy Dad had died and, instead of going back to boring maths and spelling, I was on an adventure more awesome than anything I could have imagined. My excitement must have shown on my face because the Professor smiled.

"Are we ready then?"

I nodded.

"Raise your right hand and repeat after me."

I did as he asked.

"I, Nathan Archie McMannis, do solemnly swear to keep silent the secrets of the Alexandra School of Heroic Arts. I agree to tell no one of the true nature of the school, its mission, or its activities. I shall remain silent, even under pain of death. I agree to uphold the student code of conduct and will do nothing to bring dishonour or discredit unto the school. I understand that the penalty for disloyalty to the school is death, and that once convicted of disloyalty of any kind by the headmaster, I have no recourse for appeal and must abide by his decision."

My eyes widened in horror at the significance of the last sentence. Professor Drachenmorder smiled. "It's just a formality." He dismissed it with a wave. "Now. You will begin classes on Monday. Each student pursues an individual course of study, but you will attend classes with the other first-years. Some of the first-years are nearing the end of their year, and will seem quite accomplished to you. But some are quite new to the school, like you, so you needn't worry about feeling stupid. Anyway, I'm sure your father taught you a great deal, eh?"

"No. He didn't teach me anything. I didn't even know he was a dragon slayer until...until..."

"Perfect." Drachenmorder smiled.

"Huh?"

Drachenmorder's smile vanished, replaced by a blank, businesslike face. "I mean, there's nothing wrong with that. You will do fine. Now, you've got the whole weekend to get to know the other students. Go and enjoy yourself. Classes start Monday at nine."

Something about Professor Drachenmorder's look and the words he'd uttered bothered me. I must have been frowning about it when I stepped out of his office because Sir Magnus, who was sitting at the reception desk typing on a computer, hailed me with, "Have you been expelled already, Nathan?"

I smiled at his laughing face.

"You're working today? On Saturday?"

"Nah, just catching up with my nephews on Facebook. Thought I'd head out for a little rabbit shooting. Want to come with me?"

I shrugged. "Sure."

We stepped out of the office into bright sunshine. The fog had burned off to reveal a cloudless sky. I climbed into the passenger seat of Sir Magnus' SUV, and we headed away from the row of chalets and up a steep, switchbacked farm track. As we crested the hill, the mountains beyond caught my gaze. "Wow!"

Sir Magnus grinned. "Not a bad view, eh?"

A broad rolling plain of tussock spread out before us, and jagged snow-capped peaks rose behind it. Mist still hovered in patches, swirling and shifting before slowly vanishing in the sunshine.

"Those are the Hector Mountains over there," Sir Magnus said, pointing. "And the Horn Range, with the Remarkables peeking up behind them. This tussocky wetland we're in now is called The Old Woman Range—I tell my wife it's named after her." He laughed at his own joke.

The farm track continued across the tussock and eventually petered out at a broad fan of gravel.

"On foot from here. It's a nice hike down the valley. Keep your eyes open—a nice sunny day like today, and there'll be lots of lizards out."

"By lizards, do you mean, like, skinks? Or do you mean dragons?"

Sir Magnus laughed. "No dragons here. Lots of skinks, though. And geckos."

"So, where *are* the dragons?" I asked as we followed a faint path through the tussocks.

"The closest ones to us are in the Hector Mountains. They prefer the remote areas. Tend to avoid people, when they can."

"In Professor Drachenmorder's office there was a giant green dragon head…"

"Ah. Lightning. She lived in the Remarkables. Got a little too fond of skiers."

"You knew her by name?"

"I didn't know her. None of us really knew her. It took Professor Drachenmorder three days of clever talking to get her into a position to kill her. He learned quite a bit about her during those days."

I tried to imagine killing an animal I'd spent three days talking to. It would be like killing a friend. Who could do that? Had my father done it?

"Sir Magnus? What do you know about my father?"

Sir Magnus sighed. "He really told you nothing about dragon slaying then?"

"Nothing. He joked about slaying dragons, but it was always a joke. Just something he said when he left for work in the morning."

"Nathan, your father was a good man. He earned his knighthood the first year after school. Killed a southern blue up in the Marlborough Sounds that had been taking after the ferries between Wellington and Picton. He was one of the best dragon slayers I've ever seen. I think he had eight successful missions before he reached the age of twenty-five. He was made Patriarch of the Fraternal Order of Dragon Slayers International at the age of thirty— youngest Patriarch ever. He consulted on tricky dragon situations all over the world and was called in regularly to deal with dragons outside New Zealand."

"Is that why he went on all those overseas trips? He told me he was going to plant biology conferences."

"Oh, I'm sure he went to some plant biology conferences, too. But, yeah, some of those trips were probably dragon slaying trips."

"Why didn't Dad tell me about all of this? Why did he keep it secret?"

"I don't know, Nathan. Only your dad could explain his reasons."

But he was dead, so he couldn't explain anything to me. We lapsed into silence.

"Rabbit," whispered Sir Magnus, stopping in his tracks and raising his gun. He never fired it, though, because the moment he raised the barrel, a shot went off behind us. Gravel sprayed up around our feet as a bullet pinged off the ground close by. The rabbit bounded away, and both Sir Magnus and I turned to identify the culprit.

The hill behind us was bare except for the tussocks waving in the wind.

"Bloody idiot! What was he thinking, shooting past us at that rabbit?" Sir Magnus stalked up the hill at a fair pace. I scampered along behind. "It'll be a kid, no doubt. They're up here all the time—from Alexandra, I guess— eighteen, nineteen years old, causing trouble." But we saw no one when we crested the hill.

Sir Magnus grumbled, "Scarpered, did he? No surprise." He sighed. "I probably couldn't have caught him anyway, not with this limp." He looked down at me. "I sure hope that when you get to that age, Nathan, you're a bit more responsible. Come on. Let's carry on. Maybe I'll have a shot at that rabbit later."

"Do you think it's safe?" I asked, feeling a bit shaken.

"Aw, that kid's miles away by now. We won't see *him* again."

We walked for an hour or two, making a loop down the valley and back up to the car via the ridge. Sir Magnus never once shot a rabbit, though we saw several more. He seemed more interested in the walk, the scenery, and the lizards that skittered across our path. He knew a lot about lizards.

"Keep your eyes open for Otago skinks. They're incredibly rare, but I've seen 'em up here. Big things, black with yellow spots."

We didn't see any of those, but a bunch of common geckos were out sunning themselves. Their lichen-like colours blended well with the rocks, so that when a movement gave them away, they seemed to materialise out of nowhere. Sir Magnus was great at spotting them, even when they sat stock-still in the sunshine.

The sun was high and warm on my back by the time we reached the car. My stomach growled as we clambered in.

"That must be the lunch bell." Sir Magnus laughed. "We'll get back to school just in time."

Chapter 4
Dad's Letter

The afternoon passed in a whirl. The sun brought everyone outside to the big lawn at the back of the Lodge. It led down to a small creek tumbled with boulders and thick with scrub. After lunch, I went with Oliver and the Mitchell twins to the creek where we played rock-hopping games until Marcus fell in and got soaked in the freezing water.

On our way back up to the Lodge, Will asked if we wanted to play rugby. Oliver laughed.

"Yeah, right. With you big guys?"

He had a point. All the boys on the field looked older than me.

"Just touch, right?"

"Of course. You play?"

"Yeah." I'd played rugby after school. I wasn't great, but I enjoyed it. I let Will pull me onto the pitch.

He introduced me to the other boys, who I hadn't met yet—all second-years but, as it turned out, some of them were my age. I didn't remember all their names, but one boy stood out from the others—Hunter Godfry. I could tell right away by how the others reacted to him that he was trouble. He was a big, blond kid, maybe sixteen or seventeen years old. I imagined him growing up on a beef farm and blending right in with the animals—he had the same square face and over-muscled shoulders as a bull.

Hunter was on the opposing team and, though I hope I never have to say we're on the same side, being his opponent was no fun. He didn't know the meaning of the word 'touch'. The first time I got the ball, he came at me from my left. It was like being hit by a truck—my head snapped sideways as the impact lifted me off my feet and threw me into the air. I landed with a grunt, and the ball flew out of my hands. Every touch was a full-out tackle with Hunter.

"C'mon, Hunter. Take it easy," called Dylan, who was on my side.

"Yeah, there's no need to flatten our team. You're beating us already," added Finn.

"Hey, is it my fault the munchkin can't even stay on his feet? Good thing it isn't windy today, or he wouldn't even be able to stand up." Hunter was the only one who laughed at his lame joke.

Maybe it was my imagination, but Hunter seemed to tackle me more than any of the other players on my team. It seemed like every time I got the ball, he would materialise—hurtling towards me like a runaway bull. I probably should have quit, but stubborn pride made me stay in the game. We were going to lose—there was no question about that—but I wanted to beat Hunter to the goal just once.

And I did—I managed to score, with Hunter nipping at my heels. After I'd crossed the line, I turned back to him and laughed in his face. It was probably lucky for me Hunter's team scored immediately afterwards, winning the game. He looked ready to stomp me into the ground.

As my team trudged wearily back inside, Will came up beside me and, glancing around first, said, "Uh, just a warning—I wouldn't go out of your way to irritate Hunter, okay?"

I laughed and said I'd figured that out already.

"Yeah, but laughing at him after you scored?"

"I know. Probably a bad idea. It felt so good, though."

Will smiled at that. "He deserved it, for sure. But I wouldn't do it again, eh?"

"I take it he's the school bully?"

"Well, that…and he's Drachenmorder's nephew."

"So he can get away with it."

"Yep. No expulsion for him if he disobeys the rules."

"Nor death, I expect."

"Death?" replied Will, looking at me questioningly. "That'd be a bit extreme for breaking the school rules, wouldn't it?"

"But didn't you—" My question was cut short by Oliver racing down the lawn toward us.

"Guys! Guys! You've got to come see this! Tui's balanced five full water glasses on her nose! Come on, before they fall!"

Laughing, Will and I joined Oliver, sprinting to the dining hall, where, instead of finding Tui balancing water glasses on her nose, we found her on her hands and knees with a towel, mopping the floor.

That night, I lay in bed aching from all the bruises Hunter had given me. I thought about him being Drachenmorder's nephew. I remembered the headmaster's comment about my father not telling me anything about dragon slaying—*perfect*, he'd said. And Will's reaction when I mentioned the penalty of death for disobeying the rules. Hadn't he pledged the same thing when he'd arrived?

I was missing something.

I lay for a long time, wondering what it could be. Eventually, I came back to everything my father hadn't told me about. He could have explained everything to me, but he hadn't.

Only your dad could explain, Sir Magnus had said.

My dad. I sat up in the dark and fumbled around as quietly as I could to find my torch. Then I opened the drawer in my wardrobe and slipped an envelope from underneath my clothes.

Sliding back into bed, I pulled the covers all the way up over my head and, hunched in the cave-like space, with my torch on, I opened Dad's letter.

My Dear Son,

If you are reading this, then I am dead. And worse, I am dead without having told you the truth of my life. The truth of your life.

I'm sorry.

I always meant to tell you when the time was right. But first, you were a little boy whose mother had run away. I couldn't tell you then. You needed to believe that I would always be around for you.

And the years went by, and you were happy and well-adjusted. How could I ruin that for you?

I grew up knowing my father was a dragon slayer. I grew up knowing that every time he walked out the door, it could be the last time I ever saw him. I grew up having to lie for him at school whenever someone asked what my dad did. I grew up knowing that no matter what I decided to 'be' when I grew up, I would become a dragon slayer, and eventually I would die a dragon slayer's death. It was a heavy burden for a child. I didn't want you to have to bear that burden. I wanted you to be carefree and oblivious to your fate for as long as possible.

But I did hope I would be able to tell you in person.

But by now you know. By now, you'll have received the letter telling you I will not return. By now you'll have been summoned to the Alexandra School of Heroic Arts.

31

And now, you can no longer afford to be ignorant of what I am about to tell you.

I am a dragon slayer. As was my father before me, and his father before him, for more generations than we can account for. It is a profession that once played an important role in human safety. When human populations were small and isolated, and dragons roamed everywhere, dragon slayers saved many people, protecting whole villages and towns.

Those days are long gone. The tables have been turned, and now, humans are everywhere and dragons live in small, isolated populations.

I would be happy about this if I didn't feel strongly that we've been wrong about dragons for hundreds of years. Dragons are a bit like wolves—they're predators with the potential to kill people and livestock. In our zeal to protect our families and sheep, we went on a rampage against wolves and dragons alike. But today, we know that wolves prefer to eat wild animals, not people and sheep. And it's because we encroached on their habitat that they ever bothered with us in the first place. Today, of course, we've made our peace with wolves, and we protect them and their habitat, and understand how important they are to the natural world.

Well, dragons are the same as wolves, except that they are intelligent, sentient beings, too.

And because they live for hundreds of years, they have wisdom and knowledge that we don't.

I am convinced we need to preserve dragons, not kill them. We need dragons. And they need us. They need you, Nathan.

Most dragon slayers do not think as I do. Most are blinded by tradition and the thrill of the hunt. Others see dragon slaying as a way to riches and influence. Only a handful of us believe dragons have value as living, breathing, thinking animals.

As Patriarch of the Fraternal Order of Dragon Slayers International, I have been working to try to change the attitude toward dragons. I believe we need to lift the secrecy around them, acknowledge their existence, and begin working to protect the few that remain. I believe they have much to teach us.

Unfortunately, those who think differently are doing their best to silence me. It's possible they are behind my death. I have been on good terms with the dragons for many years now, and I know most of them support my efforts—I doubt a dragon would kill me.

With me gone, my enemies will naturally turn their attention to you, assuming you will continue my work. I hope you will, son, but you must proceed with the utmost caution.

Whatever happens, DO NOT GO TO THE ALEXANDRA SCHOOL OF HEROIC ARTS. Professor Drachenmorder is a traditionalist or, at least, he appears to be. In truth, he runs a high-end safari business, charging rich clients huge sums of money (which he pockets himself) to hunt dragons. He provides his clients with military assault rifles, which is strictly against the dragon slaying code, that demands a fair fight between human and dragon. He has been leading the fight against the changes I've proposed to the dragon slaying profession. Any enquiry into his actions by the Fraternal Order of Dragon Slayers, or by government authorities, would send him to jail for a host of illegal activities. He has much to hide, and I fear he will go to any lengths to hide it.

They will come to get you and take you to the school. DO NOT GO. Once under Drachenmorder's roof, I fear for your safety. Run away. A colleague of mine, Dr. Scott Williams, can help you. He is not a dragon slayer, but he is a zoologist at Otago University who knows about dragons. He knows you might be coming and is prepared to help. You will need to act quickly. Nan cannot know where you have gone. She will be questioned.

Again, I am sorry I could not tell you all this myself. I'm sorry you are learning of it all under difficult circumstances when you've got so much else to take in. Please know I kept this all from you because I love you. Because I wanted you to be happy, not because I didn't think you could handle it. Indeed, you have grown into a fine young man who I am proud to call my son.

Most dragon slayers dream of their sons following in their footsteps. I am asking you to lead rather than follow. You are a dragon slayer's son. Do not become a dragon slayer. Become a dragon saver. It will not be easy. It will be dangerous. But I believe you have it in you. You are brave. A leader. You will make me proud.

Stay safe, son. Know that I loved you.
Dad

I could barely read the last few sentences, for the tears clouding my eyes. I hoped the other boys hadn't heard my sniffles. All the anger toward my father had evaporated. Now it was directed at myself. Because I'd refused to read this letter earlier, I had done exactly what my father wanted me to avoid. I was at the School of Heroic Arts. And I'd sworn loyalty to the school under pain of death.

The pieces started to fall into place. Drachenmorder's response when he found out I knew nothing of my father's activities, and Will's surprise at my mention of death as the punishment for breaking the rules—I bet Drachenmorder had put that in just for me.

Did Drachenmorder want to kill me?

I thought about Hunter Godfry. Did he pick on me during our rugby game because Drachenmorder asked him to?

I remembered my hike with Sir Magnus. That stray bullet—had it been meant for me, not the rabbit? And if so, had Sir Magnus been involved? Had he lured me out 'rabbit hunting' in order to put me in danger? He seemed to genuinely like my dad, but he worked for the school. Did he know what Drachenmorder was up to? He had been so friendly and understanding. He had talked so respectfully of my father. Surely, he couldn't be in league with Drachenmorder. Or maybe he was just a really good actor. Questions crowded my brain, but I had no answers for them.

I read the letter again, hoping to learn more from it, but the second reading only confirmed what I'd already gathered—I was in serious trouble.

Chapter 5
Slayers and Savers

I lay awake in bed for a long time that night. Should I run away? How would I get home? Maybe Nan could come and pick me up, with some excuse about why I needed to leave the school. But, no. Dad said not to tell Nan anything because she'd be in danger then. Maybe I could ring the professor Dad mentioned. Would he be willing to come and get me? Would Drachenmorder let me leave with a stranger? Would he let me leave at all? I doubted it. I would have to sneak out.

I jumped out of bed, ready to escape immediately. I grabbed my backpack and started to shove clothing into it.

"What're you doing, Nathan?" mumbled Oliver. "Quit making so much noise." He rolled over and pulled the blanket over his head.

What *was* I doing? Did I really think I could simply walk out of the dorms without anyone noticing?

The Lodge was peppered with CCTV cameras—it was how the teachers supervised us at night. The duty teacher slept in a small room off the kitchen and kept an eye on the cameras. If I slipped away after dark, my escape would be noticed immediately or recorded, and the teachers would see it first thing in the morning. I expected they had cameras installed on the other buildings too, and on the long driveway to the school. I wouldn't get far before they caught me, and then it would be…death?

I slowly took the clothes out of my backpack and crawled back into bed. Running away without any planning wasn't going to work. And what was I going to do if I did get away? I wished I could talk to Dad. I blinked back tears as I realised I could never talk to him again.

I went over the letter in my head again. Dad wanted me to continue in his footsteps, to change the dragon slaying profession to a dragon saving one. He thought I would be safer doing that from outside the school of heroic arts. But now that I was here at the school, I would just have to make the best of it. The thought of being a student of someone who might have killed my father made me shiver with fear. Could I really do it? Did I have a choice?

Dad had said I was brave. A leader. That's what I needed to be. I needed to forget my fear and make a plan. What did I need to do in order to continue Dad's work? I hardly knew where to begin—I knew almost nothing about dragons or the dragon slaying profession. I needed to know more before I could hope to save the creatures.

And the best place to learn about dragons and dragon slaying was the Alexandra School of Heroic Arts. Therefore, the best thing I could do was to go to my classes—learn sword fighting, learn how to talk to dragons, learn more about Drachenmorder and his activities. Maybe I was better off because I hadn't read Dad's letter until now. My ignorance during my interview with Drachenmorder had been genuine and, hopefully, it would put him off his guard. I could learn a lot at school to help me save the dragons.

I glanced at the clock—2:55 a.m. Suddenly, exhaustion overwhelmed me. I had a plan, and now it was time to get some sleep. I put Dad's letter back in its envelope and, in the dark, I slipped the envelope underneath my mattress, so no one would find it.

I woke late the next morning. The other boys were already at breakfast. I smiled to myself. Dad had loved me. He'd believed I had the ability to save the dragons.

I hopped out of bed. If I was going to save the dragons, I'd better get to it. I would need allies and information, and I thought I knew the perfect place to find them.

Tui, Ella, Will, Oliver, and Josh were sitting together in the dining hall when I arrived, the remains of toast and jam on their plates. Everyone but Josh was embroiled in a heated discussion and hardly acknowledged me as I sat down with my own toast and a glass of orange juice. Josh didn't acknowledge me either. He was focused on his breakfast.

"But, if they're *sentient*, doesn't that mean they have souls?" asked Ella.

"Being sentient doesn't mean they conform to your Judeo-Christian idea of a soul," retorted Will. "It just means they are self-aware. Your average house cat is self-aware."

"Well, maybe your average house cat has a soul, too," said Tui. "Did you ever think of that? Huh?"

"I'm just saying that the idea of a soul is a religious one, it's not a biological one—it has no basis in fact. So we can argue all day whether dragons have souls, but it doesn't change the fact that, as far as we know, souls don't exist."

Ella and Tui both harrumphed at Will. Oliver leaned in and whispered, "Soul or not, I think it's going to be awfully hard to kill an animal that can talk."

The other three nodded their agreement, and the argument was dropped.

"Nathan!" said Oliver with a grin. "You were a sleepyhead this morning!"

"I'm beginning to think you don't sleep at all, Oliver," I said, returning his grin. "You never stop."

38

"Yep, that's Oliver," laughed Will. "Not only does he never sleep, but he never stops talking either."

Oliver blushed, but Will's jibe had been good-natured, and it was clear that all three of the older kids were fond of the boy.

"Oliver, how old are you?" I asked.

"Eight. I'll be nine in September."

"Are you the youngest student here?"

"Yep. Normally the school won't take students until they're ten years old, but they made an exception for me because I'm precocious."

Will answered my question before I could ask it.

"That means he's smarter than is good for him. I just want to know what a little bloke like Oliver is going to do when faced with a thirty-metre-long dragon."

"Dad was small too," declared Oliver, drawing himself up. "Dragon slaying isn't all about brawn."

I didn't point out that Oliver's dad was dead. All our dads were dead, no matter how brawny they'd been.

"I expect that, to a thirty-metre-long dragon, we all look about the same size," I said.

"Yeah, snack-sized," added Tui. We all laughed, though, when I thought about it later, it was probably not very funny.

Most of the students had homework to do on Sunday, so there were no rugby games, for which I was secretly grateful. The bruises Hunter gave me had blossomed overnight into ugly dark patches. Since it was a perfect opportunity to start learning about dragons, I spent most of the day in the library with Oliver.

The book selection was like something out of a fantasy novel. I hardly knew where to start, but Oliver directed me to *An Illustrated Guide to Dragons of the World.*

"You'll need to be able to recite that one backwards and forwards by the end of the year—may as well start in on it. Besides, it's got great pictures!"

It was my first introduction to dragons, and it was epic. The book was written like a field guide to birds. The pictures were detailed, and the descriptions for each species included little range maps to show where they lived. It also included some great stories about famous dragon slayers.

On the page titled the North African Sand Dragon was the story of the only dragon slayer I'd ever heard of before—St. George.

In about 300 AD, St. George killed a North African Sand Dragon that was living at a spring outside the town of Silene. I had always thought of St. George as a heroic figure—I'd imagined him facing down a huge black beast with ravening claws. But, according to the book, North African Sand Dragons are small, as dragons go—about the size of a big crocodile. And they have poor fire-breathing abilities—enough to singe the feathers off the birds they like to eat, but not enough to really roast a person. And St. George went after it on horseback and wielding a long spear, so he wasn't in much danger, though his horse probably could have been hurt. According to the book, there had been no witnesses to the event, which made some critics think he'd actually killed a crocodile and then pretended it was a dragon in order to gain his DSE (Dragon Slayer Extraordinaire) credentials. "A poor dragon slayer with a good publicist" was how the book described St. George.

I tucked this knowledge into the growing list of things that defied my understanding of the world, and carried on with the book.

I read about the Black Dragons of Austria—huge beasts over forty metres long that once terrorised much of Europe but are now considered extinct.

I read about tiny Flower Dragons from the Amazon—so small you can hold them in your hand. They come in all colours of the rainbow, and it is not known whether they are one species with many colour variations, or many species, each a different colour. They use their fire to soften fruit before eating it and are the only living herbivorous dragons known to exist.

But the dragon that captivated me most was the New Zealand green dragon. The head mounted in Professor Drachenmorder's office was everything I thought a dragon should be—huge and scary—and they lived practically in my back yard. And even though Dad said he didn't think any dragon would harm him, I thought that if he *had* been killed by a dragon, this would have been the one to do it.

I read that the New Zealand greens, ranging up to thirty metres long, are New Zealand's largest dragons. Their flames can shoot nearly ten metres, and their wingspan can reach to over forty metres. Apparently, before humans arrived, they used to eat moa. After the moa were hunted to extinction by humans, the dragons started eating people instead. When Europeans arrived with sheep, deer and cattle, the greens turned their attention to livestock. "The first dragon slayer in New Zealand, Mr. Chang Wan Ng, was sent to the country to deal with the threat from these impressive beasts."

"Hey, Oliver," I said, interrupting his studies. "Is this your relative?"

Oliver grinned. "Yeah! Chang Wan Ng was my great-great-great-great grandfather!"

"Wow! He's famous."

"And I will be, too!"

I thought about Oliver and his enthusiasm for everything, including dragon slaying. I thought about the conversation at breakfast—what did he really think about dragons? At heart, was he a dragon slayer or a dragon saver?

"What do you think you'll be famous for? Dragon slaying?" I asked.

"Hardly." Oliver sighed. "Will's right. I'm too small. I don't know...I was hoping, maybe, to go into sports medicine actually. I know, it sounds dumb..."

"No, it sounds cool."

Oliver sighed again. "The trick will be to survive long enough to do it."

So Oliver might be a saver after all. I was beginning to categorise my fellow students, making a list in my head of who I thought might ultimately be on my dad's side. On *my* side. Tui and Ella most definitely were dragon savers or, at least, they could be turned into savers. And probably Oliver. I wasn't sure about Will. I really liked Will. He was a great guy, but he didn't seem to view dragons as anything but animals. I thought it might be best if I kept my dad's ideas about dragons to myself around him, at least for now.

Chapter 6
Classes

"Horsemanship first this morning, then tracking," said Oliver on Monday morning. "Dress for outdoors."

"Sunblock too," said Will, tossing a bottle onto my bed.

"At this time of year?" Dad made me use sunblock in the summer, but in September, he didn't bother.

"Alpine conditions," answered Will. "Sun's more intense up here. As a dragon slayer, chances are you won't live long enough to get cancer, but wouldn't you feel stupid if you survived the dragons and then died of skin cancer at age sixty?" He shrugged.

He had a point.

"Besides, it's school policy," said Oliver. He put on his best serious face and added, "The Alexandra School of Heroic Arts is a Sun Safe school—remember to slip, slop and slap." We all laughed.

Will, Oliver, and I met up with Tui and Ella at the front door and started toward the stables.

"Where's Josh?" asked Ella. Joshua Robinson was the sixth member of what the students referred to as the noob class—those first-years who had been at the school less than six months.

"He was still eating," said Will.

I had already noticed that Josh appreciated his food. He was first in line at meals and last to leave the dining hall. He didn't talk much, but he ate as though every meal was his last.

"Well, he'd better hurry. Marshall will give him Flip if he's late," remarked Ella, turning to look back toward the Lodge.

"What's Flip?" I asked.

Everyone laughed, and Tui began, "Flip is one of the horses—"

"The meanest horse, ever," interrupted Oliver.

"—and if Professor Marshall wants to give someone a hard time, he makes him ride Flip."

"Flip isn't her real name—she's a purebred something-or-other with a fancy name like Magic Star Dancer or something equally dumb," explained Will. "We call her Flip because she has this way of bucking that makes you fly off and do a flip in the air before landing on your back."

"You don't want to get Flip," warned Ella. "But, if you do, hang on for dear life."

Josh came jogging across the gravel just as we were entering the stables. Professor Marshall, who was waiting for us, gave him a disapproving look. Marshall was tall and angular, clean-shaven, with silver hair and a face that looked like old leather. He was a caricature of an Australian stockman, so it was no surprise when he greeted us with a broad Ozzie drawl.

He wasted no time on formalities.

"Saddle up, then. Will, stall one. Tui, stall two. Ella, three. Oliver, four. Joshua, five." The students entered their respective stalls to saddle their horses. Hands on hips, Professor Marshall sized me up. "And you're Nathan, eh? Ever ridden a horse?" I shook my head before I remembered. "Well, once, at a birthday party—"

Professor Marshall scoffed. "That's not worth a Zack. Right. I'm gonna show you this once, and I expect you to get it." I nodded. The professor led me to stall number six where a chestnut-coloured mare stood patiently. He showed me how to put the saddle on and position the bit and bridle correctly. Then he told me to lead her out into the yard with the other students and their horses.

I could tell right away who had Flip—Josh struggled to keep hold of his horse, which was a big brown animal with one white back foot. She jerked her head, and snorted and stamped, pulling Josh around the small yard in front of the stable.

"Keep control of your horse, Mister Robinson." barked Professor Marshall.

"But she won't stay still. She's too big for me," replied the boy as Flip tossed her head again.

"Don't be a sook. Stand your ground and show her who's boss." Marshall opened the gate into the paddock and gave each student instructions as they filed out past him.

"Tui and Will, practise your backing and sidestepping—I'll be testing you later in the week. Ella, work on trotting—you need to improve your posting. Oliver, you can do what you'd like, but I want to see you stay in the saddle for a full class period for once. Joshua and Nathan, you'll work with me on mounting and dismounting."

The professor led Joshua and me to a pair of mounting blocks—overturned concrete sinks—at the side of the paddock and showed us how to mount our horses. He used Flip for his demonstration, and the mare stood perfectly still for him, looking almost as bored as my placid horse. But as soon as Josh was on the block, Flip fidgeted and stamped, stepping forward then back, so that Josh had no chance of hooking his foot into the stirrup.

"Don't just stand there, McMannis—get on your horse." Marshall's order made me realise I had been staring anxiously at Josh and doing nothing. I tore my gaze from his troubles and focused on my own mount. Foot into the stirrup, swing myself up, and hey, I was sitting on a horse. I grinned, pleased at my accomplishment. My mare stood and stared into the middle distance, unimpressed.

"Hold the reins properly, McMannis. Not too high. No, don't pull so tight. Back straight. Good. Now dismount." Marshall was at my side, ignoring the struggle going on next to me.

Actually, that's not true. I think he was paying close attention to Joshua's struggle with Flip, and enjoyed watching the boy's failed attempts to mount the jittery beast.

I mounted and dismounted several more times while Josh fought with Flip. Finally, he managed to hook his foot into the stirrup and swing himself onto the horse's back, at which Flip took off at a gallop.

"Aaaaaaaaaaa! Stop! Stop! Stop!" Josh hauled back on the reins in a desperate attempt to stop Flip's headlong rush. His efforts were effective. Too effective. Flip made a sudden halt, deftly lowering her head and raising her hindquarters to propel Josh head over heels into the air. He landed with a loud "Ooof!" and lay whimpering on the ground. Flip, looking extremely pleased with herself, walked calmly back to the mounting block and stood stock-still beside it.

Everyone stopped to watch as Professor Marshall bent over Joshua's prostrate form.

"What did you think you were doing, taking off like that? You've got kangaroos loose in the top paddock, boy."

"I didn't mean to," Josh moaned. "She took off on her own."

"You must have spooked her with your prancing around on the block. She's standing calm as anything now. Get up. Go back and try again."

Josh whimpered, but he slowly sat up. He worked his right wrist around a few times, rubbed his head, then got to his feet and limped to the mounting block.

Marshall turned his attention to the other students, so when Josh reached my side, tears streaking the dirt on his face, I took pity on him.

"Here, take my horse."

"You sure?"

"Go on. Unless you want to try her again." I gestured at Flip, who had resumed her prancing now Josh was back.

"You don't want Flip, Nathan. She's evil."

"I know. The others told me about her. But you don't want her either."

Josh admitted that he didn't and thanked me as we switched horses.

He had much better luck with my horse, mounting and dismounting with relative ease, although with no grace.

I stood, palms sweating, assessing the fidgety Flip. She was clearly sizing me up as well.

First rule of dragon slaying is to show no fear. That's what Sir Magnus had told me. I figured the same was probably true of horse riding too, so I took a deep breath and swung myself into the saddle.

But my bottom never reached it because it was no longer there. Flip had moved so quickly that, if I'd been a cartoon character, I would have hung suspended for a moment in mid-air, looking down at the empty space below. Not being so fortunate, I fell unceremoniously on my bum. I cried out when I landed, and rolled to my side to ease the pain in my tailbone. My roll landed me in a fresh pile of horse poo. Flip looked back at me, and I swear she grinned.

Show no fear. I was going to ride this horse. I knew she could stand still. She'd done so for Professor

Marshall. I clambered to my feet, wiped the horse poo off my arm, pulled Flip back into position and climbed up onto the block. I didn't give her any time to react and practically leapt onto her back.

Then we were off. I knew enough not to try and stop her, as Josh had done, but I wondered if she would try the same move even if I didn't haul on the reins. I focused on staying in the saddle, clutching the reins and pressing my knees against the horse's flanks. She would have to slow down sometime, right? If only I could hang on until then.

I knew nothing about riding, so staying in the saddle for even a minute was sheer luck. Unfortunately, that minute was the most punishing one I'd ever experienced. It was almost a relief when Flip tossed me over her head onto the ground. The ground might have hit harder, but it only hit once then was done beating me up.

I lay on my back trying to regain the breath knocked out of me by the blow. I hoped no one had seen me fall, but the sound of Oliver's laughter came wafting over the field.

If anyone else had laughed at me, I would have been pretty angry about it, but Oliver's laugh was so genuine, so full of mirth and free of malice, that the only thing to do was to laugh along with him.

So, as soon as I got my breath back, I was sitting up and giggling, and before anyone could say 'Flip', we were all laughing.

Professor Marshall, who had been adjusting a strap on Ella's saddle, looked up at the sound of our laughter.

"What's going on here?" he growled. We all fell silent. He looked at me, sitting on the ground, and then at Josh, sitting on my horse. "Robinson, where's your horse? Get off McMannis' and back on your own."

"But, Professor, we were just—" began Josh, but he was cut off by a look from Marshall.

Thankfully, our session was nearly over, and before Josh could be thrown again, Professor Marshall sent us all back to the stables to unsaddle and groom the horses.

"You are completely insane, Nathan!" said Oliver as we walked back to the Lodge for morning tea. "Voluntarily getting on Flip?"

"He was being nice to Josh," said Ella. "I thought it was brave."

My cheeks grew hot and I shrugged. "It wasn't fair for him to make Josh ride Flip, just because he was later than the rest of us. He wasn't even late to class. And why is he making any student ride that animal? She's gonna kill someone."

"That's why you're completely insane to have volunteered to ride her," said Will.

"Well, insane or not, I appreciated it," said Josh. "Thanks, mate." His face brightened. "And did you see that? I had no trouble mounting Nathan's horse. It's that stupid Flip, not me."

"Marshall has something against Josh," explained Tui. "Unless one of the rest of us has made him particularly mad, Josh is the one who gets stuck with Flip."

Tracking, after morning tea, was taught by Professor West. It was awesome. Professor West was awesome. He seemed to be hardly any older than the oldest students at the school and showed up to class in cargo shorts and a flannel shirt. But the most striking thing about West was that he was missing an arm and a leg. He had prosthetics for both, but he moved around like…well, like everyone else. If he'd been wearing long pants and a jacket, I might not even have noticed the fake limbs.

Professor West sent us outside in two teams—Ella, Oliver, and me; and Will, Josh, and Tui. My team had a five minute head start, and we ran around trying to throw the other team off our trail. The other team had to track us. We could go wherever we wanted. Oliver and I took off at a run up the hill behind the stables. Ella trudged along behind.

"Why do we have to go uphill?" she asked breathlessly when she caught up to us at the top.

"Because it's fun!" cried Oliver as he plunged down the other side. We wound our way through the scrub at the bottom of the hill, leaving a trail as broad as a highway, I'm sure. On the other side, we came to the farm track that passed the faculty chalets.

"Wait," panted Ella. "We can't outrun them. We need to cover our tracks."

Oliver and I, who were having great fun running, reluctantly agreed, and we set about discussing a plan.

First, we made a mass of confusing tracks around all the chalets. We ended up on Professor West's porch. From there, we jumped to a boulder, then to another and another until we were a good ten metres behind the chalet, in the middle of a field of tussocks. One final big leap and we were off running again, wending our way through the tussocks toward the stream below.

"Of course, you know they're going to assume we've come to the stream," said Oliver as we rock-hopped down the bank to avoid leaving skid marks. "That's the classic place to confuse your trail."

"Well, it must work then, right?" I said.

"Upstream or down?" asked Ella. "I vote for upstream."

"That'll take us right back to the Lodge. We can't go upstream," I said.

"Exactly. We go back to the Lodge and hang out in the atrium with our feet up while the others stumble around out here looking for us."

Oliver and I both squashed that idea. Professor West had given us free rein to go anywhere we wanted, and Ella wanted to go back to the Lodge? This was an opportunity to explore places that were off limits at rec time. We weren't about to pass that up. We overruled her and headed downstream.

The stream was swift and rocky, angling steeply downhill. Oliver giggled madly as he leapt from boulder to boulder, until I told him he needed to be quiet or it wouldn't matter how well we covered our tracks—the others would just follow his laughter.

Ella followed sullenly, grumbling and reminding us that every step we took downhill would have to be repeated uphill later. Oliver and I ignored her.

Eventually, even Oliver and I thought we'd gone far enough. We stopped to let Ella catch up for a consultation.

"Looks like we could climb up the other bank here without leaving much of a trail," Oliver suggested.

"It's about time," replied Ella. "I thought you guys would never turn around!"

Suddenly, a shout rang out behind us.

"That was Josh," I said.

The discussion ended. We took off up the bank—carefully, to avoid leaving any sign we'd left the stream bed there. When we reached the ridge above, we stopped and crouched behind a boulder. The other team was close enough that, if we were to move, the rustling grasses and shrubs would give us away.

"How did they find us?" I whispered.

"Tui is really good at tracking," replied Ella. "Like, creepily good."

Oliver nodded agreement. We could hear nothing of the group below us, but they had to be close by now. We waited, straining our ears and trying not to breathe too loudly.

A minute passed. Oliver looked at me with a question in his eyes.

"Wait," I mouthed. Oliver leaned against the rock.

Another minute passed. All was silent. Ella made to stand, but I grabbed her arm and kept her still. We listened but heard no sound of our pursuers.

"Boo!"

Ella screamed, I jumped, and Oliver laughed.

"Ha! Gotcha!" cried Will.

"I can't believe you were able to track us," I said.

"It was actually pretty hard," Will admitted. "You did a good job. The bit around the chalets had us stumped for a while."

"If it hadn't been for Tui and her sniffer, we'd never have found you," added Josh.

We all walked back to the Lodge together, chatting and laughing. It was the best class I'd ever had.

Chapter 7
Fighting

After lunch we had Combat class with Sir Christopher Grehan. Sir Christopher was a small, stocky man, balding, with sandy hair. He wore wool trousers, a crisp white button-down shirt and a red tie, which seemed out of place in the sheep-scented shearing shed.

Combat class wasn't as amazing as tracking, but it still beat year eight maths back at Lincoln Primary. By a lot.

"Ah, Nathan McMannis," said Sir Christopher when I entered the shed. "What a pleasure to see you here, though it's such a shame about your father. He was a strong man."

I looked at the floor, blinking hard.

"Well, as we have a new student, why don't we review the basics of tameshigiri? You could all use a refresher, I think. Who would like to explain to Nathan what tameshigiri is?"

Oliver raised his hand.

"Tameshigiri is test cutting. It was traditionally used in Japan to test the quality of a sword, but today it tests the quality of the sword fighter and is practiced as a sport."

"Well done, Oliver. For our purposes, tameshigiri is a way of practicing the cutting motions you might use to incapacitate or kill some of the lesser dragons—generally, those under ten metres long. Now, if you will all please select a sword and take your places, we'll review the basic cuts."

A row of long, slightly curved swords lay on a table, each one safely sheathed. I recognised the lettering on the scabbards.

"Japanese swords?" I asked. "Why Japanese? I think of dragon slaying as a European thing."

"Japan used to be full of cool dragons," Oliver explained. "They're all extinct now—I guess their dragon slayers were really good at it."

"Sir Christopher studied under an old Japanese guy," added Will. "I guess that's what he knows."

"I learned swordplay from Kuro Takahashi, one of Japan's last dragon slayers," said Sir Christopher, who must have overheard our conversation. "It is said, he himself slew the last Japanese dragon. He was in his nineties when he taught me. It's true, the Japanese *were* the best of the dragon slayers but, once their own dragons were gone, they simply stopped hunting them anymore. They were never part of the Fraternal Order of Dragon Slayers International but, nonetheless, the Order sent me to Japan to learn their arts from the old man. That is why we practise tameshigiri. Why do we use Japanese swords?" He shrugged. "I get them cheap from a Japanese friend of mine. And they're basically the equivalent of the European longsword."

We spread out across the shearing shed floor, and Sir Christopher took us slowly through the motions of the four cuts of tameshigiri. Then, he demonstrated the cuts on a post that looked like a giant sausage wrapped in tinfoil.

"What is that?" I asked.

"The target I'm using is a tatami mat wrapped around a bamboo core, and then wrapped twelve times in aluminium foil. The bamboo core simulates bone, the mat is the consistency of flesh, and the foil simulates the dragon's scales."

Drawing his sword and taking up a fighting stance, he sliced and diced the target as neatly as if he were cutting a carrot. When he'd finished, he set up another one and let us each have a go at it.

"Nathan first, because he's new."

First? I supposed it didn't matter, but I my palms were sweating as I approached the target. I took a deep breath like Sir Christopher had shown us, to compose my nerves, then I took a swipe at it, putting everything I had behind my swing.

My sword practically bounced off the target. I managed to cut through the foil, but that was all. My face went hot as the other students stifled giggles. But as I stepped back, Oliver leaned over to whisper in my ear.

"Pretty good for your first."

"Good? It was pathetic."

Tui stepped up next. I knew she had been here almost six months, so I expected a good show. She had a fierce expression on her face as she closed with the target—that alone would have scared off a dragon. She swung and hit the target with a loud thwack.

Her sword penetrated to the bamboo core and stuck.

"Yes!" She raised her arms and grinned.

Will was next. He stepped into position, but before he took his swing, Sir Christopher spoke.

"Will, your six-month exams are next week. If you'd like, we can count this as part of your sword practical."

A nervous look flitted across Will's face. "Sure." He stepped away from the target, closed his eyes, and took a deep breath. When he opened them again, he was all concentration. One more deep breath, and then he launched himself at the target, slicing all the way through. The top of the target toppled to the floor, and we all broke out in applause, clapping and whistling. Will beamed.

"I take it he passed," I said to Oliver. He grinned and nodded in answer.

Oliver didn't even make a dent in the aluminium.

Josh and Ella made it through the aluminium, but no farther.

Maybe I wasn't so bad after all.

Sir Christopher was smiling.

"Well done, all of you, though I wouldn't go taking on any dragons quite yet. Will and Tui, you carry on practicing with the tatami targets. And the rest of you, shall we get some more realistic targets for you to try?"

We all nodded, and Sir Christopher produced an armload of foam pool noodles. We fitted these over short stakes set upright in the ground, and spent the rest of the session whacking them. Even Oliver could slice through a pool noodle, and his giggle as he did so rang out through the shed.

Perhaps Oliver and I got a little over-enthusiastic. We *were* telling our targets to 'take that, vile beast!' and other nonsense. When Sir Christopher's stern voice rose over our shouts, I knew exactly who he was going to yell at.

"Nathan and Oliver. This is not a play. You are not actors. You are learning a skill that will someday save your life and the lives of countless innocent victims of dragons. You are training in the most honourable profession on Earth. A profession that your fathers died for. This is not a joke. Do not treat it as one."

"Yes, Sir Christopher," we both said, staring at the floor. Oliver still smiled, but we both finished the session in silence.

"So, why do we use swords, anyway?" I asked Sir Christopher as we were cleaning and oiling our blades at the end of class. "Wouldn't guns be safer and more effective?"

"It's all about maintaining honour. Dragon slaying has a long and venerable tradition of pitting man and beast against one another in a fair fight. It is the only honourable way to challenge a dragon. We are knighted upon slaying our first dragon because to slay a dragon is a noble deed. It requires placing oneself in danger. It requires not only physical, but also mental prowess, for dragons are cunning and deadly. And it is all done for the greater good—those we protect may not even know they are in danger. Thus, dragon slaying is an honourable profession. If we merely shot a dragon from a distance with a modern armour-piercing bullet, it would be slaughter, not slaying. Slaughter is not honourable. It is the work of cowards. Do you want to be a coward, Nathan?"

I shook my head. "No, Sir Christopher."

We filed out of the shearing shed in silence, but half way to the Lodge, Oliver started giggling, and all the other students followed his lead.

"What?" I asked.

"Sorry, we should have warned you not to ask about guns," said Will.

"Every new student asks," said Oliver.

"Well, it makes sense. Why wouldn't you use the best tools available to do the job?" I asked.

"But Sir Christopher makes the same speech every time," said Josh. "Honour. It's all about honour." he added, mimicking Sir Christopher's voice.

"I suppose he's right," I said. "It wouldn't be sporting to use a rifle. It'd be like scooping up trout with a net instead of fishing with a rod."

"Besides, swords are so much cooler than guns!" Oliver slashed through the air with an invisible sword.

"And if you shoot a dragon from far away, you don't get the chance to talk to it," said Tui.

"*Talk* to it?" asked Will. "Why would you want to do that?"

"Well, they're highly intelligent, and...aren't you curious? I mean, we've got these incredible animals right here in New Zealand." She lowered her voice. "Why aren't we studying them? Why aren't we trying to learn to live with them rather than kill them? We do that with tigers and lions, and all sorts of other dangerous animals. All the teachers talk about is killing." She was blushing now, as if she was embarrassed by her own thoughts. "It's like…you know, the Māori taniwha. They're made out to be monsters, but not all taniwha are bad. They're guardians. Some of them protect sacred places and important resources. Some of them warn us of danger. What if dragons are actually taniwha? What if we need dragons like we need taniwha?"

"Need dragons? Yeah, like we need a hole in the head," said Will. "Come on, let's get dinner."

"Yeah, I'm starving," said Josh. Will and Josh jogged ahead to the Lodge. The rest of us stopped walking.

"Can I tell you a secret?" I asked. Tui, Ella, and Oliver nodded, and I motioned them close, keeping my voice low. "My dad, before he died, was trying to change the dragon slaying profession into a dragon *saving* profession. He believed that dragons are like any other wildlife, only even more so because they're so smart. He wanted to give them the same protections that other endangered species have. I think he had even befriended some dragons. He warned me not to come to this school. He said Professor Drachenmorder—" Someone was coming, crunching across the gravel toward us. I raised my voice. "So then I just popped the whole bug into my mouth."

Oliver took the hint. "Ew! You ate the bug?" The others picked up on what was happening and started to express their disgust. It was pretty poor acting, if you ask me, but as Sir Magnus passed close by, he waved and greeted us as usual.

"You'll be late for dinner if you don't hurry, boys…and, er, girls."

We finished our walk to the Lodge in silence.

"Study group tonight in classroom one? Eight o'clock?" asked Oliver pointedly as we climbed the steps. We all agreed, and I knew I'd found my allies.

The time between dinner and our eight o'clock meeting might have dragged, but there was plenty of excitement to distract us.

After dinner, most of the students were socialising in the atrium. Eventually, we would all get down to our homework, but we took an hour or so to blow off steam first. I challenged Josh to a game of pool. We both took a light-hearted view of the game—neither of us was very good at it, and our matches were mostly just excuses to goof off.

I went first and broke with a dramatic flourish that was largely ineffective at scattering the balls but made Josh laugh. He ploughed the cue ball through the thicket, knocking two balls into the pockets by sheer luck. We both cheered. I pocketed one ball on my next turn. Never mind it wasn't the one I'd been aiming for. Then Josh made a big show of a behind-the-back shot that sent the cue ball flying right off the table.

The ball rolled across the floor and under an armchair. Josh ran after it, and I cringed.

Sitting in the armchair was Hunter Godfry. Josh pulled up short in front of him.

"Um…"

Hunter looked up with a sneer.

"Um, excuse me, but can you get up? I lost a ball under your chair."

"You lost a *ball* under my chair? What were your balls doing under my chair in the first place?" Hunter guffawed, and Josh's face went red.

"No, a ball from the pool table. Please. I need to move the chair to get it."

Hunter stood. He towered over Josh.

"Go ahead. Get your ball." He didn't step away from the chair.

Josh swallowed then stepped toward the chair past Hunter. He bent, pushed the chair away, and snatched the cue ball from under it. Before he could rise again, Hunter grabbed his hair and pulled him upright. Josh called out in pain.

"Next time, keep your *balls* away from me, or I'll—"

Tui streaked toward Hunter and punched him full in the face. Hunter dropped Josh, who scurried away.

"Leave him alone!"

Hunter rubbed his face and turned on Tui. By now, everyone was watching. I held my breath. She was no match for him. He probably weighed twice what she did, and he was angry.

"Oh? Is Josh your little boyfriend?"

"Josh is *not* my boyfriend, but you are a jerk!"

He snarled and lunged at her.

I expected her to jump away, but I had clearly underestimated her courage. She ducked his punch then kicked him hard in the crotch. He doubled over, and she brought up her knee, cracking him soundly on the nose with it.

Hunter crumpled to the floor.

"You...you b—"

"Pick on someone your own size next time, Hunter." Tui turned and stalked back to the fireplace, picking up her book and flopping down on a couch. Applause broke out among the watching students.

Tui looked up, and I followed her gaze to see Professor West among the crowd. A flicker of dismay crossed her face when she realised she'd been caught beating up another student. Then Professor West winked at her and began clapping himself. She grinned.

Chapter 8
The Dragon Defence League

"Who's on duty tonight?" asked Oliver as we assembled in classroom one.

"Professor West." Tui set a stack of books onto the table.

"If we get caught..." warned Ella.

"Don't worry," said Tui. "You know West will be playing ping pong until lights out. And when has he ever paid attention to the cameras? Besides, we're not doing anything wrong. We're studying."

There was a camera in the classroom, and we made a show of bringing out our books and notes and pretending to refer to them as we talked, in case West was watching.

"So, what did your dad say about Drachenmorder?" asked Ella. "That guy gives me the creeps." She shuddered.

"He says Drachenmorder is using the school as a front for a high-end safari business."

"What, tahr hunting?"

"Dragon hunting. Have you been in his office?" The others shook their heads, and I wondered again whether I had been treated differently than the other students. "His office wall is filled with pictures of famous people with the dragons they've bagged. He told me they're the school's benefactors, who are allowed to accompany dragon slayers on their missions, but I think they're his clients."

"So he's getting non dragon slayers to kill dragons. Why is that a problem? Aren't we supposed to be slaying dragons too?" asked Oliver with a shrug.

"They use military assault rifles. It has nothing to do with dragon slaying; it's dragon slaughtering, like Sir Christopher said. And Drachenmorder is pocketing the money for himself. It's not going to the school. And who knows what else he's up to? Dad said Drachenmorder would end up in jail for all sorts of reasons if anyone found out what he was doing."

"And what does this have to do with us?" asked Ella.

"My dad considered Drachenmorder his enemy. He told me his enemies were trying to silence him, to keep him from saving the dragons. Dad's dead now, but he was counting on me to continue his work. He wanted me to become a dragon *saver*. I guess that makes Drachenmorder my enemy too. And yours, if you become dragon savers with me."

"Dragon saver," echoed Tui. "I like that."

Oliver nodded thoughtfully. "Chang Wan Ng will turn over in his grave, but Dad would understand. He always talked of dragons as individuals." He laughed. "And, let's face it, how am I ever going to kill a dragon? It'd be like a flea trying to kill a dog."

We looked at Ella. She frowned. "You do realise we'll get into heaps of trouble if anyone finds out." She sighed. "I can't say I've ever looked forward to becoming a dragon slayer; I hate camping and hiking. The only good thing about it is the horses. Yeah, I'm in."

"We need a name," said Tui. "Like a secret society."

"How about the Fraternal Order of Dragon Savers?" suggested Oliver.

Tui rolled her eyes, "*Fraternal*? Do Ella and I look like your brothers?"

Oliver shrugged. "It was only a suggestion."

"Dragon Savers International?" said Ella.

"Are we *international*?" I asked.

"Kids for Dragons!" said Oliver.

We all wrinkled our noses at that one.

"The Dragon Conservancy?" said Tui.

That one wasn't too bad.

"Defenders of Dragons?" said Oliver.

"The Dragon Defence League," said Ella.

"That's it," agreed Tui.

"The DDL," I said. "Perfect."

Coming up with a name was the easy part. Deciding what we were going to do was a bit harder.

"Your dad must have worked with others, right? Did he tell you who?" asked Oliver.

"The only person he mentioned was Dr. Scott Williams. But he's not a dragon slayer; he's a professor at Otago University. That's where he wanted me to go to instead of here. Apparently, Dr. Williams knows about dragons."

"Well, let's see if we can find this Williams guy," said Oliver.

"I can do that," I said. "He was expecting me to contact him if Dad…died. I think we also need to find out more about what Drachenmorder is up to."

"And who's working with him," added Tui. "You can bet that some, maybe all, of the staff are involved, as well."

"Should we be doing this?" asked Ella. "I mean, we're just kids. Maybe we should get out of here. Leave the school. Can't we simply not become dragon slayers rather than trying to save them all?"

"I can't," I said. "Dad wanted me to continue his work, and that's what I'm going to do. Anyway, I don't know if they'd let us leave. When your parent dies, you *have* to become a dragon slayer—my nan was quite clear about that. They'll find you and bring you to the school no matter what. When I first read the letter my dad left for me, I thought about running away that night. But I knew I'd be caught on camera. There are cameras all over this place."

"Yeah, but only in the buildings," said Oliver.

"Are you sure?"

"There's one on the main gate," said Tui. "I saw it during tracking class one day."

"And you can bet there are others. No, whatever we do will be seen. If we try to escape, they'll catch us."

"Well, what can they do to us? Expel us? Then we'd get to go anyway," Ella remarked.

I frowned. "My first day here, Drachenmorder called me into his office. He made me swear to obey the school rules."

"Yeah, we all took that pledge," said Ella. "So? We'll be expelled."

"The oath I took said the penalty for dishonouring the school was death."

"What?"

"That's not what I pledged."

"No way!"

I nodded.

"Why would Drachenmorder do that? Make you agree to be killed for breaking curfew or something?" asked Tui.

"It must have something to do with my dad. He wants to make sure I don't carry on Dad's work."

"He wouldn't really kill you, would he?" asked Ella.

I remembered my strange meeting with Drachenmorder and the creepy feeling I'd had when I left his office. I shuddered. "I don't know. We need to take some time and gather information. Find out more about Drachenmorder and talk to this Williams guy. We need to keep our eyes and ears open. I don't think we can do anything yet because we don't know enough."

"I agree," said Oliver.

"I also think we need to keep up our dragon slaying studies because it's the best way we're going to learn about dragons. Dad was obviously working with them. At some point, we're going to have to find out about that, too. We're going to have to introduce ourselves to the dragons." The others shifted uneasily and cast worried looks at me. I tried to smile, but I expect I looked as terrified as they did.

We decided the Dragon Defence League should meet once a week to share what we'd all learned.

"And if anyone asks, we can say we're studying— DDL stands for Dedicated Dragon Learners," suggested Oliver.

"That is the stupidest name," replied Tui.

But Oliver was right. We had to keep it a secret and, if a stupid name helped us do it, that was fine by me.

"What about Josh and Will?" I asked. "Should we tell them about it? They'll wonder why we're all studying together without them if we don't."

"I don't know what Josh thinks about dragon slaying," said Tui. "But Will is totally into it."

I nodded. "But do you think we could change his mind? He's…" I wasn't sure how to express the thought that I wanted an older kid with us. Someone who knew more and was more…confident. Now that it was really happening, I felt nervous about leading a group of kids in an endeavour so dangerous it had killed my father.

"Will's really nice, but he plays by the rules. If he knew what we were doing, I think he'd feel compelled to tell someone. We can't include Will," said Ella. "But he's out of the noob class next week, anyway, assuming he passes all his exams, so that's not a big deal."

"And Josh?" asked Oliver.

"Can you imagine him slaying dragons?" asked Tui. "He can barely ride a horse, and he's been here for four months already."

"It's not a matter of his ability but his attitude," I said, though I did think that having Josh on our side might be more of a liability than an asset. Still, it would look less suspicious if the whole noob class studied together.

"I think we need to invite him," said Ella.

"I think you're right, but let's see if we can feel him out first, to make sure he won't go directly to Drachenmorder and tell him what we're up to."

As we cemented our plans, classes continued. I have to admit, while I knew I wanted to see dragon slaying stop, the classes at the Alexandra School of Heroic Arts were the best ever.

Dragons of the World and Draconic Language were taught by Sir Leandro Justo. Sir Leandro was from Peru, and he always wore a colourful knit hat with tasselled ear flaps. The effect would have been cheerful if it hadn't been for his face, which was an ugly mass of scars that pulled his mouth into a permanent grimace. He wore a patch over his left eye. Will said he was also missing an ear, and that's why he always wore the hat.

I was terrified of him that first class. He walked briskly into the room, plugged in a laptop, and turned on the data projector.

"Ella, where would I go to see a Humpbacked Ice Dragon?"

"Antarctica," she replied quickly.

"And where else? Oliver?"

"Parque Nacional Cabo de Hornos."

"Cabo de -*ornos*. Remember the H is silent. Yes. Cape Horn National Park, in Chile. Good." He adjusted the data projector and brought up an image of a long, skinny dragon with no wings and very short legs. "And what is this creature's name, Will?"

"The scaly sewer rat?"

Sir Leandro laughed, and I watched his good eye crinkle with humour, "Only if you live in London. What's its real name? Tui?"

"The fringed burrowing dragon."

"Correct. A small and innocuous dragon, and one of the few that has possibly increased in number over the last few hundred years. Why? Will?" There was a twinkle in his eye.

"Because it likes living in sewers, feeding on the rats."

I raised my hand.

"Yes, Nathan." Sir Leandro's good eye crinkled kindly at me.

"Is that why people think there are alligators in the sewers in America?"

He laughed. "No. I'm afraid there are, in fact, alligators in the sewers in America. The fringed burrowing dragon is strictly European. But your point is well-made. Dragons that show up in unusual places...no...any dragons seen by the general public are often mistaken for other animals. Reports of reptiles glimpsed where they shouldn't be are very often actually dragons in their proper habitat."

"Like the Loch Ness Monster?"

Sir Leandro laughed again. "Ah, now that is an interesting case. As far as I know, there has never been a dragon in Loch Ness. Although the surrounding lochs are swarming with northern copper dragons, they don't seem to like the deep waters of Loch Ness. You really only find them in the shallower, warmer lakes. So why people keep seeing a monster in Loch Ness and nowhere else in the region is truly a mystery."

Sir Leandro's classes were almost entirely a lecture, and they should have been frightfully boring, but the disfigured dragon slayer somehow made memorising facts about all the dragons fascinating. His good eye smiled all the time, and he related a personal story about nearly every dragon he introduced to us. His hour-and-a-half class felt like fifteen minutes. And by the end of the first class, I didn't even see his scars anymore.

Chapter 9
Plans

It was easy to track down Dr. Williams at Otago University. I simply googled him and got the university's staff directory. But when I rang the number, someone else answered the phone.

"Dr. Williams? I'm afraid he's no longer with us."

"Oh. Where does he work now?"

"No. You don't understand. Dr. Williams passed away last week."

I hung up and googled again. There it was in the Otago Daily Times—*Otago University Professor Dies in Suspicious House Fire*.

The police blamed the fire on the students living in the flat next door. Apparently someone had thrown a burning chair through the professor's window in the middle of the night. The students denied the charges but admitted they had all been drinking that night and couldn't remember clearly what had happened.

I was pretty certain the students were innocent.

It couldn't be a coincidence that both my dad and Dr. Williams had died within a week of each other.

Especially not after what happened on Friday.

Fridays were field days. Instead of having separate classes around the school, Miss Brumby made us packed lunches, and all the first-years headed offsite for the day. Professors West and Marshall taught the field days. The outings usually involved riding to some rock outcrop and climbing it or tracking rabbits across the tussock lands.

Tui was the first to know something was up. Unfortunately, she didn't have a chance to tell anyone until later. She was saddling her horse on Friday morning when Sir Leandro came into the stables and pulled Professor West aside. Tui heard their conversation from the other side of the stall door.

"Daniel, is Marshall coming with you today?" Sir Leandro asked in a low voice.

"Yes. Why?"

"I just…just wondered. Hey, the new boy, Nathan. Will you keep a good eye on him today?"

"I always look after the students, Leandro."

"Of course, but I'm…I'm worried about him."

"How so?"

"We'll talk later. Just keep him safe, eh?" said Sir Leandro earnestly.

"I'll keep a close eye on him."

Friday was fantastic. I didn't know what Tui had overheard, so I had no worries at all. I saddled up and led my mare out of the stable. Poor Josh had Flip, until West told Marshall he had to give the boy a better horse. We all waited while Marshall grudgingly brought out a grizzled old gelding for him. When Josh was finally seated on his horse, we rode up a narrow track farther into the mountains. Along the way, Professor Marshall barked orders at us.

"Side step. Turn to your left. All the way round." He kept us so busy with manoeuvres it was a wonder we actually covered any ground. Only a few of us were skilled enough to do everything he directed us to do, but

71

we all tried. And the horses were used to students. If we made a mistake, they stood their ground until we worked it out or gave up.

Professor West stuck beside me the whole way. I didn't really notice at the time, but Tui mentioned it later. We followed a ridge toward a massive tor in the distance. The large rock outcrop didn't seem all that far away, but we had to drop down into two valleys and climb back up in order to get to it, and it was lunchtime before we arrived.

The tor was impressive up close, and everyone was chatting excitedly about the climb after lunch. Everyone, that is, except Ella. She was rubbing her legs and grumbling about having to come all the way out here just to climb a rock.

I dismounted and was about to sit down at the base of the rocks to eat lunch with everyone else, when Tui came up behind me. "Nathan. Let's sit over here." She pointed to a pair of rocks a few metres away from the rest of the group.

"Can I come with you?" asked Oliver.

"Sure," said Tui.

As we settled on the rocks and opened our lunches, I asked, "So how did you do with those riding moves on the way out here?"

Oliver laughed. "I nearly fell off twice! Didn't you see me?"

"Are you kidding? I was too busy trying to stay in the saddle myself." We both laughed.

"Hey, Nathan," said Tui. "This morning I—"

"Mind if I sit here?" asked Professor West, coming up behind us.

"No. Not at all," I said. Professor West sat down.

"I noticed you were having trouble with your horse this morning, Oliver," said the professor. Oliver giggled.

"Yeah, a little."

72

Professor West smiled. "It's hard for the younger ones. I remember once we took on a ten-year-old who must have been even smaller than you. Poor kid had a heck of a time controlling a horse." The professor talked as he ate, regaling us with stories of past students. When he'd finished the last of his sandwich, he brushed the crumbs off his shirt and stood.

"Well, shall we climb some rocks?" he said, loudly enough for everyone to hear.

A cheer arose from the students, and we all jumped to our feet. All except Ella, who heaved a sigh as she hefted herself off the ground.

Professor Marshall lay down in the grass, pulled his hat over his eyes, and appeared to fall asleep. Professor West led us to where he had set out the climbing equipment. He showed me how to put on a harness and reminded the other students of the safety rules while they donned their own harnesses.

"Now, when I teach you rock climbing, we will always use the appropriate safety gear, and you will never be in a position where you can fall—at least, not far. That won't always be the case when you're out doing your job. Sometimes, there won't be time to pull out your gear—maybe the dragon is right there, ready to roast you." He backed up to the rock face. "Maybe he's got you up against the rocks, and you've got nowhere to go but up. Can you just say, 'Excuse me Mister Dragon while I put on my safety gear?'"

We all laughed.

Professor West continued, "Of course not. You've got to act immediately." And with that, Professor West turned and leapt at the rock face, grabbing a handhold with his good arm and a foothold with his prosthetic leg. But he didn't stay there long. In an instant, he was moving, scrambling like a spider up the sheer cliff.

"Awesome," I breathed.

73

West climbed about five metres, then shimmied back down. Everyone clapped.

"That was epic!" said Oliver.

West laughed. "You think that was good?" In a moment, he had removed his prosthetics and turned back to the rocks. This time, he was slower, but we all watched in amazement as he inched his way up the rocks like a caterpillar, one-armed and one-legged.

He hopped back down to our cries of amazement, took a bow and, grinning, replaced his limbs.

Then his face became serious.

"Now you've seen that, you know there is no excuse for any of you. Climbing might save your life one day, and you *will* learn how to do it. And I expect you to be good at it, even though you're all handicapped by having two arms and legs."

We spent the afternoon climbing the rock face. After Professor West's demonstration, I was keen to prove myself. I climbed until my arms and legs were shaking and did pretty well, I thought. Will, however, rocketed past all of us. It was clear to me he would pass his mountaineering practical the next week.

Mid-afternoon, when we took a short break, I removed my harness to go off into the bush and 'use the facilities'. Afterward, I put my harness back on, and asked Professor West to check I'd done it properly.

"Hold it, mate. What's this?" I looked down to where the professor had grabbed my waist strap, thinking I'd done something wrong. "Take it off, Nathan." I stepped out of the harness and handed it to him. He examined the waist. "This strap is damaged. You're lucky it held you at all." He shook his head, frowning. "I checked these over this morning—can't believe I didn't see that. Well, no worries. There's an extra harness in my saddlebag. Go and get that one."

Professor West spent a long time looking over the gear before letting me put it on and resume climbing.

I noticed Tui looking at me with a frown on her face.

"All good. I've got a new one," I said.

It wasn't until late Friday evening that Tui had a chance to tell me what she had overheard. Then, I understood her earlier frown.

"Somebody cut your harness," she whispered. We were sitting on a couch near the fire, pretending to look at photos of Tui's dogs while most of the other students were engaged in a noisy ping-pong tournament in the dining hall.

"What?" I asked.

"West would never have let anyone climb with a damaged harness—he's obsessed with safety. Someone cut your harness while you had it off."

"But everyone was there. Who could have done it without being seen?"

"While you were off…doing your business, Oliver saw a lizard. We all ran over to look at it. All of us, except Professor Marshall."

"Yeah, but he was asleep. He hardly moved all day." It was hard to believe anyone would want to kill me. But then, Marshall was a man who made students ride a dangerous horse, simply because they were late to class.

"He could have easily messed with your harness and lain back down before any of us noticed. He was sleeping only a few steps from where you dropped it on the ground."

"Why would he do that?" I asked, but I knew the answer. "Because of my father. But why risk getting caught doing that when he could just make me ride Flip?"

"I don't know," replied Tui with a frown. "It doesn't make sense, does it?"

"Maybe someone else was there. Someone who followed us. It would have been easy to find out where we were headed or to follow our tracks. What if Drachenmorder had been hiding in the bush nearby, waiting for his chance?"

Tui sighed. "I don't know. Either way, that harness was damaged on purpose. I'm sure of it. You need to be extra careful, Nathan."

"Yeah. I'm beginning to think that too."

Just then, Oliver came over, pressing an ice pack to his eye. He flopped down on the couch next to Tui.

"What happened to you?" I asked.

"Hunter Godfry. That's what. Punched me in the eye."

"What did he do that for?"

"Hunter doesn't need an excuse," said Tui. "He's a bloody bully."

Oliver chuckled. "Oh, he had an excuse this time, I suppose. I beat him at ping-pong. Twice." He laughed again, though it was clear it hurt him to do so. "It was almost worth getting punched to see his face when I won the second time."

"Ooo! I should go over and punch him," snarled Tui.

"You're only half his size."

"Of course. You wouldn't see him picking on anyone bigger than himself, would you?"

"*Is* there anyone bigger than him?" I asked. Hunter wasn't the oldest student at the school, but he towered over most of them.

"Luke is probably taller," mused Tui, "but he's such a bean pole, he probably only weighs half of what Hunter does."

"So, did you tell one of the staff about it?" I asked Oliver.

Oliver laughed again. "Nah. Didn't have to. Sir Christopher was on duty. Saw it on the cameras and was on Hunter in five seconds. Gave him the whole 'honour' speech and made him scrub the kitchen floor for Miss

Brumby. And"— he unwrapped the serviette he clutched, —"Miss Brumby saw it, and gave me cookies!"

Oliver shared his prize with Tui and me. They were chocolate chip, still warm from the oven.

"You should get hit by Hunter more often," I said. Tui punched me in the arm, but Oliver only laughed.

Before the weekend was over, I was also sporting fresh bruises from Hunter. There had been another rugby game, and I couldn't resist. However, I managed to keep away from Hunter for most of the match, so I wasn't as badly off as Oliver. His eye swelled shut and turned a disgusting shade of green.

Later in the day, I approached Josh and Ella in the atrium where they sat playing Uno. Josh looked up from his cards and winced at the sight of the bruises on my arms and legs.

"You know, Nathan, you really shouldn't play rugby with Hunter."

I sat down next to him and grinned. "Yes, but it's so fun when we beat his team."

"You won today? Well done. That might be a first."

"You know, I almost feel sorry for Hunter," said Ella.

"What?" Josh looked at her like she'd gone mad.

"No, really, I do." She screwed up her face. "He doesn't have any friends."

"Who would be his friend when he bullies everyone?"

Ella sighed. "When my dad died, I got really mad. I was mad because he went and got himself killed. I was mad because it meant I had to come here. I was mad because my little sister didn't have to become a dragon slayer, but I did." She sniffed, and I pretended I didn't see the tears welling in her eyes. "I punched my sister when she said something about moving into my room when I'd gone." She laughed ruefully. "It felt really good at the time, but Mum wasn't amused. It wasn't a very good way of expressing my grief, she said. And I realised that's what it was. I wasn't mad at my sister, I was upset because Dad was dead."

"What's that got to do with Hunter?" asked Josh.

"I wonder if Hunter is just stuck in that mad stage. His dad died too, like ours did. Maybe he started punching people after his dad died, and now he can't figure out how to stop. Maybe he didn't want to come here. And he's got no friends here. And being Drachenmorder's nephew has to come with a certain expectation of excellence in dragon slaying. Maybe he's under a lot of pressure." Ella sighed. "Or maybe he's just a jerk. I don't know, and I'm not about to and go ask him."

"I can sympathise with not wanting to be here," said Josh with a sigh. "I was fine with it at first. Thought it would be a great adventure. Me, a daring dragon slayer, rescuing damsels in distress." He barked a laugh. "Yeah, right. It would be the damsels rescuing me, like Tui did the other day with Hunter. I'm such a coward." He dropped his head into his hands. Ella and I glanced at each other over his head and nodded.

"Josh," I said. "What would you say if I told you there might be another option?"

"An option that takes a different sort of bravery than the kind needed to stand up to Hunter," added Ella.

The DDL met on Sunday afternoon, with the addition of Josh, who was eager to be part of the group. We discussed the issue of my harness and Dr. Williams' suspicious death.

"So someone set Dr. Williams' house on fire, and someone tried to kill Nathan on Friday," Tui recapped. "Nathan, your dad wasn't killed by a dragon."

"He was murdered," said Josh.

I knew that. I had known ever since I read Dad's letter. But I had refused to think about it. Refused to put the word 'murder' next to my dad's name. I burst into tears.

"Josh! Look what you've done!" Ella glared across the table at Josh.

He shrugged, looking a bit miserable. "I was only saying what we were all thinking."

"Yeah, but you didn't have to blurt it out like that!"

"No," I said, bringing my sobs under control and wiping my eyes on my sleeve. "Josh is right. Dad was murdered, and I've known it for a while. I guess...I guess I didn't want to admit it to myself."

"If you're not up to it, we can meet some other time," suggested Ella.

"No, I'm okay," I said. "We need to come up with a plan for this week. What's our priority? What's our goal?"

"We need to find out who killed your dad," said Oliver. "Whoever did it is probably behind Dr. Williams' death, and the attempt on your life."

"But I thought this was the Dragon Defence League?" said Josh. "Aren't we supposed to be saving dragons, not tracking down murderers?"

"But the murderers are also probably the people who are against saving the dragons," said Oliver. "Why else would they go after Sir Archibald? He was Patriarch of the Fraternal Order of Dragon Slayers International. He was well-respected and well-liked."

I looked at Oliver in wonder. "You knew my dad?"

"No. Not really. But my dad talked about him a lot. I guess they did some missions together when they were younger."

My eyes were threatening to leak tears again. Oliver knew more about my dad than I did. My throat tightened, and I looked down to see my hands balled into fists. Dad had told me nothing. He'd lied to me. Why should I bother to try to find his killer? I took a deep breath and remembered his letter. He'd done it because he loved me. He'd done it to protect me. He'd trusted me to carry on with his work. And Oliver was right. Whoever had killed Dad was killing dragons too.

"You're right, Oliver. So if the person who killed Dad is also the person who cut my harness, who might it be?"

"It's got to be Professor Marshall, like I said to you on Friday," said Tui. "He's the only one who could have done it."

"I don't agree. Anyone could have followed us. All the staff knew where we were going and what we were doing," I said.

"But you have to admit that Marshall is the most likely culprit," said Ella.

"For sure. But who else could have done it?"

"Tui, you said that Sir Leandro told Professor West to take special care of Nathan on Friday," said Josh. "So it couldn't be either of them, right?"

"Unless," said Oliver, "what Sir Leandro meant was that West should kill Nathan. They could have been speaking in some sort of code."

"You think West cut my harness himself?"

"Seems unlikely," said Tui. "Professor West is so...nice."

"And Sir Leandro too," said Ella.

"But you can't deny they were both talking about harm coming to Nathan on Friday," argued Oliver. "They knew something was going to happen. They could have easily made it happen."

I sighed. "He's right. We should put them on the list of suspects." The others reluctantly agreed.

"Also, Drachenmorder has to be a suspect," said Oliver. "If what your dad said is true, and he's making heaps of money from dragon hunting safaris, he would have had a strong motive to stop your dad." We all readily agreed.

"And if Drachenmorder is a suspect, we have to include Sir Magnus," I said reluctantly.

"But I like Sir Magnus," said Oliver.

"I do too, but he does all the financial stuff for the school and a whole lot of other things. He must know what Drachenmorder is doing and be covering it up for him, doctoring the books. Besides..." I told them about the stray bullet when Sir Magnus took me rabbit shooting. "At the time, I didn't think he'd had anything to do with it. I still think maybe it was simply what he said it had been—a local kid being stupid—but given what we know now..."

Sir Magnus went onto the list, as well.

"At this rate, we're going to have everyone on our list of suspects," cried Ella.

"Well, I'm pretty sure it wasn't Miss Brumby," I said. Everyone agreed. Miss Brumby, the mother hen who fed us all, couldn't have killed anyone.

"That leaves Sir Christopher as the only one we haven't considered," I said. We sat in silence for a moment. Finally, Tui spoke up.

"I can't see Sir Christopher's sense of honour letting him commit murder."

"He's really good with a sword, though," said Oliver.

"They all are," said Ella. "They're dragon slayers."

We went back and forth on Sir Christopher, finally concluding we had no reason at this point to suspect him, and he didn't seem like the sort to commit murder.

Our long deliberation did little to narrow things down, especially after Oliver pointed out what we hadn't discussed yet.

"It could be someone we don't know. Someone unconnected with the school."

I sighed. "We need more information. We need to investigate the suspects on our list. Follow them. Eavesdrop on their conversations. Find out what they do when they're not in class."

We divided up our list, assigning each of us to a suspect. Josh immediately claimed Professor Marshall—he seemed eager to find out if Marshall was up to no good. Tui would focus on Professor Drachenmorder. Oliver took Sir Leandro. Ella claimed Professor West. I chose Sir Magnus.

"Good luck," I told everyone. "Stay safe, whatever you do. Don't get caught doing anything you shouldn't be."

"You too, Nathan," said Tui. "You're the one they're still after."

Chapter 10
A Change of Plans

Sir Leandro was technically Oliver's target, but I had a perfect opportunity to size him up myself on Tuesday.

"Nathan, do you have a minute?" he asked at the end of class. "Walk with me. I need to drop my laptop off in my office."

We crunched along the drive toward the chalets. Sir Leandro was silent for a minute, and I wondered what he was up to. After Friday's harness incident, I was on high alert and didn't like the idea of going anywhere alone with a staff member.

"Nathan, I don't know how much you understand about your father's activities." He paused, but I decided not to tell him anything. He carried on. "But his work was…controversial. In recent years, he spent much of his time seeking out dragons. Spending time with them. He became fluent in Draconic and came to view dragons not as monsters, but as individuals."

I let Sir Leandro talk, not knowing exactly what his words were leading up to.

"He was a visionary. Ahead of his time. He believed dragons should be preserved, not killed, and he used his position as Patriarch of FODSI to try to push his ideas. He wanted us all to become dragon savers instead of dragon slayers." Sir Leandro sighed. "Of course, he made enemies. People stuck in the old ways; people who, rightly or wrongly, benefit from the dragon slaying profession. When your father disappeared, I thought he must have been murdered. But now I'm not so sure."

"You think a dragon killed him?"

"No. A dragon would never kill your father, Nathan." Sir Leandro stopped walking and glanced around before leaning in close and whispering, "Nathan. Your father isn't dead."

"What?" It was the last thing I'd expected to hear.

"When your father went missing, I suspected foul play. I went looking for him. I found his companion's body but not his."

"What?" I said again, my mind reeling.

Sir Leandro took me by the arm. "Come. You should sit down." I let him lead me into his chalet and sit me down in an armchair in the lounge. He sat in an identical chair facing me. He leaned forward, elbows on his knees and his hands clasped in front of him.

"Your father's last mission was a diplomatic one. It was a meeting between him, the head of the Royal Society of Dragon Slayers, and a representative from the New Zealand Draconic Council."

"He met with a dragon?"

Sir Leandro nodded. "He was hoping to persuade the Royal Society of Dragon Slayers to back his plans for a gradual 'reveal' of the existence of dragons to the general public. The head of the Royal Society of Dragon Slayers was killed during that mission—slain by a sword. Your father wasn't. I'm quite sure of that. When I got to the scene, I found the tracks of five different men—your father, his companion, and three others. As far as I could tell, one of the men arrived alone and engaged Archie and his companion in a sword fight. In that fight, your father was forced off a cliff."

"But he's alive?"

Sir Leandro held up a finger. "The man who attacked them ran from the scene in the direction he'd come from. The other two sets of tracks arrived on the scene from a different route and led to the edge of the cliff. Two sets of tracks led to the cliff and three came back." He stared hard at me. "Your father went with them."

"How did he survive the cliff?" I asked.

Sir Leandro laughed. "I wondered the same, so I peeked over the edge. A few metres down I could see a wide ledge. He must have landed on it. Why his pursuer didn't check to see he was dead, I don't know. But clearly he didn't. His tracks never went near the edge."

"So the other two men? They rescued Dad?"

"It would seem so."

"Then why is he still missing?"

"I can only assume they kidnapped him. He got into a car with the men, and they drove off. Once they got to the road, I couldn't track them anymore. They could be anywhere by now."

"Who would kidnap him? And why?"

"I don't know. Your father had plenty of enemies, none more set against him than Claus Drachenmorder."

"So Drachenmorder did it?"

Sir Leandro shook his head. "I think Drachenmorder was behind the attempt on his life. The kidnapping? It makes no sense at all."

I took a deep breath.

"Dad's alive."

Sir Leandro held his hand up. "Was alive, Nathan. I don't know where he is, who kidnapped him or why."

"But you think he's alive."

"I do. Why would you rescue someone you wanted dead when all you had to do was push him the rest of the way off the cliff?" He lifted his eyes to the clock on the wall. "You're late for your next class."

"Traps and Tricks with Professor Marshall," I said.

Sir Leandro made a face like he'd just bitten into a lemon.

"Sir Leandro, my climbing harness was cut on Friday. Could Professor Marshall have done it?"

"I've been wondering the same thing. Marshall never liked your father, and he was clearly pleased when Archie vanished. But I wouldn't have thought of him as the murdering type." He smiled. "Of course, it's hard to imagine anyone committing murder, isn't it? I suppose only murderers can imagine it." He shuddered. "This is a lot to take in, Nathan. Skip Marshall's class this morning. I'll talk to him. I'll tell him you became ill after my class, and I sent you to bed. Take some time to digest all of this."

"Thanks," I said, rising to go.

"Oh, and Nathan."

"Yes?"

"Be very careful. Don't trust Professor Drachenmorder."

I nodded and stepped out the door.

I was lying in bed, staring at the ceiling, turning over in my head the idea that Dad was still alive, when Tui burst into my dorm room along with all the other members of the DDL.

"Oh my god! You're okay."

"You're not supposed to be in here," I said, sitting up. The girls were strictly forbidden to enter the boys' rooms and vice versa. "What's going on?"

"That's what we want to know," said Oliver.

"When Sir Leandro came into Marshall's class and said you'd gotten sick—" began Tui.

"We thought he'd poisoned you or something," finished Ella.

"You weren't sick in class, that's for sure," said Josh.

"And we saw you walking with him. That was a really stupid thing to do, you know? He's on our suspect list."

"Not anymore," I said. They all sat down on Oliver's and my beds, and I told them what Sir Leandro had said about my father.

I'd just finished my story when Professor Marshall stormed into the room.

"Girls are not allowed in the boys' dormitory. Out. Kitchen duty for all of you. And Mister McMannis, why were you not in class this morning?"

"I was sick. Stomach ache. I'm feeling a bit better now."

"We came in to see how he was doing," explained Tui. Professor Marshall gave her a withering look.

"You know the rules. Kitchen duty for you. Right now. Go!"

Tui scampered out followed by the others. Marshall took a hard look at me then left, slamming the door behind him.

Dad was alive. Okay, maybe alive. But he wasn't known to be dead, and that was good enough for me. I bounced through the next couple of days almost giddy with relief.

Then the reality set in. Dad might be alive, but no one knew where he was. Unknown assailants had captured and taken him to who knew where. I had to find him.

"Guys, I've got to get out of here and find my dad," I announced at the next DDL meeting.

"Of course we do," said Oliver.

"The question is, do we have enough information yet? Drachenmorder seems to be at the centre of it all. We shouldn't leave here until we're sure we've gotten all the information we can," said Tui.

"We?" I asked.

"Of course!" said Oliver. "You don't think we'd let you go without us, do you?"

"I just thought, since he's my dad..."

"We've all lost our dads, Nathan," said Ella, blinking furiously. "If we can get even one back, we will."

"Besides," said Oliver, "your dad is...like...our leader. He's the one who changed our thinking about dragons. He's the one who befriended dragons."

"Befriended dragons..." I said. "Befriended dragons. Guys! What if the dragons know where my dad is?"

"You want to ask the dragons about your dad?" asked Josh. "Isn't that sort of...dangerous?"

"But they were friendly with him."

"Yeah, but they don't know *us*. And we haven't even been taught how to approach a dragon yet—that's second-year material. And how's your Draconic coming, eh?"

"Josh is right," said Tui. "We aren't equipped to seek out dragons."

I slumped in my chair, defeated.

"Yep. We'll have to do some extra studying," said Oliver.

"If we divide up the material and each focus on one thing, it'll go faster," said Tui. "I can already track just about everything else, so it wouldn't take me long to learn how to track dragons."

I smiled. We were going to do it. We were going to find Dad.

"So, if it took us a month to get ready," I said, "that would mean starting out to find the dragons in mid-November."

"We'll still have to worry about avalanches, and we'll be snowed on, for sure, but it could be worse," said Oliver.

"Couldn't we wait until December?" asked Ella.

"No," I said. "Who knows what they're doing to Dad? Who knows how long he has before they kill him? We've got to go as soon as we're ready."

The others nodded and, soon, we were making our plans. Two 'experts' per subject, in case something should happen to one of us.

Naturally, Tui was our first choice for a tracking expert. Oliver volunteered to join her.

Ella and I were to focus on Draconic and how to approach a dragon.

Oliver and Josh took on mountaineering.

"Can you handle both of them, Oliver?" I asked.

"Of course I can, I'm precocious!" He grinned, and Tui rolled her eyes.

"I already know some mountaineering—my dad taught me. But everyone needs to learn the climbing part. Josh and I will learn how to choose a route and everything, but we can't carry you," warned Oliver.

"And we all need to keep trying to find out as much as possible about what Drachenmorder is up to. And probably Marshall, too. The more information we have when we leave, the better," I said. "Keep your eyes and ears open."

"And whatever you do," added Tui, "Don't breathe a word of this to anyone else."

We all nodded grimly. I didn't want to think what would happen if Professor Drachenmorder found out what we were planning.

Chapter 11
Allies and Enemies

A month wasn't enough time to learn an entire language. Draconic was full of harsh and strange sounds, and the sentence structure was baffling.

"So, if I say 'Dog bite me was', that means 'I bit the dog'?" asked Ella as we pored over the Draconic textbook.

"But if I say 'Me dog bite was', that's 'The dog bit me'." I sighed. "This is impossible."

So, instead of trying to learn the entire language, we focused at first on the words and phrases we thought we might need.

We come in peace.
I am Sir Archibald's son.
We are friends.
Help us find Sir Archibald.
Do you know where my dad is?
Please don't eat us.

Pronunciation was tricky too, as we found out in Draconic class when we tried out our new words on Sir Leandro.

"*Skrgleyit.*" I called as I entered the classroom. Sir Leandro raised his good eyebrow, and I saw the hint of a smile in his eye.

"That's 'good afternoon', right?" I said.

"Not quite," said Sir Leandro. "*Skrgleyīt* is 'good afternoon'. *Skrgleyit*—what you said—means 'good tasting'."

I gulped.

"Not exactly something you'd want to say when meeting a dragon, huh?" I said weakly, sitting down.

Sir Leandro smiled. "That is why you have two full years studying Draconic before we send you out to meet a dragon. Don't worry, Nathan. It's a common mistake for beginners. But in two years, you'll have no problems."

I glanced at Ella, who looked about as pale as I felt. We had one month.

In addition to our extra studies, we still needed to find out who was working with Drachenmorder, and how he had been involved in my dad's disappearance. We could take Sir Leandro off our list of suspects, but I still didn't know what to make of Sir Magnus. He was clearly right in the middle of Drachenmorder's schemes, but he also seemed to really like my dad and went out of his way to make sure I was doing okay. I took advantage of his attentions and went 'rabbit shooting' with him as often as he offered to take me.

Mostly, we talked about my dad.

"He took a real academic view of dragons," Sir Magnus said one day. "Always took a long time over his missions. I think he did a lot more studying than killing, actually. He'd have made a good teacher, if he'd made it to retirement. I encouraged him to apply for the headmaster position here about fifteen years ago when it opened up last. He didn't want it. Said he wasn't cut out for administration." He shrugged. "He was probably right.

He wouldn't have done as good a job as Professor Drachenmorder has."

It was the perfect opening.

"What does Professor Drachenmorder do all the time? He only teaches the one class, doesn't he? And I almost never see him around the school," I said.

"Well, there's a lot more to running a school than teaching. Professor Drachenmorder's primary job is to secure funding to keep the school running."

"The sheep don't bring in enough?" I feigned ignorance of Drachenmorder's sideline.

Sir Magnus laughed. "Not by a long shot. No, the school depends upon donors."

"Donors? But isn't the school supposed to be secret? Are the donors dragon slayers?"

"No, we dragon slayers are rarely wealthy. The donors are a…select group…mostly wealthy businessmen who know how to keep their mouths shut."

"So what's in it for the donors if they can't even say they've donated the money?"

Sir Magnus chuckled. "That's Professor Drachenmorder's genius, you see. He lets the donors go out on a mission with a real dragon slayer."

"Isn't that dangerous?"

"Oh, when they get close, the donor just stands back and watches from a safe distance. And then, for an extra donation, they can have their picture taken with the dragon once it's been slain." Sir Magnus smiled. "It's all terribly clever, and a great way to secure funds for the school."

"So does Professor Drachenmorder take the donors out himself?"

"He acts as host for all the missions with donors. His role is to keep the donor safe. There is always another dragon slayer who leads the mission, although Professor Drachenmorder has done the slaying a couple of times, when the primary dragon slayer…er…didn't make it."

"If Professor Drachenmorder has killed dragons, why isn't he knighted?"

"Ah, he's so modest. Says that dragon slaying is merely his job, and he won't accept a knighthood just for doing his job. He's quite the man."

"Did he know my dad?"

Sir Magnus frowned. "He and your dad never saw eye to eye. I don't know why. You know, your dad actually tried to dissuade me from taking this job—didn't want me working for Professor Drachenmorder." He shrugged. "I think he just didn't give the professor a chance to show him what a good bloke he is."

As far as I could tell, Sir Magnus believed everything he said about Drachenmorder and everything he said about my dad. Drachenmorder was a genius and could do no wrong in his eyes. Dad had been a great man and a model dragon slayer. It was almost a relief to me. If I thought Sir Magnus was only pretending to have been my father's friend, and he knew all about Drachenmorder's unsavoury activities, I would never have been able to trust anyone again.

Sir Magnus might be a fool, but he wasn't our enemy.

Of course, on top of all our 'extracurricular' activities, we still had to go to classes. But now, we had a real incentive to do well at them while also appearing to be enthusiastic about the profession of dragon slaying.

Fortunately, in mountaineering class, Professor West was teaching us about lead climbing—a skill we were going to need if we were to find any dragons.

"So far, I've always had a rope ready for you, so you've just clipped into the rope and climbed. That's fine, if you're the second member of a climbing party. But if you're first, you have to attach the rope as you go. That means you're climbing above your rope. This is what we call lead climbing."

Oliver and Josh gave a thumbs-up behind Professor West's back. They had been reading up on lead climbing and were excited to have a chance to practise in class. When Professor West pulled out a cam, Josh identified it right away.

"That's used for protection. You stick it into cracks in the rock and attach the rope to it."

"Well done, Josh." The professor looked surprised. Josh didn't normally volunteer information in class. "Can you show everyone how it works?"

Josh blushed. "Well, I've never actually done it. I've only read about it."

Professor West laughed, "That's okay. Here, I'll walk you through it."

Josh and Oliver asked detailed questions throughout the lesson. Afterwards, Professor West praised them.

"Josh and Oliver win the prize for most well-prepared for class today. Good work. Keep it up, and you'll be excellent lead climbers."

Both boys beamed.

Ella leaned in close and whispered in my ear. "Look at Josh. Might be the first compliment he's gotten from a teacher here. He's standing taller."

I hadn't noticed, but Ella was right. Josh looked different. I glanced around at the rest of the group. We all looked different. More focused on the task at hand. More determined. These classes weren't merely training us for some romantic ideal of a dragon slaying job—they were for real. Now, they were training us for an actual mission we all believed in. A mission that would save my father…we hoped.

In combat class, Oliver and I played the part of dragon-slayers-in-training with genuine enthusiasm. Not that either of us ever wanted to kill a dragon, but what pre-teen boy doesn't dream of swashbuckling adventures with a sword? I guess we got a little out of hand.

"I name thee Slash," I cried one day as I picked up my sword at the beginning of class.

"I name thee Sharpie!" cried Oliver as he selected his.

Tui snorted. "*Sharpie?*"

"Don't ever name your sword." Sir Christopher's voice made us jump. It was authoritative and commanding. "You name it, and you get too close to it. You start to believe it is a living thing. It starts to possess you. The next thing you know, you are doing unspeakable atrocities with it. A sword is nothing but steel. There are good swords and there are ones that are not so good, but the only bad swords are the ones with names."

We regained our seriousness then, and even Oliver was quiet for much of the class.

Sir Christopher showed us how to demolish two targets in quick succession, with one cut flowing seamlessly into the next. It looked like dancing when he did it.

It looked like stumbling when we tried it. After an hour, I could make the first cut perfectly and make it flow into the second, but by then there was no power behind my arm, and I couldn't even slice through a pool noodle.

"Put more attitude into it, Nathan," encouraged Sir Christopher. "Your form is not bad, but you lack conviction. The key to a good strike is conviction. When the form is good and the cause is honourable, your conviction will bring the blade home."

I tried to muster some of the professor's conviction. Given my previous performance it wasn't easy but, by the end of class, I could slice through two targets. Not gracefully, but I could do it.

I can't say I liked Sir Christopher—he was too gruff and formal—but I respected him. After class, I felt like I needed to apologise for our childish behaviour. While the others walked out the door, I lingered behind. Sir Christopher didn't see me standing there—his back to us, he was unbuckling the sword he wore every day for class. He set it gently on the table and gave it a pat.

"Well done, my dear Dragonbiter. Well done."

I turned and ran out the door.

"Just because he talks to his sword doesn't mean he's a murderer," said Tui.

"But he gave us that speech about not naming your sword."

I had caught up to Tui before she entered the dining hall and told her what I'd overheard. The others were already inside.

"Relax, Nathan. Sir Christopher isn't even on our list of suspects."

"Maybe he should be."

"That's ridiculous. Sir Christopher? No way. Come on, I'm starving." She pulled me into the dining hall where loud cheering chased all thoughts of Sir Christopher out of my head. Will had passed his final six-month exam. Tui and I hurried to join the festivities as Miss Brumby carried out a giant cake from the kitchen.

Chapter 12
The Client

On Saturday morning, Ella and I were in the library practicing Draconic. We looked up briefly when we heard a helicopter fly low over the building. A few minutes later, Tui raced in to tell us what was happening.

"A client," she hissed breathlessly. "Drachenmorder's got a client. They're going to his office."

"Who?"

"I don't know who it is—some short guy in a suit. Come on. I need your help. I'm going to eavesdrop, but I need you to keep watch."

"What?" said Ella. "You're going to sneak into Drachenmorder's office? You'll get caught."

"Not if you guys keep a lookout. Come on." She slammed our books shut.

"What about Oliver and Josh?" I asked as we scurried through the tussocks behind the staff chalets.

"They're already here."

As we crept toward the back of Drachenmorder's chalet, I saw the two boys crouched underneath the building's back porch. Oliver smiled and waved. Josh looked left and right, then waved us forward.

With a quick glance at the windows, we sprinted across the open space between the tall tussocks and the chalet, and ducked under the porch with the others.

"Are they in there?" whispered Tui.

"They've just gone into his office," replied Oliver. "Josh and I did what you suggested and ran past them like we were playing tag or something."

"Yeah, and Oliver nearly smashed right into them," said Josh.

"And?" asked Tui.

"It's Graziano Neroni!"

We all gave Oliver blank looks. He rolled his eyes.

"Sorry, Oliver. We're not all precocious like you," said Ella. "Who is Graziano Neroni?"

Oliver sighed. "He's some mafia guy from Chicago. He was convicted of rigging the U.S. presidential election last year, but he bribed his way out of jail. It was in all the papers. Didn't you see it? He's considered one of the most powerful people in the world. He's super rich."

"The perfect type for a dragon safari," I commented.

"Come on, let's get in there." Tui started to rise, but I held her back.

"What's our plan?"

Tui rolled her eyes, but I continued. "We can't simply march into Drachenmorder's office. We need to be stealthy. We can't be seen. Has anyone been into the back of Drachenmorder's chalet before?"

"I haven't been in the back, but I have seen it through the door from the reception area. There's a kitchen behind Drachenmorder's office, and the back door opens into it. I was going to go in and see if I could listen through the wall. If I can't hear from there, I'll go and listen through the door." Tui seemed to think she had it covered.

"No, you won't be doing that," said Oliver. "Sir Magnus is in the reception area right now."

"Well, then I'd better be able to hear something through the wall. I need lookouts."

"I'll stay out here and keep an eye out for anyone approaching from another building," volunteered Josh.

"Great. Oliver, can you station yourself at the door to the reception area? If Sir Magnus decides to come to the kitchen, we'll need your innocent face and clever lies to explain our presence or to give the rest of us time to vanish."

Oliver grinned and saluted Tui.

"I'll watch the back door," said Ella. "Josh, if you see anyone, just signal to me. Don't come to the door."

"That leaves me," I said.

"You come listen with me. That way, we can catch as much as possible of the conversation."

I nodded. "Sounds like a plan. Ready?" Everyone nodded, and we crept out from under the porch to take up our positions. We tiptoed up the steps, and Tui eased the back door open. It scraped against the sill at one point and we all froze, holding our breath. When nothing happened, we slipped in through the door.

It was a bachelor's kitchen—breakfast dishes lay piled in the sink, a dirty coffee mug sat on the table surrounded by crumbs, and an open packet of cookies formed the table's centrepiece.

"Ooo! Tim Tams!" mouthed Oliver as we padded past. Tui gave him a withering look.

Oliver and Ella took up their stations by the doors. Tui and I found our access to the wall between the kitchen and Drachenmorder's office hindered by cabinetry. I frowned, but Tui deftly hopped onto the benchtop and crouched there with her ear pressed to the wall. I followed her lead, and soon our heads were bent close together against the wall.

I could hear Drachenmorder's voice, but it was so muffled I couldn't make out what he was saying.

"Can you understand?" I mouthed to Tui. She shook her head.

I remembered a spy story I'd read years ago. I opened the cabinet above my head and drew out two tall water glasses.

Tui smiled. She knew what to do. We placed the open end of the glasses against the wall and our ears to the bottom.

"It works," whispered Tui, surprise in her voice. I couldn't believe it either, but I said nothing. I could understand the men's words now, and I didn't want to miss anything. Drachenmorder was speaking.

"For you, I've scoped out a nice southern blue dragon."

Neroni's flat Chicago accent would have made me laugh if I hadn't been so nervous about what we were doing. "How about one of those?" he said. I could picture him pointing toward the massive green dragon head near the ceiling.

"Ha! Ha! I think you'll find the southern blue to your liking. She is not as large as the green, but she is vicious. And..." I heard Drachenmorder walk across the room and open a cabinet. "I have a new toy for you to play with."

"Oh ho! What is this?"

"A little gift from a friend in the American military."

"This is more than a little gift."

"A very nice little gift. It's an XM25 CDTE. Also known as the Punisher. Fires twenty-five millimetre grenades. Can pierce armour fifty millimetres thick and has an effective firing range of five hundred metres against a dragon."

Neroni whistled appreciatively. "Illegal?"

Drachenmorder laughed. "Not even deployed yet. Still in testing, but it's a beauty."

Both men laughed, and Neroni said, "I like you, Claus. You're my kind of guy. So, what does it cost to use this new toy of yours?"

"That depends in part on how good a shot you are. Every round for this thing costs a thousand U.S. dollars. That's in addition to the standard safari fee."

"Naturally."

"Then, of course, there is a surcharge to help cover any...issues, if you should accidentally mention the existence of this weapon to anyone."

"Of course."

"I would think that six hundred and fifty thousand U.S. dollars should cover it. Ah, plus twenty bucks if you want the 'I killed a dragon' T-shirt."

"Oh, surely you can throw in the T-shirt for free?"

"Perhaps I can." Drachenmorder laughed. "We'll leave in the morning. Let's have a drink while we fill out the paperwork, eh?"

Tui and I looked at each other.

"Drinks," she mouthed at me. My eyes flew to the sideboard where bottles of all shapes and sizes were lined up. Then I looked at Oliver, whose eyes had widened at the sound of the men leaving the office. We eased ourselves off the benchtop as quietly and quickly as we could, but we weren't fast enough. Drachenmorder was at the kitchen door giving instructions to Sir Magnus about the contract for Neroni.

Oliver waved us out the back door. "I'll stall them," he mouthed. "Go!"

There was a thump as Drachenmorder pushed on the door and Oliver resisted his efforts.

"Go!" he hissed.

We sprinted out the door. I sent Ella and Tui to the Lodge with Josh.

"Act normally. Pretend Oliver and I are...I don't know...studying. I'm going to stay here and make sure Oliver is okay."

While the others ran for safety, I ducked under the back porch and held my breath. In our haste, we had left the back door wide open. I was thankful we had because it allowed me to hear what was going on inside.

There was another thump on the kitchen door, and then Oliver must have let it open because I heard heavy steps as Drachenmorder stumbled into the room. Oliver didn't give him time to ask what he was doing there. His words were rapid and excited.

"Professor Drachenmorder! Oh! You *are* here! I couldn't get the front door open, and I was worried no one was around. Professor, one of the toilets is clogged. It's flooding our whole room!"

Drachenmorder made a sound of disgust then called to Sir Magnus.

"Magnus, go see what you can do about the toilet. And if it's clogged with anything…unnatural…find out who the culprit is. That's the *third* clogged toilet this year."

"Certainly," replied Sir Magnus. "Oliver, run along. I need to grab my tools and a mop. I'll be there in a minute."

"Thanks, Sir Magnus!"

I was pressed against the side of the chalet waiting for Oliver when he dashed down the porch steps. Spotting me there, he grinned and gave me a thumbs-up. I fell into step beside him.

"That was brilliant, Oliver."

"Yeah, and the best part is that now we get to go upstairs and flood the bathroom!" He caught my shocked look. "Well, we've got to make it look real, right?"

I grinned back.

The DDL met that evening for an emergency 'study' session. As I walked into classroom one with Oliver, I tried not to glance nervously at the camera.

"Who's on duty?" I asked.

"Marshall," replied Oliver with a fake smile.

"Lovely."

We sat down and opened our books. Tui and Ella arrived shortly afterward.

"What are we studying tonight?" Tui asked.

"Plumbing," I replied. Oliver laughed.

"Okay. Tell us everything," said Ella. "What *was* the toilet overflow all about?"

I held up a hand. "Wait until Josh gets here. Then we'll tell you."

"Where is Josh, anyway?" asked Oliver.

Josh's entrance answered his question.

"What happened to you?" asked Ella. Josh's face was streaked with mud, and there was a cut on his right ear, dripping blood. His shirt was torn.

"Guess," he said, flopping heavily into a chair.

Ella pulled a tissue out of her bag and handed it to him. "Your ear is dripping."

"Thanks." Josh pressed the tissue against his ear.

"Hunter again?" asked Tui. Josh nodded.

"Did you tell someone this time?" asked Ella. "You can't just put up with this forever."

Josh laughed. "Yeah, I thought West was on duty tonight, so I went to the duty office."

"And found Marshall, instead," said Oliver.

"And?"

Josh sighed. "Marshall sent Hunter to Drachenmorder's office."

Tui snorted. "Yeah, that'll do a lot of good. Hunter and Uncle Claus are probably in his office right now laughing about it." Her hands balled into fists and, for a moment, I was worried she was going to punch

103

something. Instead she pasted on a smile and waved at the security camera. Jaw clenched, she muttered, "Way to go, Marshall. Well done."

"Forget it," said Josh. "Tell us what happened this morning."

Tui and I related the conversation between Drachenmorder and Neroni. At the mention of the illegal, experimental, military grenade launcher, everyone's eyes widened.

Ella shook her head. "I wonder what else he's got in that gun cabinet in his office."

"Doesn't matter, does it," said Tui. "That one weapon is probably enough to put him in jail."

"Tui's right. We could have him in jail tomorrow. All we have to do is call the police," said Oliver.

"Let's do it right now." Tui pulled out her phone. She dialled 111 and put the mobile to her ear. A moment later, she spoke. "Police...um...no, but..." She frowned. "Oh...okay. Thank you." She hung up, scowling. "It's not an emergency, so we have to call the local police station."

I pulled out my own phone and googled. "There's a station in Alexandra." I dialled the number. It rang, and rang. Eventually, an answering machine picked up.

"You have reached the Alexandra police station. Hours of operation are nine a.m. to five p.m. Outside of these hours, please dial 111 for emergency services."

I sighed. "We'll have to wait until tomorrow morning."

We lapsed into silence. "So, if we can get Drachenmorder arrested, he wouldn't be able to be headmaster anymore, would he?" Oliver's words shook me out of my thoughts.

"And Sir Leandro would take his place, since he's the deputy headmaster," said Ella with a smile.

I smiled back. "That would make it a lot easier to leave here and search for my dad." My mind raced

104

through the possibilities. If Drachenmorder was in jail, we might even be able to get Sir Leandro to help search for Dad. We could openly prepare to rescue him. Everything would be easier. Hope blossomed in my chest.

"Right. We've got to make that phone call tomorrow," declared Tui.

Chapter 13
Another Change of Plans

I woke confused. Sir Leandro was shaking me. It was still dark outside.

"Wake up, Nathan," he hissed in my ear. "Wake up."

"Huh?" I said.

"Shh. Nathan, you and your friends need to get out of here. Now."

I sat up, wide awake.

"Joshua told Professor Drachenmorder about your plans."

"What?" I almost shouted it, and Sir Leandro clapped his hand over my mouth.

"I walked into Drachenmorder's chalet earlier this evening to see about taking some annual leave, but from the waiting room, I heard Joshua with him. I listened. I know what you are planning. Drachenmorder knows what you're planning. He knows that you know about the illegal gun, and he knows you're planning to search for your father. None of you is safe here anymore. You have to leave."

"But the cameras."

"I'm on duty tonight. I've cut power to the whole place to kill the cameras. But I can't give you long. Maybe fifteen minutes."

I woke Oliver and sent him to the girls' room to get them up. Then I shoved clothing into my backpack while Sir Leandro gave me instructions.

"Best place to start is the place where your father disappeared. I've marked it on here." He handed me a folded map, which I stowed in my pack. "You'll need to avoid leaving tracks—Drachenmorder will follow you. You should have rope and climbing gear and tents...but there's not time. Here is my own gear. Take it. It will help." He thrust a bag into my hands.

"Thank you. But, why are you helping us?"

Sir Leandro put his hands on my shoulders. "Nathan. If your father is alive, he will be expecting you."

The last thing I did before leaving was to lift my mattress and retrieve my father's letter.

Sir Leandro ushered us all down the steps. By the door was another bag, which he gave to Ella.

"Food." Then, one by one, he shook our hands. "Go safely, my friends. I'll do what I can here to slow down the search party. Don't stop anywhere tonight. Get as far away as possible before dawn. Upstream is good. However, I suggest a few downstream tracks first."

We stumbled silently across the grass toward the water, making plenty of tracks, and heading downstream. Ten minutes later, we turned and scrambled upstream. In the darkness, we moved more slowly than I had hoped. I could hear Ella sniffling—she didn't like doing this sort of thing even in daylight. I imagined how loudly she would be complaining if we weren't all terrified of being caught.

A million questions knocked around in my head as we hopped from rock to rock in the moonlight. Why did Josh tell Drachenmorder what we were doing? How much did he tell? Did Drachenmorder know Dad was still alive? How long before someone started after us? What was happening to Josh now? Where were we going to go? How were we going to find Dad? Were we ready for this?

The only question I knew the answer to was the last one. We were definitely not ready.

After a couple of hours, the stream vanished. We continued for a short way up the dry creek bed before that, too, gave way to tussock dotted with rocks.

"Can we take a break?" asked Oliver, panting. It was the first time any of us had spoken since we left the Lodge. We all sat down on a broad boulder. I looked up for the first time.

"Oh, wow," I whispered. The moon, which had lighted our way until now, had just set behind the mountains, and the pitch black sky sparkled with more stars than I'd ever seen.

"That's awesome," said Tui. Oliver murmured his agreement.

"My feet hurt," complained Ella.

We sat for only a few minutes. I checked the time on my phone.

"It's three a.m. We've still got a few more hours before we'll need to find a hiding spot."

"Where are we going, anyway?" asked Tui.

"For tonight, we're simply trying to get as far away from school as possible. Sir Leandro gave me a map that shows the place where Dad disappeared. Tomorrow, we'll head there to start our search."

"We'd better make sure we don't get lost in the dark tonight," said Oliver. "Even with a map, if we don't know where we are, we won't be able to find where we need to go."

"Well, we've come right up that creek. So we know where we are now."

"But from here?" asked Tui. The land spread out in a series of featureless mounds and dips, all covered in tussock. "None of this is going to show up on the map to tell us where we are."

"Maybe we should just stay here?" suggested Ella.

"No. We need to keep moving. Sir Leandro said to go as far as we could tonight." I thought if we could find a distant landmark and walk toward it, we could get our bearings in the morning. But, with the moon gone, I couldn't even see a landmark. "I think we need to go straight across this and hope we come to some obvious feature we can find on the map."

"Right, then," said Tui, rising. "Let's go. I'm getting cold sitting still."

We carried on through the tussocks. Where there were rocks we stayed on the rocks, but much of the way was swampy. I was sure we were leaving a trail, but there was no other way to go. I only hoped that by the time someone found our trail we would be long gone.

After about half an hour, Tui spotted a tor, and we made toward it. We stopped briefly at the outcrop, sheltering from the wind. No one spoke much. Oliver yawned.

From there, we headed downhill and ended up in a swampy area that got wetter and wetter the farther we went.

"We can't go on like this." Ella's voice shook. "My feet are soaked."

"We need to keep going," I replied. "It's bound to get drier up ahead."

It didn't.

"There has to be a better way," cried Ella, stopping and crossing her arms.

"Fine, you tell us which way we should go." Ella had been grumbling ever since we'd left the creek bed. I was tired, and my feet were wet too. I was sick of listening to her.

"Well, I don't know," she said, throwing up her arms. "I wasn't the one focusing on mountaineering skills, I was learning Draconic."

Oliver yawned. "Josh and I were supposed to be the mountaineering experts. But I've mostly been walking with my eyes closed. Can you sleepwalk if you try to?"

In different circumstances, Oliver might have gotten us out of the mess, but he seemed too tired to think straight. So we kept on, wading through the muck for another half hour.

When Oliver sank to his knees in the mud, we turned around.

By the time we made it back to the tor, the sky was beginning to lighten in the east. With a little more light, it was easy to see that if we'd gone a bit further to our right where a slight, but rocky, ridge curved off from the tor, we could have avoided all the swampy areas.

We made good time on firm ground with the growing light, but we were out in the open. We would be easily visible once the sun was up.

"Keep your eyes open for somewhere we can hide. It'll be fully light soon." Tui's nerves showed in her voice and echoed my own fears. "Stay on the rocks, so we're harder to follow."

Twenty minutes later, Oliver pointed down a steep slope to a brush-filled gully. "Down there?"

We stumbled down the slope. I was dead on my feet. Suddenly Tui, who was in front, disappeared with a cry. It took me a moment to realise that she'd slipped and tumbled over a drop-off, invisible in the half-light.

"Tui!" I gingerly made my way with the others to where she'd disappeared.

"Tui!"

Tui's voice floated up from the darkness below. "I'm okay. It's only a short drop." I heard her moving around. "I actually think this would be a great place for us to stop. It's really sheltered, and there's water."

The rest of us carefully climbed down the rock face into a room-like space under the arching branches of the stunted trees in the gully. A tiny rivulet wound through the area, but there was still plenty of room for us to spread out.

"Can we sleep, now?" asked Oliver, who looked like he was going to drop off no matter what I said.

"Yes, let's get some sleep. This is as safe a spot as we're going to find."

It was cold, even in the shelter of the gully. I was glad we were all dragon slayer's children—it meant we were well prepared for the outdoors. Even Ella, who preferred the mall to the wilderness, had a proper down sleeping bag and mat. Within minutes, we were all stretched out in our sleeping bags and, in spite of the excitement and fear of the night, I slept soundly.

Chapter 14
Flight

When I woke, blinking against a ray of sunlight peeking through the branches above, Oliver was standing and stretching. Tui was sitting, wrapped in her sleeping bag, with her back against a tree. Ella was still asleep.

"What time is it?" I asked.

Oliver pulled his phone out of his backpack. "Eleven twenty-three."

"I'm starving," I said. "Sir Leandro gave us some food?"

"Ella's got it," said Tui.

At the sound of her name, Ella stirred.

"Do I have to get up?" she mumbled. "There's an eel in the bathtub, Mum."

We all giggled.

"Ella?" Tui called.

Ella snorted and shook her head then opened her eyes. She blinked, a confused look creasing her face, and then dismay spread across her features.

"I really hoped last night had been a dream." She sighed and sat up.

"We were wondering about the food Sir Leandro gave us," I said.

"In my pack. You can get it." She waved an arm at her pack and yawned. Tui pulled the bag from Ella's pack and opened it.

"Plenty of food but, unless someone's got a stove and a pot, it won't do us a lot of good. Porridge and hot cocoa mix is what he gave us for breakfast. There's crackers and peanut butter, and a block of cheese, and a couple of packets of instant ramen noodles too. Oh, and chocolate," she added, waving a large Caramello bar in the air.

"He gave me a bag of gear. Let's see what we've got."

I hauled out the bag Sir Leandro had passed me in the dark. In it were two climbing harnesses loaded with the necessary hardware, a long hank of rope, a fully stocked first aid kit, a personal locator beacon, a roll of toilet paper, a tiny backpacking stove, a pair of nesting pots, and plastic dinnerware for two.

"Just what we need," I said, handing the cooking equipment to Tui, who'd offered to prepare our breakfast.

I took another look in the bag. At the bottom was an envelope. I pulled it out and opened it.

"He gave us money too," I said in wonder. "Two hundred dollars."

"What are we going to do with money out here?" asked Ella, finally crawling out of her sleeping bag.

"Who knows where we'll have to go to find Nathan's dad?" said Tui. "If he got into a car with his kidnappers, he's not likely to still be out here in the mountains."

"Excellent." Ella snatched the envelope from me. "Let's get out of here and find somewhere with hot, running water. Do you think this is enough for a hotel room?"

"Ella, we didn't run away from the school to go on holiday. Remember, someone tried to kill my dad, and then he was kidnapped. We're here to find him."

Ella sighed and threw the envelope back at me. "I know." She ran her fingers through her hair, then rummaged in her pack. "Aw! Anybody have a comb? I forgot mine."

"Comb?" I asked. "What's wrong with your fingers?"

"Here, you can use mine," said Tui, tossing a blue one to Ella.

"Thanks," replied Ella, taking the comb to her hair with enthusiasm.

"Oh, Ella," called Oliver. "Tui didn't tell you, did she?"

"Tell me what?"

"She's got lice."

Ella picked up a stick and threw it at him. Oliver giggled.

With our limited dishes, we took turns eating porridge and drinking hot chocolate. While we ate, we discussed what was on all of our minds.

"How could Josh have given us away to Drachenmorder?" began Tui.

"Yeah, I thought he was one of us," said Ella.

"He seemed a bit jumpy the last couple of days," mused Oliver.

"No surprise," I said. "Hunter beat him up three times last week. If Hunter had decided to make a hobby of giving *me* black eyes, I would have been jumpy too."

"Hunter," said Oliver.

"Of course," said Tui. "He's Drachenmorder's nephew."

It took no stretch of the imagination to realise Drachenmorder had figured out we were up to *something*. I knew he'd kept a close eye on me. Once he suspected the noob class was working together, all he had to do was get Hunter to rough up the weakest member of the group until he got some answers.

"What do you think he's done with Josh?" asked Ella.

"I expect Drachenmorder agreed to go easy on him in exchange for a full account of our activities," I said.

"I wish we knew exactly what Josh has told him," said Oliver. "It'd make a big difference if we knew."

114

I thought back to Sir Leandro's words the night before.

"Sir Leandro knew only what Josh had said about our plans, and he knew we were going after my father. So we can assume Drachenmorder knows that too."

"That means, he also now knows your father isn't dead," said Oliver.

"And it probably means he's not only looking for us but for your dad as well," added Tui. "In which case," she said, rising, "we need to get moving. Sir Leandro gave you a map?"

I nodded, pulled out the map, and spread it on the ground. The others gathered around. Someone had drawn a star on a spot in the Hector Mountains.

"James Peak," read Oliver. There was an arrow curving from the mountain across a small stream to a broad ridge, where Sir Leandro had made a heavy dot and had written the word 'car'.

"So, where are we?" asked Ella.

"Well, last night, we came up this creek," said Oliver, running a finger over the map. "We crossed this ridge and, here, this must be the boggy area we got stuck in. Then we must have come back this way and down this ridge. I'd guess we're right here, at this little stream."

"If that's true, all we have to do is cross the stream and go down the hill on the other side to Lower Nevis. This little farm track should take us almost to the car's location," said Tui, plotting the route with her finger. "That's easy."

"Yeah, but it's at least two days of hiking, just to reach the car," warned Oliver. "Are we going all the way to James Peak?"

"I think we have to," I said. "We need to see if there are any clues as to what happened." The others nodded.

"I think we'll need a whole day for the bit from the car to the peak," said Oliver.

"But it's such a short distance," said Ella.

"But it's all uphill," said Oliver. "Look how steep it gets here too. And we won't want to spend a night up there, that's for sure. At over 2,000 metres, it'll be cold and exposed. We'll want to be able to get back off the mountain before dark."

"Okay," I said. "So today, we'll go as far as Lower Nevis. There's a hut marked on the map near there where we can stay the night. We'll hike up to the car tomorrow, and then to the peak the following day."

"We're going to hike during the day?" asked Tui. "There's nothing but tussock on these slopes, and we'll be easy to spot."

"You're right," I said. "I suppose we'll have to travel at night. Even if they didn't find out we'd gone until this morning, they're almost certainly after us by now. And they've got cars. They'll catch up to us quickly once they know which way we've gone."

"I am *not* hiking in the dark again," said Ella. "We're lucky Tui didn't kill herself when she fell last night. And, if I have to slog through another swamp..."

"Ella's right, Nathan," said Oliver. "It really isn't safe to hike at night. Even if we didn't stumble off a cliff, we can't navigate at night."

"All we have to do is go down this hill. We can follow this stream right here," I said, pointing at the map. "We won't get lost."

"It's not as easy as that, Nathan. It looks neat and tidy on the map but, in reality, it's not. And I'm not even certain that we are in this spot exactly. Another night of hiking in the dark, and we could be hopelessly lost."

"But if we're seen, we're worse than lost," argued Tui.

"I don't know if it will matter, actually," said Ella. She had stepped away from our discussion and clambered up the cliff to take a peek around. Now she jumped back

116

down into our sheltered nook. "You can't feel it at all down here, but there's a nor'wester picking up."

We all knew what that meant—driving rain and gale force winds. It would make hiking miserable, but it would also lower visibility enough to give us some protection.

"Let's get going then," said Tui. "Let's get as far as we can while visibility is good, and hope the rain hides us by the time Drachenmorder discovers where we've gone."

We packed our things, put on our rain gear, and climbed away from the stream.

At the top of the rise, the wind hit us full force.

"You weren't kidding," I shouted to Ella.

"It's going to be nasty," she grumbled.

Oliver pointed off to our left. "If we slept where I think we did, we should circle to our left around that peak and head down the second stream we come to."

"You're our mountaineering expert," I said. "Lead on."

The weather closed in rapidly and, within fifteen minutes, we could no longer see the peak we were supposed to be circling. The rain lashed us side-on, driven in billowing waves by the howling wind.

"The peak," yelled Ella, pointing into the grey nothingness where our landmark should have been. She cast a questioning look at Oliver.

He shrugged and smiled. "No one can see us either!"

"But how will we find our way?"

"We'll manage. Here's the first stream."

We hopped across what might have once been a stream but now had no water in it.

"Are you sure this is the first?" asked Tui.

"No, but I'm pretty sure," replied Oliver. "Let's start angling downhill now. When we hit the next stream, we'll follow it down."

We trudged after Oliver, slogging through the tussocks. No one spoke—it was too hard to hear above the wind and rain. The wet tussock leaves grew slick, and our downhill trudge became a slide. Oliver was the first to end up on his bottom. He laughed and hopped back up. As the slope got steeper and wetter, we all went down—Tui, me, and finally Ella.

But when Ella fell, she didn't get up again. Instead, she lay on her back, face to the sky, bawling.

"I'm soaked. I'm cold. I'm tired. And I'm hungry," she cried. "I don't want to be a dragon slayer, or a dragon saver. I want to go home. This is stupid. How are we supposed to find Nathan's dad when Sir Leandro couldn't do it? We're just kids. Can't we go home?" She rolled onto her side and curled up into a ball.

Tui scrambled down and crouched next to her. I couldn't hear what she said to her friend, but I saw Ella shake her head and cover her ears with her hands. Tui stood and came over to me.

"She says she's not going anywhere. I don't know what to do."

"Well, we can't stay here."

"That's what I told her, but she wouldn't listen."

I sighed and went to Ella myself.

"Ella, you've got to get up."

"No."

"We can't stay here. There's no shelter. We're all cold and wet and tired and hungry. I'm sure we're near the hut. When we get there we'll make some hot chocolate and put dry clothes on, and then you'll feel better."

"No."

"Well, the rest of us are going on. If you stay here, you'll stay alone." I stood and motioned everyone else onward. They all gave me questioning looks, when Ella made no move to follow. "I told her the rest of us are going to the hut."

"We can't just leave her," said Tui.

"We also can't stand here in the rain all day. If you haven't noticed, the weather is terrible and getting worse. Do you want to still be out here when night hits?"

"But she could die out here," said Tui.

"We're all going to die out here if we don't move on. We need to find some shelter." I lowered my voice. "Surely, she'll follow us eventually, won't she?" I started down the hill again. Oliver followed. Tui lingered for a moment, bending over Ella, then she jogged after us.

Despite the cold, my hands were sweating. We had left Ella alone on an exposed alpine slope in the middle of nowhere during a storm. I looked at the others for some sign I'd made the right decision, but their faces were grim and worried. I didn't know if I'd done the right thing, but we *had* to find that hut or none of us would make it. The sky lit up, and a peal of thunder shook the ground. We all started, and Tui yelped.

A moment later, Ella came scrambling down the slope behind us. She was still crying, but she was moving. I breathed a sigh of relief.

For five hours, we slid and scrambled through wet tussocks. Finally the land flattened out a little, and we could see the Nevis River below us.

"The hut!" Oliver grinned as he pointed across the flat to a tiny building clad in corrugated iron. The grey building was almost invisible in the driving rain, but it stood out like a beacon for us. Exhausted though we were, we picked up our pace.

The river brought us up short. The Nevis wasn't like the small mountain streams we had crossed earlier. In the downpour, it had become a raging torrent.

119

"No," cried Ella in despair. "How are we going to get across?"

"I have no idea," I said. It was agonising being able to see the hut but not reach it.

"Well, I can make it, I'm sure," said Tui, stepping toward the churning water.

"No!" said Oliver. "It's dangerous."

"Maybe for you, but I'm bigger," replied Tui. "I'll get to the other side, and then...we'll use the rope to pull the rest of you across."

"No, that's not the way you cross a river, Tui," said Oliver. "Josh and I read all about it when we were—"

"I've crossed rivers with my dad before," interrupted Tui. "I can do this." She took another step.

"Don't go, Tui," implored Oliver. "Just wait. Let me find a good place for us to cross, and then I'll show you how."

"You're going to show me how to cross? I don't think so."

"Stop it." I said. "Tui, we divided up our studies for a reason. Oliver and Josh focused their effort on mountaineering. If he says he knows how to do it safely, we should listen to him."

"But he's eight years old. He's a little kid."

Oliver's perpetual smile turned to a scowl. "Just because I'm small, doesn't mean—"

"Oliver has successfully guided us this far, Tui."

"Getting stuck in that swamp and having to turn around last night was successful?"

"We're going to have to stay here," said Ella.

"No," said Oliver. "If we work together and find the right spot, we can cross safely."

"Like I said. I'll cross, and we'll use the rope—"

"That won't work." I had never seen Oliver angry before. Unfortunately, it only made him seem younger.

"I am not going through that water," said Ella.

"It's not that bad."

"If you'd just listen."

"I've done this before."

"We can't cross."

Tui stood menacingly over Oliver. Oliver wagged his finger at Tui. Ella paced hysterically, listing her complaints. All the while, the wind blew stinging rain into our faces. I had to take charge.

"Shut up!" I bellowed. Everyone stopped and turned to me. "Look, we are all wet and tired, and want to get to that hut. Yelling at each other is not helping us to get there. Tui, maybe you could cross the river by yourself but, if you slipped and fell, none of us could save you. And the rest of us will need your help getting across." As she opened her mouth to argue, I raised my hand and continued. "We split up our studies so we would have an expert in our group. Oliver is our mountaineering expert. We will wait here until Oliver has determined where to cross, and then we'll follow his directions."

"But I'm cold and—"

I cut her off. "We're all cold, Ella. Complaining about it doesn't help anyone."

It was the first real test of my leadership and I knew it. I held my breath to see how my friends would react. There was a moment of strained silence in which everyone seemed suspended in their irritation. Then Tui sighed, and Oliver smiled.

"Just give me a couple of minutes to find the right place."

The rest of us huddled on the riverbank, staring numbly into the foaming water while Oliver clambered upstream.

"Do you really think we can get across?" asked Ella.

"Oliver is our expert. If he says we can, then I believe him."

"Have you ever crossed a river like this?"

"No."

Oliver came back a few minutes later.

"It widens out just up here a ways. It'll be shallower there, and I think we can make it."

We followed him to a spot about five minutes upstream, and Oliver showed us how to create a tight chain of our bodies by holding onto one another's belts.

"That way, if one of us loses our footing, the others will keep them from falling."

I was nervous. Everyone else was nervous too, even Oliver. But, unlike the rest of us, he still wore a grin. I smiled back at him, but the way I felt, it probably looked more like a grimace. We had to cross the river. There was no shelter on this side. If we didn't reach the hut, I didn't know how we'd make it through the night.

We put Oliver in the middle of the chain. He might be the one who knew all about river crossing, but he was also the smallest of the group and the one most likely to be swept away by the current. Oliver situated Tui at the upstream end of our group.

"Because you've done this before and are more likely to be stable in the water, you'll break the current for the rest of us," he said. The move placated Tui somewhat, and I wondered if it was actually something Oliver had learned in his mountaineering studies, or whether he had simply made it up for Tui's sake.

I took a deep breath, and we stepped into the water as one. Tui's grip on me tightened. Ella screamed.

"It's freezing."

It was. I thought I'd been cold before, but this was ten times worse. My teeth started chattering, though I think that could have been as much out of fear as from cold.

Slowly, we inched our way across. The water rose to our knees, then to our thighs. Poor Oliver was up to his waist. He kept a grin on his face the whole time, but I could see his lips were turning blue. Tui slipped, and her weight nearly pulled me down with her before I managed to steady us both. I could hear Ella whining over the rush of water.

It probably only took three minutes to cross the river but, by the time we stepped out, we were all shivering. But now, it was just a short flat walk to the hut. We scrambled up the bank with relief.

Only to find ourselves knee deep in mud.

"Oh, not mud," cried Ella.

"We're already soaked. Let's just keep going," I said. "We can dry off when we get to the hut."

So we waded through the swampy ground, doing our best to hop from tussock to tussock. It took nearly twenty minutes to make it through the muck. When we stepped out onto the gravel road that ran the length of the valley, we broke into a jog.

Chapter 15
To James Peak

We tumbled into the hut with relief. It was small and draughty. Two grimy windows let in gusts of wind, and the loose iron cladding shuddered. But it was dry, and I was thrilled to see a bucket of coal next to a small pot-bellied stove in a corner.

"Fire first," I said.

"I'll light it," volunteered Tui.

We shucked our wet clothes and assessed our situation. There were six bunks in the hut, and a small table with benches. It had no running water, but there was a stream out the back. A lean-to held plenty of coal and some brushy kindling. There was little else in the hut, aside from half a dozen well-used candles and a pack of matches.

An hour later, the hut was warm and steamy as our dripping clothes hung drying over the stove. We drank hot chocolate and made some ramen noodles. Not having stopped for a rest or eaten anything since breakfast, we were exhausted and starving. While we ate, it grew dark outside, so Tui lit the candles. I was thankful we weren't still out in the rain. Crossing the river in the dark would have been all but impossible.

Most of our conversation, so far, had focused on the necessities—food, heat, water. But with our bellies full and our toes finally thawing, our talk turned to other things.

"Well done, Oliver, for getting us across the river," I said.

Tui looked at the floor. "You were right, Oliver. My way wouldn't have worked."

Oliver shrugged. "To be honest, I wasn't convinced my way would work either, not until we'd got across. But it was awesome!"

"It was awful," said Ella.

"Well, we did get across safely," I said. "Thanks to Oliver. Tomorrow, we'll go up the other side of this valley. We should be able to make it to the spot where Sir Leandro says dad got into a car."

"Up?" whimpered Ella.

"But we'll be on a farm track. It'll be easier than it was today, going through the tussock."

"I hope so," said Ella. "Let's hope the weather's better tomorrow too."

"It probably worked in our favour today," said Tui. "Not only could no one spot us from a distance, but our tracks were almost certainly washed away. Drachenmorder won't be able to find us."

"Unless he guesses where we've gone," I cautioned. "Remember, he probably knows we're going after my dad. And it would be logical we'd start our search at the place where he was last seen."

"Except, he may not know that *we* know your dad was last seen near James Peak," said Tui. "Josh couldn't have told him that because we didn't know about it until this morning."

"So where else might he think we've gone?" asked Oliver.

"Where else would it be logical to start our search?" asked Tui.

"Well, if I didn't know where to look, I'd probably start by going through Dad's desk at home," I said. I sucked in my breath. "Home. Nan's staying there. I need to warn her. She doesn't even know that Dad might still be alive." I rummaged in my pack for my phone and pulled it out, only to discover there was no cell phone reception. Of course there wasn't, not out here in a remote valley. Even at the school cell phone reception hadn't been reliable. Frowning in frustration, I shoved the phone back into my bag.

"She'll be all right," said Tui.

"Maybe." I shrugged. There was nothing I could do about it. But that didn't stop me worrying.

Oliver yawned.

"We're all tired," I said. "Let's get some sleep. We've got another long hike ahead of us tomorrow."

The wind howled and rattled the roof all night but, by morning, it had calmed a little. We ate breakfast slowly, savouring the warmth and dryness of the hut.

"Well, we should get going while the weather is good," I said finally.

"You call this good?" asked Ella. "It's still raining out there. Can't we stay here another day before we move out again?"

I shook my head. "We can't waste time. Drachenmorder could be on our tail. Dad could be...anywhere. We've got to keep moving."

The others nodded, and we began to pack up our things. Within half an hour, we were trudging up a little-used farm track and looking back down on the hut.

It was much easier going than the day before, even though it was uphill. The wind wasn't quite as bad and, although it was still raining, at least now it was coming down vertically.

That didn't last long.

Within an hour of starting out, the wind had picked up and was threatening to blow us back down the mountain. Bent nearly double against the slope and the rain, my world was soon reduced to the effort of putting one foot in front of the other. I was so focused on the rhythm of hiking, that when the farm track petered out, it caught me by surprise. Not long after, we crested the top of the hill and took a break, crouching behind a scattering of large rock outcrops. While we rested, the wind and rain slackened. Ella passed around the chocolate bar.

"Not too far, now," I said. "Sir Leandro said the car that took Dad away was parked near the top of that hill over there." The broad saddle between the two peaks looked like an easy stroll and, with the wind and rain abating, everyone's mood seemed to improve. We walked more confidently, and even Ella managed a smile when Oliver told a joke.

An hour later, we were standing at the spot indicated on the map.

"What do we do now?" asked Ella.

"We look for clues," I said.

"Any tracks will be long gone," said Tui.

"Still, we need to look for anything that might tell us where the men took him."

We fanned out over the area, scanning the ground all around us. The sun peeked from behind the clouds, and we threw back our hoods.

With our eyes on the ground, we didn't notice the black clouds piling up to the south. When the first gust of icy wind hit, I looked up.

"Oh no," I cried. The others raised their eyes, just as the rain started splatting on the rocks.

"Naturally," said Tui. "A southerly always follows a strong nor'wester. We should have guessed we were in for this."

"We don't want to be up here in a southerly," warned Oliver.

The wind picked up, and more rain fell. The temperature dropped ten degrees. I continued scanning the ground and rocks for any sign of my dad, not even knowing what I was looking for.

"There's nothing here," said Ella. "We need to go back to the hut."

"But we've got to get to James Peak," I said. "There may be clues there."

Tui eyed the clouds and pulled up her hood. "Nathan, there's nothing here."

"We'll never make it to James Peak in this weather," said Oliver.

"So let's stay here for the night, like we planned, and wait till this blows over. We'll go to the peak tomorrow."

"On these rocks, and with the rain, even I won't be able to find tracks," said Tui.

The sky opened up, and the rain turned to hail.

"I'm not staying here in this weather," yelled Ella over the rising noise of the storm. She produced a hat from her pocket and pulled it low over her ears. I shivered and did the same.

"Let's look for shelter," I urged. "There's got to be somewhere we can get out of this."

Once again, we spread out, searching for even the smallest overhang where we could take cover.

There was nothing. The hill was bare and windswept. I sat down on a rock and bowed my head, so the others couldn't see my face. Ella was right. There was nothing here. Tui was right. Any traces of my dad were long gone. Oliver was right. We couldn't stay up here in a storm. I had been so sure we'd find something. In hindsight, it had been a foolish hope. Did I think there would be a sign post here saying, 'Nathan's dad, this way', and an arrow pointing to his location? A tear slid down my nose, and I watched it drip onto the rocks. Then, something white caught my eye, tucked under the rock I was sitting on. A tiny corner of paper.

I stood and heaved on the rock, rolling it over, and snatched at the folded notebook page before it blew away. I turned my back to the wind and fingered the paper. It was waterproof—the same stuff Dad used for his field notes. On it was written, 'Storm Cloud, Mt. Crosscut'.

It was my father's handwriting.

"Guys! Guys! There's a note from my dad!"

Eagerly, they gathered around and read the note. Their excitement turned to bewilderment.

"What does it mean?" asked Tui.

"I don't know," I admitted.

"So we found something. Can we go now?" pleaded Ella.

"She's right," agreed Oliver. "We have to go."

It was true—rain and hail had given way to snow. The temperature was dropping fast, and there was no shelter up here. I tucked my dad's note in my pocket, and we started trudging back down to the hut.

At least it was downhill. Otherwise, we wouldn't have made it. The snow came down so fast that, before we even made it across the saddle, there were three centimetres of it on the ground. The farm track was already masked with snow by the time we reached it, and it was only visible because of the deep ruts it cut into the slope.

We moved as fast as we could, but we were all exhausted. Rocks hidden in the snow made the descent treacherous, as we slid and stumbled our way down the hill. Thankfully, the snow lessened the further we descended, and the track became easier to follow. We stopped once for more chocolate but didn't dare linger, though we were all hungry and tired. We hadn't planned to return to the hut today, and turning back had doubled the day's hike. It was long after dark when we finally stumbled back into the building.

We lit the fire and ate a cold dinner of crackers and peanut butter before collapsing into bed. Even with the words of Dad's note bouncing around in my head, I fell asleep instantly.

Chapter 16
Mt. Crosscut

"But what does it mean?" asked Tui.

It was morning. A light blanket of snow covered the valley, and the peaks above groaned under a heavy load. The sky was blue and clear, and the air still. The four of us had finished breakfast and were sitting around the table, my dad's note spread out before us.

"Is this somewhere he wants us to go?" asked Tui. "Mt. Crosscut?"

"Where's Mt. Crosscut?" asked Oliver.

"And what's with the storm cloud?" added Tui.

I glanced at Ella.

"Are you thinking what I'm thinking?" I asked her.

"About Storm Cloud? Yeah."

"So are you going to tell us, or wait for us to figure it out too?" asked Tui.

"New Zealand green dragon names are all weather-related. Famous ones include Zephyr, who once terrorised the town of Haast; Thunderclap, who spent a season picking skiers off the slopes at the Remarkables; and—"

"Are you saying that Storm Cloud is a dragon?" asked Tui.

I nodded.

"Awesome!" said Oliver with a grin.

"And Storm Cloud must live on Mt. Crosscut," said Ella.

"What are we waiting for?" said Oliver. "Let's go!"

"We don't even know where Mt. Crosscut is," said Tui.

"We need the Internet," I said. "We need to get out of here and back to civilisation."

"Yes!" cheered Ella.

"It's a long hike out," said Oliver, pulling out the map. The gravel road next to the hut went all the way to the end of the valley, and then climbed over the tail end of the Hector Mountains and down to Garston, which was on Route 6. That would be the closest place to get Wi-Fi or even cell phone reception. "It's thirty-six kilometres."

"But look," I said, pointing at the little icons, "There are huts along the way. Three days, and we'll be in Garston."

"Three days?"

"I'm a little worried about sticking to the road," said Tui. "That will make it easier for Drachenmorder to find us."

"Would you rather go up here, over the Hector Mountains where they're 2,000 metres tall?" asked Oliver, placing a finger on the map. "We were up there yesterday—no shelter, and now there must be half a metre of snow to wade through. I think Nathan's right. We have to go by the road."

"And if Drachenmorder comes driving down it?"

Oliver shrugged. "We've got no chance going up over the mountains, and we don't know for certain Drachenmorder will come looking for us here. Our odds are better on the road."

Nobody argued. Walking up the gentle slope of the river valley on a road, with huts to stay in along the way, sounded almost like a holiday compared to finding our way through the mountains.

The air was crisp, but not cold, and the sun sparkled off the snow as we started out that morning. Oliver was in high spirits, laughing and skipping as he went, and Ella didn't complain once. Tui tried to prevent us from making tracks, but it was hopeless in the snow. Instead, we threw snowballs at each other as we hurried along.

The snow didn't last long in the valley and, by noon, when we stopped for lunch, the road was a slurry of mud—better if Drachenmorder was trying to follow us, but not nearly as much fun as snow. The afternoon was less cheerful. We were still tired from the day before and, because we had to ration our food to make it last three more days, by mid-afternoon, we were hiking on empty stomachs.

"Aren't we near the hut yet?" complained Ella. "My feet are wet, and I think I've got a blister."

"We can't be too far, now," I replied.

"But my feet hurt. And I'm hungry."

"What do you want me to do? Call you a cab?"

"Well, if you had at least warned me we'd be walking half way across the world—"

"Guys, be quiet," said Tui.

"Don't tell me to be quiet—"

"Ella, *shut up!* Listen."

Looking a bit put out, Ella closed her mouth. Everyone stopped walking, and then I heard it, coming from behind.

"A car."

"Drachenmorder?"

"Could be."

"Where can we hide?" The valley was barren— nothing but tussocks and a few sparse bushes here and there.

We scanned the area.

"There." Tui pointed to the remains of a stone fireplace up ahead—the remnants of some miner's cottage from the mid 1800s. In spite of our hunger and exhaustion, we ran. When we neared the ruin, it was tempting to veer off the road, but Tui stopped us.

"Our tracks. We don't want it to be obvious where we've left the road."

We spread out and each made our own careful way to the fireplace. The car was nearer now, but we still couldn't see it. We ducked behind the crumbling stones. It was hardly enough cover for four, but it was all we had. As the car came nearer, we pressed ourselves against the chimney, not daring to even peek out to see who was coming.

The vehicle was moving slowly. No surprise, given the state of the road. It felt like we'd waited for years before it crested a small rise and passed the ruin. We listened as it motored past. Then it stopped and backed up.

Tui, who had shut her eyes, opened them, a look of horror on her face. "He's stopping," she hissed.

"What do we do?" squeaked Oliver.

"Shh!" I said, hoping the car had stopped for some unrelated reason.

I heard the car door open and close. Then there was the crunch of boots on gravel, followed by footsteps in the tussocks. There was nowhere to run, nowhere to hide. As the sounds came closer, we shuffled around the corner of the fireplace, hoping to stay hidden. It was useless. We were all primed to run when a man appeared around the chimney.

"Kids!" he exclaimed, his eyebrows raised in surprise. "What the hell are you doing here? I thought you were rabbits." He raised the gun in his right hand to illustrate.

"Um…" began Ella.

"We were on a school field trip. History," said Oliver, patting the chimney. "We're studying the mining history of Otago."

"Just the four of you? Alone?"

"Well, we got lost. Separated from the others. I'm sure they'll be by soon."

134

"This isn't a place for kids to be wandering around in. Weather's not bad today, but it can turn in a minute."

"Oh, we're prepared for the weather," said Oliver with a smile.

"Since when does a school trip go out with tramping packs?" asked the man.

"It was a school tramping trip," said Tui, stepping forward and looking authoritative.

"Was it?"

I could tell the man wasn't buying our story. I would have been surprised if he had—it was as full of holes as a sieve.

"So, where were you headed when you got...separated from your group?"

"We were on our way back out. To Garston," I said.

"It's a long way to Garston."

We nodded.

"And I've got blisters already," whined Ella.

There was an awkward silence as the man sized us up. He obviously didn't believe we were a school group, but he didn't ask us any more questions. He sighed and rolled his eyes.

"Get in the truck. I'll take you to Garston."

The ride to Garston was crowded. The back of the white ute was already filled with bales of hay, a rusty wheelbarrow, and a shovel. Ella and Oliver rode in the cab, while Tui and I perched on top of the hay in the back.

When we arrived in Garston, the man pulled into the car park at the Garston Hotel. We thanked him and hopped out before he could stop us or ask any awkward questions.

"Do you think they have Wi-Fi?" asked Oliver, looking at the 1930s art-deco building.

"Don't count on it," said Ella.

I pulled out my phone. "There's cell phone reception, so we're good either way. I get twenty megs of data with my phone plan."

"Twenty megs! Lucky!" said Oliver.

"Forget the Wi-Fi. Let's get something to eat." Ella had perked up at the prospect of food.

We stepped into the hotel's restaurant, only then realising how muddy and dishevelled we looked. But the waitress took it in her stride. She showed us to a table in the corner where there was plenty of room to stow our packs. We ordered and ate our burgers and chips in high spirits, our quest taking second place, for the moment, to the enjoyment of being indoors and well-fed.

But the day was getting on. It was already nearly six, and we still didn't know where we would be going next. I pulled out my phone and typed in 'Mt. Crosscut'.

"Well Ella, you'll be glad to note we won't be walking to Mt. Crosscut," I said, showing the others the map I'd pulled up.

"Just before the Homer Tunnel. That's at least two and a half hours' drive from here," said Oliver. "Dad and I went tramping near there once."

"Well, how are we going to get there?" asked Tui.

"I could ring my mum!" said Oliver. "She could drive us!"

"And what's your mum going to say when you tell her you're going to climb Mt. Crosscut to visit a dragon?" I asked.

Oliver deflated. "You're right. She wouldn't even take us there."

"Besides, I think it's best if our families don't know anything about where we've gone or what we're doing, don't you?"

136

"You mean, so they don't come and make us go home?" asked Ella.

"I mean, so that when Drachenmorder knocks on their doors and asks if they know where we are, they can honestly say no."

"Do you think he'll do that?" asked Tui.

"I'm sure he will."

"But, then our parents will think we're missing," said Oliver.

"They will. But they won't be able to tell Drachenmorder anything."

"But—"

"All the more reason for us to find my dad as quickly as possible."

The others nodded.

"So how are we going to get there?" asked Ella. "Too bad we don't have a car."

"Yeah, like any of us could drive it anyway," I said.

"Isn't there a bus that goes from Queenstown to Milford Sound?" asked Oliver.

I did a quick Google search.

"Yes, the InterCity does."

Just then, the waitress returned to ask us if we needed anything more.

"Does the InterCity bus stop near here?" I asked.

"Yes, it stops right here at the hotel."

"What time?"

"About quarter past eleven."

"Tonight?"

She smiled. "No, quarter past eleven in the morning."

"Oh."

"You kids travelling alone?" she asked. "You seem awfully young to be by yourselves."

"She's our chaperone," I said, pointing at Ella, who was the largest of us.

"I'm eighteen," she lied.

"So, if you're catching the bus tomorrow morning, you'll be wanting a room tonight, eh? There's no freedom camping here in Garston." She eyed our packs.

I thought about our two hundred dollars. We'd blown a fair bit of it already, on dinner, and if we had to pay for the bus too…I noticed Ella's pleading eyes and Oliver's eager grin.

"How much is a room?"

"A hundred dollars a night."

Half our money. Still, a night in a hotel would be great. I was exhausted. Ella and Oliver looked desperate. Even stoic Tui was caving in to the lure of a night indoors. We booked a room.

The next morning, after we'd eaten a hearty breakfast and paid for the room, we had exactly twelve dollars left of our two hundred. It wasn't going to pay for four of us to take a bus to the Homer Tunnel.

"We could hitchhike," suggested Oliver.

"Four of us?" Who's got room for four in their car?" replied Tui.

"We shouldn't have gotten the hotel room," I said.

"Or breakfast," said Tui. "We did have some porridge left."

"Let's try the bus. What have we got to lose?" asked Oliver.

When the bus pulled up in front of the hotel, a few passengers hopped out to use the toilets, and the driver leaned on the front of the vehicle smoking a cigarette. He was a big man, wearing an InterCity Bus Line uniform and a scowl. It wasn't promising. We had decided Ella would do the talking, as she could pass for an adult—sort of.

"Well, here goes nothing," she said, and walked over to the driver. The rest of us followed.

"Excuse me, sir," she began. The man took the cigarette out of his mouth.

"Yeah?"

"Is there room for four more? We're going to Milford Sound."

"You kids?" the driver asked, looking dubiously at us.

"Yes, the four of us," explained Ella, waving a hand our way.

"There's room, but we don't usually take on passengers unless they've booked in advance." He heaved himself upright. "That'll be two hundred and fifty dollars for the four of you."

Ella's polite smile vanished, as did everyone else's. *Two hundred and fifty dollars?* Even if we hadn't spent any of our money, we still wouldn't have been able to afford the bus.

Oliver pushed forward, his smile wide.

"But we need to meet up with Mum and Dad. Me and my brother and sisters are going to meet them at Milford Sound."

"You four are siblings?" The man looked from Oliver, with his classic Chinese looks; to me with my ginger hair and freckles; to blond Ella; and then to Tui, who took after her Ngāti Whātua father.

"It's a blended family," explained Oliver. "Mum and Dad just got married. These guys are really my half siblings."

"Half siblings?"

"Well, I was adopted, of course," said Oliver conspiratorially. "Mum and Dad are on their honeymoon, and we're meeting them for a cruise in Milford Sound. But our car broke down, and we haven't got money to fix

139

it. Mum and Dad will be so disappointed if we don't make it."

Oliver put on a sad expression, and the rest of us did our best to join in, though I could tell Tui was having a hard time keeping her laughter in.

The bus driver's scowl flickered momentarily. He shook his head and stubbed out his cigarette on the ground.

"Get in," he said. "I think we've got four extra one-dollar fares today."

We all thanked him profusely, grabbed our packs, and boarded the bus. Ella handed the driver a five dollar bill, but he waved it away with a smile.

Tumbling into the back row of seats we all dissolved into silent laughter.

"Oliver, that was brilliant," I said.

"Siblings?" said Ella.

"Of course. Oliver, my bro." I thumped him on the back.

"I wish I were cute enough to get whatever I want," said Tui. "You must be spoiled rotten at home."

"Nah, that doesn't work on Mum *at all*," replied Oliver.

We sat back and watched the scenery pass, happy to be on our way and thankful not to be on foot.

When the bus stopped at the Homer Tunnel to let the tourists get out and take photographs, we quietly slipped away, hiding behind a massive boulder until the bus pulled away and was out of sight in the tunnel.

"There it is," I said, pointing to the snow-covered peak behind us. "Mt. Crosscut."

"We're not going up there are we?" asked Ella.

"Hope you've all been practicing your mountain climbing!" said Oliver rubbing his hands with glee.

"And somewhere up there is a dragon?" Tui sounded sceptical.

"I hope so," I said.

Chapter 17
Storm Cloud

It was an easy walk from the road to the hut at the base of Mt. Crosscut. I was eager to go up the mountain that afternoon, but Oliver and Ella vetoed the idea.

"There's a route up from the hut. From what I saw online, it's only a day trip from here."

"Yeah, a day trip if you start first thing in the morning, Nathan. It's already two o'clock. We'd be lucky to make it up before dark, and we certainly wouldn't make it back down again," said Oliver.

"And I am not spending the night on top of a mountain with a dragon," said Ella.

So we spent the night in the hut.

Next morning, we left some of our gear in the hut, taking only what we needed for the climb. None of us wanted to carry a gram more than we had to. Mt. Crosscut was formidable—all broken rock and snow-filled crags. An information sheet in the hut warned climbers not to attempt it between April and December.

"It says avalanche risk runs all the way through late December," said Tui.

"We don't have until late December. We have to go up today," I said. I was every bit as worried as Tui, but it was *my* dad we were after, and every day we didn't find him was a day he could be dead.

By eight o'clock, we were on our way. It was a clear, frosty morning, and the rocks were slick with ice. Going up the west side, we knew the sun wouldn't hit us until afternoon, so there was no point in waiting for the ice to melt. It would be there for most of the day.

Oliver and Tui took the lead—Tui was our best climber, and Oliver had the most knowledge of mountaineering. Working together, they chose the route and did our lead climbing. I was glad to see them each accepting the other's expertise. After the incident with the river crossing, I was worried they would argue all the way up.

At first, it wasn't too bad—a bit of a scramble, no more—but it wasn't long before the mountain challenged our skills.

"That's, like, completely vertical."

"No, I actually think it overhangs a bit at the top."

"Isn't there any other way?"

We did our best to avoid the steepest routes, and Tui and Oliver put in twice as much protection as they thought we might need.

"I've never done this before," explained Tui. "I don't trust any of the cams I've placed."

We inched up the rock. My fingers and toes went numb while belaying Tui. I had to massage and stamp feeling into them before climbing up myself. We didn't talk much, except to offer suggestions to whoever was struggling up the current pitch. The ascent was even more difficult than it should have been because we had only two sets of gear. Tui would go up a pitch and set the rope, and then whoever had been belaying her would go up. Then, we'd send the harnesses back down for the next two.

After two hours of climbing, we took a break on a wide ledge. We had already reached dizzying heights, but the peak seemed as far away as ever.

The view was spectacular. The sun glinted off fresh snow on the mountains around us, and we could see tiny cars moving on the road far below.

"We'll be getting into snow before long," said Oliver, looking up at our route.

"Are you sure your dad meant for us to climb this mountain?" asked Ella.

"How else are we going to find a dragon? They live at the tops of mountains," I replied. Ella sighed.

"Well, let's get on with it," said Tui, standing up and checking her harness.

Everyone groaned, but Tui was right. If we were going to make it up and back in one day, we needed to keep moving.

On the next pitch, Tui lost her footing three metres above her last cam. I was belaying her, and the momentum of her fall lifted me right off my feet. She hit the rock with a sickening thud.

"Are you okay?" I called. There was no answer. "Tui?"

"I'm fine. I think." Tui's voice was strained. "Bashed my knees, that's all." She gathered herself together and resumed her climb, more slowly this time, and with more protection.

It was about then that the wind picked up. And not gradually. One minute it was calm, and the next minute I was swinging like a barn door from one hand and one foot as the wind tried to tear me from the rock. Ella, on the ledge below me, screamed.

Our slow progress grew even slower.

"We must be near the top," panted Tui as we clawed our way up a patch of scree. But, when we got to the snow-covered shoulder above it, a huge fall of ice, not visible before now, was spread out above us. What had looked like the peak from down below was not even close to the top. And in between was the sort of terrain I was sure none of us felt confident tackling.

"Let's take a break," I said, brushing snow off a rock and sitting down. Tui and I had been first to the top of the scree. As we waited for the others, the wind rose to a gale and snow blew off the ice fall above to swirl around us.

Oliver scrambled up beside us, turning immediately to call down to Ella.

"Come on! You can do it. You're nearly there." A gust of wind made him teeter on the edge, and I grabbed the back of his jacket.

"Don't stand at the edge."

"Ella's going to need some help," said Oliver, crouching down now. "She doesn't like this wind."

"None of us do," I said. As if in response, the wind picked up even more. We all went down on our hands and knees and peered over the edge to where Ella still struggled. She was crying, her breath coming in ragged, hiccupping gulps. Looking back down the way we'd come, I could have gotten pretty hysterical too. One slip, and that would be it. I took out the rope and threw an end to her. The rest of us anchored the other end.

"Grab the rope, Ella," I called down. "Grab the rope, and we'll pull you up."

She snatched at the rope with relief, almost collapsing as we began to pull.

"Slowly," I cautioned. "Ella! You have to stand up. Lean back against the rope." She was trying to stay close to the rocks, but that meant she was being dragged up the slope on her knees.

"I can't," she yelled back.

"Yes you can."

"I can't!"

I sighed.

"Let's just get her up here," said Tui. "We'll pull slowly. If she wants to be dragged up on her face, that's her problem."

So that's what we did. Ella managed to haul herself into a crouch and stumble along on shaking legs.

When we got her to the top, she collapsed face-down onto the snow. For a while, we all sat huddled against the wind, looking up at the route to the top. No one smiled. Even the ever-confident Oliver looked pale and seemed uncertain as to our next step. I had to get us moving again soon, or we would all lose the nerve to go on. I stood up, bracing against the wind.

"Right. Let's move. Not much farther."

"I can't go any farther," sobbed Ella.

"We have to go on," I said.

"We can't. We're all going to die."

"If we don't find this dragon and find my dad, he's going to be killed."

"Better him than m—AAAAAAAA!" Ella's eyes grew wide with terror, and I had less than a moment to turn and glimpse what had frightened her before a massive gust of wind knocked me off the edge. I didn't fall far. Before I'd even registered I was airborne, a huge scaly claw snatched me from the sky.

We all screamed. My stomach lurched as the massive claw jerked me up and down. When I'd gotten my bearings, I spotted Ella, Tui, and Oliver clasped tightly in the other claws of the enormous green dragon.

The dragon soared away from Mt. Crosscut and, suddenly, we were almost two thousand metres above the ground. The wind whipped around me, threatening to tear me from the dragon's grip. My first frantic attempts to get away from the claws turned to a white-knuckled grip on them and a fervent hope the dragon wouldn't drop us. I heard Tui vomit and closed my eyes so I wouldn't do the same.

With my eyes closed, my brain started working again. We'd found Storm Cloud, but this wasn't quite how I envisioned our first meeting. We were supposed to find him in his lair and talk to him.

146

Talk to him. Could I remember any Draconic while dangling from a dragon's claw? I took a deep breath and did my best not to sound too terrified.

"We come in peace! We come in peace! Don't eat us!"

The dragon circled wide around the peak of the mountain, and then swooped toward a crevice on the eastern side. Oliver's screams turned to laughter, and I thought he'd gone mad. When we drew close to the peak, I could see a broad expanse of rock. My stomach lurched as the dragon dipped down then swooped up to land gracefully on the rock, depositing us gently as he did so.

Tui, Ella, and I lay on the rock gasping for breath. Oliver, after his initial tumbling roll, sat up with a grin on his face.

"That was awesome!"

The dragon turned to face us, its tail thrashing like an angry cat's and knocking loose stones that tumbled down the mountain. The creature was at least twenty-five metres long with scales the colour of the jade pendant Tui always wore. Its crocodile-like head was ringed with a fringe of spikes, reminding me of a triceratops. Smoke curled from its nostrils.

"We come in peace," I said again. "Please don't eat us."

The dragon slowly turned its huge head and focused its gaze on me. It regarded me with yellow eyes, and its tongue flicked out as though savouring my taste already. My knees were shaking so badly with fear, I had to steady myself on a rock.

"I'm Sir Archibald's son," I squeaked. Fitting, since I felt like a mouse that had been caught by a cat.

The dragon cocked its head and regarded me curiously. Then it snaked its head toward me. I scrambled backwards, but it caught me in its tail and brought its nose close to my face. Sweat broke out on my brow. Not from the heat of the dragon's breath, which snuffled noisily in its nostrils and blew my hair back from my face, but from the sheer terror of being a hand's breadth away from a dragon's mouth.

"Humph!" said the dragon, withdrawing slightly. "Archie's son. I can smell the family resemblance." His voice was like an earthquake rumble. It rattled my teeth, and I finally understood how Draconic was supposed to sound. I relaxed ever so slightly and glanced at my friends, giving them a brief smile.

"What did he say?" hissed Tui.

The dragon looked toward her, and she yelped and covered her head with her arms.

"Do you not all speak Draconic?" asked the dragon.

"No, Your Majestic Greenness," I said, using the formal dragon title. "We are students. Still learning. Ella and I"—I gestured to where my friend cowered—"have studied more than the others, but, even so, our Draconic is limited."

"Oh, well, then. We'll switch to English. That is little Archie's language, isn't it?"

"Yes," I said. "Yes, we all speak English." The others relaxed, and I was glad I wasn't going to have to explain everything in Draconic.

"Are you Storm Cloud?" I asked.

"I am. And you must be Nathan."

My surprise must have shown, because Storm Cloud laughed, sending a jet of smoke out each nostril.

"Archie speaks of you often. But I haven't seen Archie for some time." Storm Cloud's voice grew stern. "He missed a meeting not long ago. He and his dragon slaying friend." The dragon's tail began thrashing again, and I had to jump forward to avoid being knocked over by it.

"That's why I'm here, Your Majestic Greenness. My father was kidnapped, and the other man you were supposed to meet was killed. My father left a note with your name and…um…address…on it."

"He did what?" Storm Cloud's voice boomed and his tail thrashed wildly. "He promised never to reveal my location to anyone. ANYONE. It just goes to show, you can never trust a human, no matter how reasonable they appear to be. I suppose he sent you all here to slay me, eh?"

"No. We're here because—"

"Just like you humans. Pathetic. Resorting to deceit and trickery."

"No! We're—"

"And I was a fool. Believed what he said. Bah! Well, I know what to do this time." The dragon raised its head and inhaled deeply, preparing to roast us all with its fiery breath.

"Now wait a minute," barked Ella, taking a step forward and shaking her finger at the dragon. He froze and held his breath, his eyes widening in surprise. "We escaped the School of Heroic Arts, hiked for *days* in the rain and snow, and climbed all the way up here to see you. I have a dozen blisters on my feet, three broken fingernails, and I haven't washed my face for days. Sir Archibald has been kidnapped because he is trying to help you." As she said this, she moved forward another step and poked Storm Cloud in the chest with her finger. "He might even be dead by now, for all we know. And it's because he is friends with *you*. He told us your location because he expected you to help. He considered you a friend. He assumed that, like most dragons, you were loyal to your friends."

I couldn't help but smile. Ella was hitting Storm Cloud where it hurt—his pride—and doing a spectacular job. The dragon was visibly shrinking under her tirade.

"I suppose he was wrong about you. Maybe we've been wrong about all dragons. Maybe you're all fair-weather friends. Simply in it for whatever you can get."

"Now, wait a minute," broke in Storm Cloud. "You've got it all wrong."

"Yeah? Well, looks to me like you're about to eat us and, last I checked, friends don't go around eating each other. Not friends who are loyal to one another."

"Now look here. I never meant to—"

"No, you look here. Are you going to help us rescue Sir Archibald or not? Because if you're not, I'd like to get off this miserable rock before it gets dark. Don't waste my time."

I felt it wise to step in at this point.

"Look. We've just had a little misunderstanding. How about we calm down and discuss the situation like civilised people...er...dragons."

"Well, that's exactly what I was about to suggest, but this...this...*blarghstra* here got all huffy about it."

I could see Ella getting ready to storm again. *Blarghstra* is the Draconic word for an irritating, bossy female dragon—not a nice word either. I gave her a warning look, and she held her tongue.

"Will you help us?" I asked. "Will you help save my dad? He's counting on us. He's counting on you, Your Majes—"

"Oh, cut it with the fancy titles. Call me Storm Cloud. Yes, of course, I'll help you find Archie. But let's get out of this wind." The dragon shivered. "It's ruffling my scales."

Chapter 18
At Storm Cloud's Lair

Storm Cloud squeezed through the crevice behind him—an impressive feat for an animal that huge—and we all followed, single file. Oliver stepped through first with an enormous grin on his face. As I waited for my turn, I spoke to Ella. After her rant, my respect for her had gone way up.

"That was awesome. I thought we were all toast."

"He was being a jerk. Somebody had to be a *blarghstra*." Ella shrugged. "My dad once told me about a conversation he overheard between a female dragon and her mate—she was whiny, overbearing, and demanding."

"A *blarghstra*," I said with a grin.

Ella returned my smile. "I just pretended I was her."

"Well, you saved our lives."

"You can repay me by building a ski lift to get down off this mountain," she replied as she ducked into the crevice.

I followed the others into the dark crack. Five metres into the mountain, it opened into a large cavern. My exclamations joined those of my friends as we looked around. Even in the dim light filtering through the crack, we could see that the floor of the cave was piled high with gold and jade. The walls sparkled.

Storm Cloud took in our responses with obvious pride.

"Welcome to my home, little friends."

"Is that gold?" asked Ella, pointing to the walls.

"It's mica. Pretty as gold, but not nearly so warm." He shuffled his feet, shifting the gold and jade underneath him, then settled himself with a sigh. "Please, make yourselves comfortable."

We all sat down, and I was surprised to note the gold *was* warm. I had expected the cold touch of metal and stone, but the dragon's treasures were pleasant to sit on—more like a cosy bean bag chair than a pile of rocks.

"Now," said the dragon when we were all settled. "Tell me everything."

So we did. I started with the letter telling me of my father's death and my arrival at the Alexandra School of Heroic Arts. I told him how I'd read my father's letter too late to avoid going to the school.

"So young Archie had told you nothing about his...profession...or his activities?"

"No. I think he wanted to keep me safe. But it kind of backfired. Drachenmorder—"

"Drachenmorder," interrupted Storm Cloud. "Claus Drachenmorder?"

I nodded.

"Drachenmorder brings hunters to the mountains to kill dragons. Hunters with guns. The stinking *sharkund*! If I knew where to find him, I'd—"

"We know where he is," said Ella. "He's at the School of Heroic Arts."

"I know that, but where's the school?" Storm Cloud snaked his head down, so he was eye-to-eye with Ella. "Where's the school?"

Ella darted a nervous glance my way.

"Did my father not tell you?" I asked.

"No. He never did. I didn't press him because I assumed I could catch Drachenmorder unawares someday in the mountains. But two weeks before your father disappeared, one of Drachenmorder's hunting parties shot my sister, Southwind." Storm Cloud's voice grew thick

152

with anger and smoke rose from his nostrils. "I swore then I would find Drachenmorder's lair and burn him out of it along with his filthy friends." His tail thrashed, scattering gold, and he punctuated his declaration with a spurt of fire aimed at the ceiling.

I could see why Dad hadn't told Storm Cloud where the school was.

"Not all the people at the school are Drachenmorder's friends," I said. "It was one of the teachers who helped us escape—Sir Leandro Justo—and there may be others there who are against dragon slaying."

"You were forced to escape the school?" asked Storm Cloud, calming somewhat.

"Yeah," said Oliver. "After Nathan read his dad's letter, he told us about it, and we all decided we wanted to be dragon savers, not dragon slayers. Of course, we couldn't let Drachenmorder know. Nathan was already in danger because of his dad."

Tui took up the story, telling how someone sabotaged my climbing harness, how we found out that my father wasn't dead after all, and how Sir Leandro made it possible for us to escape.

Ella chimed in then with her rendition of the trip across the Old Woman Range to James Peak. The story was full of complaints and blisters, but none of us contradicted her—it had been a truly miserable hike.

"So young Archie left my name and location for you near James Peak," mused Storm Cloud when Ella had finished. "And you're sure Drachenmorder isn't the one who kidnapped him?"

"Yes," I said.

Tui piped up. "Drachenmorder wants Nathan's dad dead. He thought he had killed him at James Peak. Sir Leandro said that someone else took him away."

"Hmm…someone who wanted him alive."

We sat in silence while the old dragon shut his eyes. Just when I thought he must have fallen asleep, he stirred and opened them again.

"Well, I have no idea who would want to take Archie prisoner, though I suspect I know why."

"Because he knows where you live?" I ventured.

The dragon nodded. "And where to find most of the dragons remaining in New Zealand. If someone wanted to kill us all, Archie would be able to direct them to us."

"But surely he'd never do that," said Ella.

"Not willingly, no," said Storm Cloud.

"Are you saying you think…you think my dad's being…?" I couldn't bring myself to say the word *tortured*.

"We need to find him," cried Tui.

"Yes. We do. But we don't have enough information to even know where to start searching," said Storm Cloud. "We'll need help."

"From who?" asked Oliver.

"The dragons, of course."

Oliver grinned.

Storm Cloud suggested calling a Draconic Council meeting. The other dragons might have information that could help, and they would also appoint a dragon to accompany us on our search.

"It will take three or four days for everyone to gather. In the meantime, you're welcome to stay here," he said.

The cave was warm and sheltered, if a bit dark. But we had left much of our food and gear in the hut at the bottom of the mountain. I told Storm Cloud this.

"Well, that's no problem. We can go get it and bring it up here."

"I am *not* climbing this mountain twice," said Ella.

"Well, of course not," replied Storm Cloud, clearly cowed by the tone of Ella's voice. I fought to suppress a smile as Storm Cloud continued. "I'll fly one of you down to the hut after dark. You can collect your things, and I'll fly you back up."

"I'll go!" volunteered Oliver with a grin.

As soon as it was dark, Storm Cloud squeezed out through the crack, followed by Oliver. They were gone less than an hour and, when they returned, Oliver's hair was tousled, and he was breathless.

"That! Was! Awesome!"

Almost immediately, Storm Cloud took off again to alert the other council members of the meeting.

With all our gear, plus a few candles Oliver had nicked from the hut, we were able to make ourselves quite comfortable, spreading out our sleeping bags on top of Storm Cloud's hoard. We didn't have much food left, but we made a decent enough dinner from a packet of noodles and some crackers.

"I don't know what we're going to eat for the next four days," said Ella. "We'll make it through tomorrow, but after that…"

"Maybe Storm Cloud can take me down to the grocery store in Te Anau," said Oliver eagerly.

"Right. I can see a dragon just dropping into the car park at New World. That wouldn't cause any trouble," said Tui, rolling her eyes.

"Well, he could drop me nearby," said Oliver.

"And what would you buy groceries with?" I asked. "We've got twelve dollars. That's not going to buy much food."

"We're sitting on a pile of gold," said Oliver.

"Don't ever steal from a dragon!" Ella and I spoke in unison. Our studies of dragon culture had taught us that a dragon's sense of personal property was strong, and a dragon knew his hoard in intimate detail. He would know if even one grain of gold dust went missing. And it wouldn't be pretty when he discovered it.

We decided to consult with Storm Cloud when he returned. We were all exhausted and, soon after dinner, we fell asleep. None of us woke when Storm Cloud returned shortly before first light.

It was the dragon's snores a few hours later that got us all out of bed. I had heard Dad snoring before and thought he was loud, but his snores were nothing compared to the rumbling freight train sound that Storm Cloud produced. We slipped through the crack into the morning sunshine to eat breakfast in the relative quiet of the mountaintop.

"This is the end of the food," said Ella as she pulled out an odd assortment of crackers, peanut butter and chocolate. It was a strange breakfast and not particularly satisfying.

"We're also low on water," said Tui, shaking her nearly empty bottle.

"How many days did Storm Cloud say we had to wait?" asked Oliver.

I looked out over the fog-filled valley below. My dad was out there somewhere. I didn't care about the food and water—I just wanted to find Dad. Sitting here, doing nothing for four days wasn't going to be easy. I sighed.

"We'll find your dad." Ella patted my arm.

"But what if we don't? What if we find him...dead somewhere?"

The pain in Ella's eyes reminded me that I was the only one with a father who still *might* be alive.

"I'm sorry. It's just..."

"Nathan," said Tui, stepping toward me and putting a hand on my shoulder. "We're going to find your dad." She was blinking back tears. "We're going to find him and, whether he's alive or not, we're going to end dragon slaying, so no kids have to ever lose a parent that way again."

Ella and Oliver nodded their agreement.

"Thanks. All of you." I took a deep breath, fighting my own tears. "So what do we need to do in the next four days besides find food and water?"

The others shrugged. I continued.

"Well, if Storm Cloud is willing to help, I think we should all practice our Draconic as much as possible. It will come in handy at the Council meeting, I'm sure."

"It also might be worthwhile to see if we can gather more information about what Drachenmorder is up to," suggested Oliver. "Maybe Storm Cloud can drop us off near the school, so we can do some spying."

"You want to go back to the school?" asked Ella. "I thought we just escaped from there."

"He has a point," said Tui. "Drachenmorder now knows Sir Archibald is alive. I'll bet he's looking for him too. And he might have more information than we do about who kidnapped him."

"He might lead us right to him," I suggested.

"Or he might catch us and kill us," said Ella.

"Oliver is right." Storm Cloud's rumbling voice made us jump. How he'd slipped unseen out of the cave was a mystery, but he surprised us all. "I think Drachenmorder is likely to have more information about Archie's whereabouts than we do. It's worth finding out where he is and what he's doing to find your father."

"I doubt it's actually Drachenmorder doing the searching," said Ella. "He strikes me as the type to get others to do his dirty work."

"Indeed," mused Storm Cloud.

"The school is close to Alexandra," I said. "So, if Drachenmorder were going to start searching, he might send someone to Alexandra first."

157

"Or to Garston, which is the closest town to where your father disappeared," said Oliver.

"But Alexandra is where they go to get supplies for the school—petrol, and everything. They would have to go through there on their way anywhere else, even to Garston."

"Nathan is right. I think it's worth taking a trip to Alexandra," said Storm Cloud. "And perhaps you'll show me where the school is on the way," he added, a cold and menacing tone to his voice.

"Only if you promise not to torch it," I said. "There are good people there."

"Drachenmorder is there."

"But he's not the only one. Sir Leandro defied Drachenmorder to get us out. He provided us with the information and equipment we needed to start searching for my dad. And I'm sure he's not the only one who would help us against Drachenmorder. Don't attack your allies."

Storm Cloud harrumphed and snorted smoke, but he agreed not to destroy the school.

"If we go to Alexandra, can we stop by a grocery store and get some food?" asked Ella.

Chapter 19
Alexandra

To avoid being seen by anyone, Storm Cloud would only fly at night. In spite of his ability to slink silently in and out of his cave, it was wise—you couldn't exactly hide a dragon in a clear blue sky.

"But we're out of food and water," Ella reminded us.

"Oh, that's no problem. There's a spring not far down the mountain, and I picked up some food for you last night." Storm Cloud disappeared into his cave and reappeared with three dead rabbits, which he tossed onto the rocks in front of me.

"You want us to eat those?" Ella's nose wrinkled in disgust.

Tui shrugged. "Dad used to bring home rabbits now and again. They're not bad."

"But they've still got the fur on!"

"Oh, you don't like fur?" I had to jump out of the way as Storm Cloud directed a blast of fire at the rabbits. The stench of burning hair was overwhelming, and we all covered our noses with our sleeves. "There," declared the dragon. "Hair's all gone."

We looked down at the scorched but now hairless rabbits. Ella whimpered, and Oliver giggled.

Tui did her best with the rabbits, skinning and gutting them. When it came time to cook them, she enlisted Storm Cloud's help.

"Dad always marinated the meat before grilling," she said. "But this will have to do. Go ahead, Storm Cloud. Not too hot."

Storm Cloud breathed a gentle, steady flame over the prepared rabbit, stopping now and again for Tui to turn the pieces. The result was edible, but it was bland and a bit gamey. We ate rabbit for lunch and rabbit for dinner. I considered our twelve dollars and how little it would buy, and how much rabbit we'd have to eat over the coming days. It wasn't a pleasant thought.

Before dawn the next morning, Oliver and I climbed onto Storm Cloud's back. We had decided it was safer for just two of us to go to Alexandra, since we'd attract less attention that way. I carried our money and a list of grocery requests that totally outstripped our measly twelve dollars.

Riding on Storm Cloud's back was both the most amazing experience ever and the most terrifying. As Storm Cloud launched himself off the mountain, I shut my eyes and hung on tightly to his spines, my stomach lodged in my throat. He fell for so long before opening his wings to catch the wind, I thought for certain we would crash onto the rocks below. Oliver seemed to have no such fears as he whooped and laughed.

It was overcast and, even once I was able to open my eyes, there was little to be seen in the darkness. I was thankful for that. I wasn't sure I wanted to see how far from the ground we were.

"We'll have a nor'wester blowing by this afternoon," said Storm Cloud. "If it's rainy enough, I might be able to pick you up before dark. I'm pretty well-camouflaged in the rain."

"I can't imagine we'll be able to hang out in Alexandra all day without being noticed as loiterers," I said. "I expect we'll be at the pick-up spot by mid-afternoon, regardless of the weather."

Storm Cloud dropped us off in the lee of a large boulder about two kilometres outside Alexandra, then flapped off into the darkness. We waited until it was light and then struck out toward the town.

It was nearly eight before we entered Alexandra. We hiked in via the Central Otago Rail Trail, figuring we would look less out of place if someone saw us—lots of people hiked and biked the route. Unfortunately, neither of us had ever entered Alexandra from that direction, and we weren't entirely sure how to get from the rail trail to the grocery store. Nor were we entirely sure where to go for information about Drachenmorder. Now that we were here, it seemed foolish to think we would learn anything by just wandering around town.

"What day of the week is it?" I asked, suddenly thinking about how it would look for two school-aged kids to be wandering around out of school on a weekday.

"Saturday," replied Oliver. At least one thing was in our favour.

When we reached a street that crossed the rail trail, we turned toward the centre of town.

"Best place for information is going to be a cafe," said Oliver as we neared the main street.

"But we've got almost no money, and we've got to save that for food to take back. We can't just sit in a cafe without buying anything."

"We can tell them we're waiting for someone—our parents—who were behind us on the rail trail. It'll give us a few minutes, at least."

The Tin Goose Cafe looked promising. There were a few people inside and bicycles parked out front. My stomach growled at the smell of baking as we walked in.

"Oh! Blueberry muffins," cried Oliver.

"We'll have to wait 'til Mum and Dad get here," I said, loudly enough for the woman clearing a table nearby to hear. I steered Oliver to a table near the window.

"I'll get us some water. Keep your eyes and ears open."

When I returned with two full glasses, Oliver hissed at me.

"Turn away from the window." I followed his instruction and sat down, casting a questioning look his way.

"That car—the one that just pulled up in front—is one of the school staff's vehicles."

"How do you know?"

"The number plate—EVJ436—I recognise it."

"You memorised the number plate?"

Oliver shrugged, "I don't know. I have a thing about number plates. They stick in my memory."

I shook my head, mystified, but thankful for Oliver's oddities. "Do you know whose car it is?"

"No. I only remember I've seen it at school. No one has gotten out of it yet, and I can't see in because of the glare on the windscreen."

"Put your hood up. Until we know who it is, we don't want them seeing us." I pulled out my phone and pretended to show Oliver something, so our bent heads wouldn't look odd.

A moment later, the door opened, and I saw Oliver relax as he peeked out from under his hood to see who had come in.

"Sir Christopher," he whispered as he began to raise his hand to get the man's attention.

I grabbed his hand. "Don't."

"But Sir Christopher—"

"Is a complete unknown, as far as we're concerned."

"But—"

I quickly told Oliver how Sir Christopher had talked to his sword, and how I didn't entirely trust him any more.

"He might be on our side, but we don't know. Even if he's not actively working with Drachenmorder, as a teacher, he'll have to take us back to school if he finds us here."

Sir Christopher ordered a coffee, and then sat down at a table nearby. He hadn't noticed us, but already my palms were sweaty. What would happen if he did? I snuck a quick glance in his direction and was relieved to see his back turned toward us.

Oliver tapped my arm and pointed toward the street. "Drachenmorder's car," he whispered. A dark blue SUV was pulling up at the kerb. We both hunched lower over my phone.

Two men entered the cafe. We didn't dare look up, but we heard them order and saw their boots join Sir Christopher's at his table.

"Well?" began Sir Christopher.

"Nothing new." The voice was gruff, and I didn't recognise it. "It's pretty clear she's got McMannis, but we don't know where she's keeping him."

"You've searched her house in Dunedin?"

"We have. He's not there."

"Surely she didn't take him to Auckland."

"No, neither she nor any of her staff have left the South Island in the past two months."

Sir Christopher sighed. "So where has she taken him?"

There was a moment of silence. I peeked from under my hood at the trio. I didn't recognise either of the men who arrived in Drachenmorder's car. They were built like rugby players and were casually dressed, as though they had simply popped into the cafe for a coffee before a fishing trip. Sir Christopher spoke again. "And the kids?"

"We tracked them to near James Peak. They went to the top of the farm track, but looks like they got stymied by the weather."

"So they didn't make it to the peak?"

163

"No. But we tidied up your mess up there, just in case someone should come snooping around."

Oliver and I looked at each other with wide eyes. *Sir Christopher's mess.*

"Then where did they go?" asked Sir Christopher.

"They started walking up the Nevis Valley toward Garston. Looks like they were picked up by one of the locals. We asked in Garston. They were there. Took a bus to Milford Sound on Wednesday."

"And?"

"They never arrived in Milford Sound."

"Did you question the bus driver?"

"He says he never saw them get off. He said they were headed to Milford to meet up with their parents who were on their honeymoon. We got a list of everywhere he stopped along the way. He thinks they must have gotten off at Te Anau. That was the only time he was away from the bus."

"Find them," growled Sir Christopher. "I'll take over the search for McMannis. I may know where Chang has hidden him."

I didn't need to hear more, and my hands were shaking. I nodded toward the door, and Oliver and I quietly stood and walked out. We sauntered down the street, turned the first corner, and then broke into a sprint.

We didn't spend much longer in Alexandra. We picked up all the food we could afford, then sped back to the rock where Storm Cloud had dropped us off. It wasn't even lunchtime yet, but the wind was picking up, and we were hopeful for the concealing rain Storm Cloud needed if he was to collect us early.

"*Sir Christopher?*" Ella responded to the news Oliver and I brought back from Alexandra. "No way."

We were sitting in the comfort of Storm Cloud's lair, eating cheese sandwiches while rain lashed the mountainside.

"I'm sorry I didn't believe you before," said Tui.

"It doesn't matter," I said. "We wouldn't have done anything differently if we'd known. The important thing is that now we have a clue as to who kidnapped my dad."

"Yes," agreed Storm Cloud. "A woman named Chang. Hmm…" Storm Cloud hummed to himself, his brow furrowed. We all leaned forward in anticipation.

"No idea who she is."

I sighed in frustration.

"When in doubt, google it," said Tui.

"We're in the middle of nowhere," I said.

"But we're on top of a mountain. I checked earlier—there's cell phone reception up here. Outside the cave, of course."

"But it's pouring out there."

"It'll only take a minute." Tui pulled on her raincoat and slipped through the crack, phone in hand.

A few minutes later, she returned with a frustrated frown.

"A hundred and thirty people named Chang in Auckland. None in Dunedin." She flopped down with the rest of us.

"Too many to narrow it down in one place, and no sign of her in the other. Great," I said.

"Maybe one of the other council members will know her," suggested Storm Cloud. "We'll just have to wait and see."

Chapter 20
Draconic Council

Monday night, we all clambered onto Storm Cloud's back to go to the Draconic Council meeting. The journey wasn't far, as the crow flies (or as the dragon flies). Like our trip to Alexandra, the first swoop off the mountain was the worst. Oliver whooped with glee. Ella screamed. Storm Cloud cautioned us to stay quiet.

"We fly at night, but there are plenty of trampers around at this time of year, especially once we get into the Hollyford River valley. It's best if they don't know we're here." So we remained silent, tightly gripping the spikes along the dragon's back and shivering in the cold air. Storm Cloud narrated quietly as we went, describing our descent between Mt. Gifford and Mt. Gunn, where his sister had lived. We turned to the left in a graceful arc and headed up the Hollyford River over a swathe of beech forest. The moon lit our faces, though the valley was in shadow.

About fifteen minutes later, Oliver cried out, pointing to a dark form rising out of the trees below. As it gained altitude, slipping out of the shadow into moonlight, we saw it was another dragon. It was smaller than Storm Cloud, and its scales shone in the moonlight.

"That's Foggy Bottom," said Storm Cloud. "She joins us for the council meeting."

The second dragon spiralled upward, smoothly coming out of a last curve to glide alongside us.

166

"Greetings Your Majestic Greenness, Father Storm Cloud," she said in a voice only slightly less like a landslide than Storm Cloud's.

"Greetings Daughter Foggy Bottom," replied Storm Cloud. "Good to see you looking well."

Foggy Bottom cast a curious glance at us clinging to Storm Cloud's back, but neither dragon spoke again as we continued up the valley.

After passing a steep valley on our right, the dragons turned sharply uphill. Foggy Bottom climbed rapidly, and Storm Cloud followed more slowly, burdened as he was with four riders. They climbed past the shrubby edge of the forest and onto the broad, tussock-covered top of Prospector Peak. Both dragons landed gently and gracefully, which is more than I can say for how we slid off Storm Cloud's back. Oliver was the only one of us who didn't end up landing on his backside.

Four dragons waited on the peak, two so well hidden we didn't see them until Storm Cloud introduced them to us.

Night Stalker and Dawn were Fiordland fringed dragons. They were much smaller than Storm Cloud, and their scales looked copper in the moonlight. I was disappointed to note they were both females, and neither sported the bright orange neck flap that gave the Fiordland fringed dragon its name.

Rocky and Jade were South Island scree dragons. When they stopped moving, they were indistinguishable from boulders. Even in the dim light, I could see that their scales were rougher than the other dragons', and their markings mimicked lichens. Less than half Storm Cloud's size, they looked even smaller because their wings were tiny—clearly no use in flying.

We didn't wait long before two more dragons came winging toward the peak. Storm Cloud introduced them as Bluebottle and Bluette.

"Southern blue dragons have no creativity when it comes to names," he muttered quietly to me in English.

Each dragon greeted us formally in Draconic and then leaned disconcertingly close to sniff us. Oliver giggled every time, as though he was being tickled. Tui stumbled back from them the first few times, until Ella and I explained it was how dragons greeted one another.

Not that my palms didn't sweat every time an enormous dragon head snaked toward me. But I stood my ground and the sniffing didn't last long before they declared me Archie's son.

"Now, we're just waiting on Rata and Kowhai," said Storm Cloud.

Night Stalker rolled her eyes. "Those two are always late."

"Might be best to start without them," said Bluette...or maybe it was Bluebottle. I'd forgotten which was which.

"We'll wait," declared Storm Cloud.

The night was almost calm—only a light breeze rustled the tussocks. I looked out at the surrounding mountains. Snow shone brightly in the moonlight, and forested valleys looked like spilled ink. I spied a scree slope on the side of the next mountain and wondered if Rocky and Jade had come from there. Nobody spoke, and the only sound was the sigh of the wind mixed with the breath of dragons.

"Here they come," said Foggy Bottom, breaking the silence.

I scanned the sky but saw nothing. I was about to ask where they were when I heard a rapid flapping sound behind me and turned to find two tiny dragons swooping and racing up the hill. They laughed and chattered so fast in Draconic that I couldn't make out what they were saying. Moonlight sparkled off them, and I caught flashes of red and yellow as they came nearer.

They reached the top, turned circles around the other dragons' heads, and landed on a pair of lichen-covered rocks, one of which turned out to be Jade, who shook her head. The tiny dragon laughed and flitted towards me, landing on my left shoulder and peering intently into my left eye.

Sniffing loudly, the tiny dragon said, "You must be Archie's boy."

I nodded. "And you're a gold fairy dragon," I said in wonder. "But they're extinct."

The dragon laughed again. "That's exactly what your father said the first time he saw me. And with the same dumb look in his eyes."

Storm Cloud cleared his throat, and the two newcomers collected themselves enough to offer the formal greeting, "Greetings Your Majestic Greenness, Father Storm Cloud."

"Greetings Daughters Rata and Kowhai. Now that we're all here, let us begin."

"You're all Storm Cloud's children?" I whispered to Rata, who was still perched on my shoulder.

She laughed and replied, "No. The term Father is used for the council leader, and he calls the other council members Daughter and Son. I've no idea why—it's just what we do," she added in response to my curious look.

Storm Cloud cleared his throat again, and we turned our attention to him.

"I have called you all together to discuss a matter of urgency relating to Archibald McMannis. As you all know, I was to have met with Archie and a representative of the Royal Society of Dragon Slayers nearly three months ago. When I arrived at our meeting site, I found Archie's companion dead and Archie gone. I assumed he had betrayed us. Three days ago, Archie's son, Nathan, arrived at my lair with his friends and the news that Archie has been kidnapped."

169

At this, the dragons muttered, and Rata's claws gripped painfully into my shoulder.

"Who kidnapped him?" asked Jade.

"We don't know. That's why I've called you together—to see if you have any thoughts or clues as to who might have done this."

"It was obviously Drachenmorder, don't you think?" said Rocky. "I had to hide from one of his hunting parties just two weeks ago. They walked right across my scree slope."

"That was, of course, our first thought," answered Storm Cloud. "But Drachenmorder has no reason to kidnap Archie. We believe he actually tried to kill Archie along with his companion, and thought he had done so. Someone else then arrived and took Archie away."

Storm Cloud spoke in Draconic. He had apologised to us in advance, explaining that many dragons didn't speak human languages and, while all the dragons at the meeting understood a little English, they couldn't hold a Draconic Council meeting in the language.

Ella translated the conversation as best she could, not because her Draconic was much better than mine, but because she was better at catching the nuances of the conversation. She noticed things I didn't—like Rocky's sceptical eyes, Storm Cloud's irritation with Bluette, who kept fidgeting, and Night Stalker's ambivalence.

The gathered dragons asked Storm Cloud many questions about what we had told him and what he knew about the situation. When he had related everything, he asked the others if they'd heard of any recent encounters with humans that might point to Archie.

"Tealblue, who used to live near me, had a whole nest of eggs stolen just last week. We both moved our nests," said Bluette.

"Could have been rats, or dogs—" began Night Stalker.

"It was humans," said Bluette. "Their smell was all over the place."

"I surprised a pair of men near my lair about two months ago," said Dawn. "I assumed they had gotten lost, and I scared them away. But they came back the next day, snooping around the lair. I didn't have any eggs for them to steal, but I wonder now whether that's what they were looking for."

"Did you see where they went after they left your lair?" asked Storm Cloud.

Dawn smiled. "I didn't give them the opportunity to leave."

Ella blanched as she translated Dawn's words, and my palms began to sweat, in spite of the cool breeze.

Kowhai cocked her head to one side. "My grandmother used to tell stories about men who took dragons and eggs and kept them in cages." She shuddered. "They were terrible stories—most of those captured died. And those who hatched in captivity never learned how to forage so, if they were released, they died anyway."

"You think that there's someone trading in dragons as...pets?" I asked, forgetting that Storm Cloud had advised us not to speak. *Council meetings can become heated. You don't want to get into the middle of an argument between dragons.*

"I'm just saying it's been done before, and why else would people be stealing eggs?"

"For omelettes?" suggested Oliver with a giggle. His joke didn't go over well with the dragons, and Storm Cloud gave him a stern look.

"Kowhai has a point," said Foggy Bottom. "Maybe someone is looking for pets. That rules out Drachenmorder."

There was a murmur of agreement. Drachenmorder was definitely focused on killing dragons, not keeping them alive. But who would trade in pet dragons?

171

"We need to know who else has had eggs stolen, or has seen men near their nests or lairs," said Storm Cloud. "If we can find a pattern in the thefts, we may be able to pinpoint where to find the thieves."

"But how is that going to help us find Archie?" asked Rata.

"Archie knows more about dragons than any other human alive. He understands our biology and our cultures. He knows what we prefer to eat. He knows where many of us live."

"He was kidnapped for information about us," concluded Foggy Bottom.

"Precisely."

"What if *he's* the one stealing eggs?" asked Rocky, eliciting a murmur from the other dragons.

"I know you've spent less time with Archie than the rest of us, Rocky. If you knew him better, you would know he would never do such a thing," said Foggy Bottom.

"But he's *Sir* Archibald. He's killed dragons."

"And he has always regretted it," said Storm Cloud. "He hates the knighthood for what it represents, and he never uses the title himself."

"Once a dragon slayer, always a dragon slayer."

"Archie isn't a dragon slayer."

"Right, and I'm a house cat. I don't know why we're even discussing this. Humans are vermin."

The argument grew heated and so filled with what I assumed were dragon swear words, that Ella and I both lost the ability to follow the conversation. Rata flew off my shoulder to scream in Rocky's face. Rocky spurted flames at her, blasting her backwards into Foggy Bottom's chest. Foggy Bottom retaliated with her own blast of fire. But some of it scorched Night Stalker, who lashed out with her tail, clipping Bluebottle.

The Council meeting descended into a melee. We didn't need to understand Draconic to realise we didn't want to be anywhere near the action. Ella led the way, skittering down the slope to take shelter behind a large rock.

"What the…" said Tui.

"And we thought Storm Cloud had a temper," said Ella.

"Do you think every council meeting is like this?" asked Oliver.

"Well, Storm Cloud did warn us," I said.

"*Blarghstras*," said Ella. We all laughed.

"So what do we do now?" asked Oliver.

"I think we just need to wait it out. They'll come to a decision at some point," I said.

"And if they decide to eat us?" asked Tui.

"I don't think they will," said Ella. "It looked to me like Rocky was the only one who didn't want to help. Night Stalker wasn't fully convinced, but she wasn't hostile. And Storm Cloud, Foggy Bottom, Dawn, Bluette, Rata, and Kowhai were definitely on our side."

The fight didn't last long, but we stayed where we were in case tempers flared again. The rumbling of the dragons' voices was indistinct from our safe location, so we couldn't tell what was being said, but the tone had grown calm.

Half an hour later, Night Stalker and Dawn hopped down the slope past us.

"They move like rabbits." Oliver giggled.

"I don't think their wings are big enough to fly much," said Ella.

"Look! There go the southern blues," said Tui.

"The party must have broken up." I turned to walk back up the hill. "Shall we go back?"

Chapter 21
Foggy Bottom

We made our way back to the summit to find Storm Cloud stamping out a still-smouldering tussock. Foggy Bottom and Rata were the only other dragons remaining.

"Ah, there you are," said Storm Cloud. "I thought we might have to go searching for you."

"Yeah, sorry we missed the second half of the meeting," I said.

"You were wise to step away. Council meetings aren't safe for those without scales."

"So what's next?"

"Foggy Bottom and Rata will join your party."

Rata flitted to my shoulder. "An adventure! It's so exciting."

Storm Cloud gave Rata a stern look. "You have an important job to do, Rata. It's not a holiday." Then he addressed us all. "You will travel to Foggy Bottom's lair, near Haast. The other members of the council will survey the areas around the known incidences of egg theft and report any further information to you."

"Shouldn't we go to the places where eggs were stolen to look for clues?" I asked.

"There will be little there that the dragons can't pick up and tell you about," said Foggy Bottom. "I live between the locations of the two incidents we know about, so it's as good a place as any to be."

"So where do you live?"

"Mount Marks. It's just above Haast—I can look right down on the village."

"There aren't rabbits there, are there?" asked Ella.

"Oh, plenty of them."

Ella sighed, and I couldn't blame her. Our twelve dollars had barely bought us enough food for two days, and I wasn't keen to live solely on rabbit.

Foggy Bottom and Rata followed us back to Storm Cloud's lair where we packed up our things.

"Still plenty of time to get home before dawn," said Foggy Bottom. "Hop on."

We said our goodbyes to Storm Cloud and thanked him for his help.

"Just find young Archie. Meanwhile, I'll take care of Drachenmorder."

"Please don't burn the school," I begged. I had decided not to tell him where it was, but when we flew right over it on the way to Alexandra, Storm Cloud had put two and two together and figured out it was the school.

"I won't touch the school. Now I know where he is, though, it will be easier to target him."

I nodded. I believed he meant what he said, but I feared he might forget his promise in a fit of rage. Still, there was nothing I could do about it. I joined the others on Foggy Bottom's back.

Rata flitted to Foggy Bottom's head. "Yeehaa! Here we go." She giggled. Foggy Bottom shook her head and snapped at Rata as she fluttered up.

"You've got your own wings. I'm not carrying you."

Rata giggled again. "It was worth a try." Then she zipped off into the night.

Foggy Bottom flapped steadily over mountains and up valleys. At first, I tried to make sense of our route, but I wasn't used to seeing the landscape from above, and the dragon favoured remote locations, so we only occasionally passed signs of human habitation. The sky was just beginning to lighten in the east, and we were all struggling to stay awake when Foggy Bottom finally soared along a bare ridge and landed at the edge of a small lake. A cliff rose above us—the rocky peak of Mount Marks.

"Don't get off," said the dragon. "The cave entrance is high on the cliff face—you'll need to climb up my neck to reach it." She bent down to take a long drink from the lake.

"Ah! That's better. Now, to bed." She approached the cliff face, and we could see it was deeply fissured. She leaned her head into a crack about ten metres up and directed us to climb. I wondered where we were to go when we reached her head, but first Oliver, then Tui disappeared above me. It wasn't until I stepped carefully onto the bridge of Foggy Bottom's nose that I could make out the cavern.

Tui and Oliver had already pulled out their torches and were shining them around in wonder when I entered. The cavern was smaller than Storm Cloud's lair, but more sparkly. The walls were silver with mica and looked more like metal than rock. Foggy Bottom's hoard contained less jade and more gold than Storm Cloud's, and the gold was polished to a high sheen. The overall effect was one of stunning brilliance, even though the only light came from two meagre torches.

"Awesome!" was all any of us could say.

Once we were all safely inside, Foggy Bottom squeezed herself into the cave.

"Welcome to my lair." She yawned, and a burst of flame shot from her mouth. "I'm exhausted, and I assume you are too. Make yourselves comfortable. Get some sleep. We'll talk after we've rested."

I woke to a strange weight on my chest. Someone was pressing on me, making it hard to breathe. Still half asleep, I imagined Drachenmorder standing over me, his expensive hiking boot resting on my chest. My eyes flew open in terror. In the light coming through the cave entrance, I saw Rata, curled like a kitten on top of my sleeping bag. I laughed in relief. As I shifted, she woke. She yawned, displaying a purple tongue and a row of tiny needle-sharp teeth, and stretched her limbs.

Seeing her in the daylight for the first time, I understood why she was named Rata—the undersides of her wings were as red as a rata flower. She looked around the cave and sighed.

"I love Foggy Bottom's lair. See, we match!" The tiny dragon flitted off my chest and dove into the piles of gold. It wasn't a perfect match—Rata's scales tended toward coppery rather than gold—but I could see what she meant. She glittered as much as the gold. She flew back up, giggling.

"Wake up! Wake up! Wake up!" she cried. "It's afternoon already, you sleepyheads." She pounced on Oliver, who grumbled and shifted. She clambered across Tui's sleeping bag and nipped at her shoulder. She landed on Ella's head. Ella screamed and bolted upright.

Rata rolled on the ground in laughter. Then, she righted herself and flew toward Foggy Bottom's head, resting on a pillow of gold nearby. She landed on the huge dragon's nose and skittered quickly to her eyes to nip at her eyelids.

"Wake up, lard bottom." She pranced on Foggy Bottom's forehead, her claws kneading the dragon's scaly skin like cat claws. Foggy Bottom shook her head, but didn't open her eyes. Rata clambered onto one of Foggy Bottom's head spines and, clinging there with all four feet, leaned down toward her ear.

177

"Wake uuuup!" she sang. As this had no effect whatsoever, she punctuated her words with a blast of fire directly into Foggy Bottom's ear.

Foggy Bottom seemed to explode. In an instant, she raised her head and shook Rata off and then, with a bellow, she shot a jet of fire at the little dragon where she hovered.

Screams rang out in the cavern. Ella's was the loudest, but she wasn't alone. Tui scrambled for the exit, and Oliver pulled his sleeping bag over his head.

Rata's blackened body tumbled to the floor of the cave. She writhed on the ground, and it was a few moments before I realised her pained gasps were actually laughter.

"Hahahaha! That was the BEST," squealed Rata when she finally regained her voice. "You should have seen the look on your face. Hahahaha!" She collapsed again into laughter. Foggy Bottom gave a humph and a small chuckle. Tui came creeping back from the entrance, and Oliver peeked out of his sleeping bag.

Rata rolled onto her feet, still giggling. She looked down at her blackened scales.

"Aw, you got me all sooty."

"Serves you right, you little pest." growled Foggy Bottom, though with laughter in her voice. "Go wash yourself off."

Rata flitted out of the cave in a fresh bout of giggles.

Foggy Bottom sighed. "That one is nothing but trouble. Why Storm Cloud thought she should be assigned to this mission, I don't know."

"So what's the plan for today?" asked Oliver.

"Breakfast first," I said. "I'm starving."

"I think it would be lunch by now—it's nearly two in the afternoon," Ella said. "Problem is, we have no food left."

"Well, I can probably scare up some rab—" Foggy Bottom began.

"No rabbits," declared Ella. "We need regular human food."

"Rabbit isn't bad," said Tui.

"I won't eat any more rabbit. We're going down to Haast, and we're going to get some proper food."

"Ella, we don't have any money left," I said.

"Take some of my gold," offered Foggy Bottom. "I've got plenty—I'll hardly notice."

"Really?" I was surprised by the dragon's generosity. "I thought dragons were quite protective of their hoards."

"Oh, we are—don't ever try to steal from a dragon. But dragons often share with each other. Think of yourselves as honorary dragons."

"But we can't buy anything with gold nuggets," said Tui, picking up a handful and letting them run through her fingers.

"Look around," said Foggy Bottom. "I know I've got a whole lot of gold coins in here. Take what you need."

So we sifted through the drifts of gold nuggets. The coins seemed to have settled to the bottom and, once we discovered that, it was easy to sweep away the gold nuggets to find the money. Most were modern New Zealand currency, but there were a few real treasures in the mix.

"Look at this one!" cried Oliver, holding out a large battered coin. Ella took it, turning it over in her hand.

"Bonaparte…40 Francs. It's French."

"And old, too," said Tui, taking a look at it.

"Minted in 1807, I believe," said Foggy Bottom. "Brought to New Zealand by the French colonisers in Akaroa. I picked it up off the beach when I was visiting my cousin on Banks Peninsula in 1843."

"Eighteen forty-three? How old are you?" asked Tui.

"Not very old, by dragon standards—I'm one hundred and eighty-six. I was just a youngster when I picked up this coin. It was the first of my hoard." She spoke lovingly of the coin, and Tui gently replaced it in the pile.

By the time Rata came back from her bath, sparkling even more than before, we had gathered nearly a hundred and fifty dollars in one- and two-dollar coins.

"Let's go get something to eat," said Oliver.

"You're not going looking like that," said Rata. "I wouldn't be caught dead looking and smelling so bad in public. The lake is lovely for baths."

She was right. We had been hiking and sleeping rough for days. We might not notice our filth, but the people we met in Haast would.

"I suppose no one thought to grab soap when we left," said Ella with a sigh.

An hour later, Foggy Bottom dropped us off in a patch of dense bush near the township of Haast.

"Take your time. I'll pick you up here after dark."

Our first stop was the Hard Antler Bar and Restaurant where we ordered half the menu, gobbling down our food like starving wolves.

"Ah! That was delicious." Tui sighed and leaned back in her chair.

"Much better than rabbit," said Ella.

"And there's a flush toilet too. Excuse me." Tui strolled to the ladies' room, passing by the bar on her way.

It was only late afternoon, but there was a cluster of people already perched on barstools, watching a cricket match on the television. I closed my eyes—now that my stomach was full, the lack of sleep was catching up with me.

Tui bustled back from the toilet. "Come on. Let's go."

"What's the rush? We have until after dark," I said.

"Go pay our bill, and let's get out of here. Check out the tall guy with the hat, but don't let him see you looking."

The anxious look on Tui's face made me head to the cashier to pay without asking any more questions. The man with the hat wasn't hard to spot. He was half a head taller than anyone else, and the only one wearing an Aussie-style cattleman's hat. For a minute, I thought it was Professor Marshall, but this bloke was a lot beefier than him. His eyes were on the cricket game, so I was able to get a good look at his face without him noticing—clean shaven, no chin, and brown curls sticking out from under his hat. His face was flushed, like he'd already had quite a few drinks. He wore olive green convertible pants and a black T-shirt. Aside from the hat and his height, a completely unremarkable man.

"That'll be seventy-five ninety," said the cashier, bringing me back to the task at hand. I scooped a pile of coins out of my backpack and counted out the money.

"Got a few extra coins?" the tall man asked, looking over at me.

I shrugged. "Saved up my spending money."

I glanced at Tui, who was watching me with a worried look on her face. When I finished paying, she pulled us all out the door and down the street, only stopping once we had turned a corner and the restaurant was no longer in view.

"What was that all about?" I asked.

"That man—the one with the hat—when I passed him on the way to the toilet, he was talking to the woman

181

behind the bar. He asked her if she'd seen any dragons lately."

"What?" asked Oliver.

"The woman laughed and told him no, that the closest Hobbit filming sites were over near Queenstown, and besides, Smaug was all CGI. I listened from the hallway outside the toilets. He was trying to pick her up then. Said he was working in the area and wouldn't mind seeing her when she gets off work." Tui made a face.

"Do you think the guy was actually looking for dragons?" asked Ella.

"Yeah, maybe it was just a bad pick-up line," I suggested.

"I don't know, but doesn't it seem like too much of a coincidence we're here searching for dragon hunters, and we hear someone asking about dragons in the pub?"

"Maybe." I wasn't entirely convinced, but it was possible we had run into one of the very people we were looking for.

We walked to the Haast Food Centre—a tiny grocery store catering mostly to travellers. Instant meals, muesli bars, porridge—it had everything we needed. We were even able to get more fuel cartridges for the camp stove Sir Leandro had given us.

"And don't forget the soap," said Ella. "And a comb for me." She put the items on the counter next to the food.

Oliver rolled his eyes. "Girls!" Ella punched him on the arm.

Chapter 22
Clues

Rata was busy making colourful arrangements of flowers and gold all around Foggy Bottom's lair when we returned.

"Oh, you're back," she squealed. "Do you like what I've done?"

We all agreed her arrangements were lovely, but Foggy Bottom grumbled a few words about doing something useful now and again instead of focusing on frivolity.

We told the dragons what we had heard during the afternoon, and the dragons shared the information that had come in from the other members of the council.

"Bluette flew the coast, stopping in at half a dozen southern blue lairs between Milford Sound and Okarito," said Foggy Bottom. "Three of the six had either been robbed or suffered attempted robberies within the past two months."

"And I flew to the scree dragons up the Arawhata River," said Rata. "And they say they've seen at least ten men searching around the rocks up that way recently. They thought the men were looking for greenstone, but they never took any, even though there was plenty to be had." Rata turned to Foggy Bottom. "You see, I did do something useful today." She puffed a gout of flame in Foggy Bottom's direction, as if to say, "so there."

"Where's the Arawhata River?" asked Tui.

"South of us. It comes out near Jackson Bay, down the coast from Haast."

"All of the incidents have been here on the West Coast?" Oliver asked. Foggy Bottom nodded. "Tui, you might be right about that guy in the pub—he might have been looking for dragons."

We decided we needed to go back to the Hard Antler and see if we could learn more about the tall man in the hat. If we could find out where he was staying, we might be able to find the person named Chang. Or maybe Chang would show up at the restaurant too.

"But I don't think we should all go at the same time," I said.

"Why? Drachenmorder's not going to find us anytime soon—he's looking for us in Te Anau," argued Oliver.

"First off, we don't know where he's looking for us, or when he'll decide we're not in Te Anau and start looking elsewhere. But it's not really him I'm worried about," I said.

Tui was nodding. "It's so we can follow the man in the hat without being seen. If there are four of us, it's going to be impossible."

"Exactly, Tui. But two of us might be able to do it."

We ate dinner late—after our huge mid-afternoon lunch, none of us was very hungry—canned spaghetti and buttered bread.

"Ooo! What's for dinner?" asked Rata, eyeing the pot.

"Don't eat that stuff," warned Foggy Bottom. "That's people-food. It's disgusting."

Rata sighed. "I've always wondered about bread...the ducks and gulls seem to like it." She sat at our feet like a puppy, looking longingly as we ate our meal. Ella was the first to break down and toss her a piece of crust. Rata leapt to catch it.

"Mmmm! Delicious. More?"

I tossed a piece, and again she jumped at it, catching it in mid-air.

Soon, we were playing a rousing game of catch—throwing chunks of bread in unexpected directions to see if Rata could catch them before they landed. She caught every one and hardly even chewed before begging for the next.

We quit only after Rata had devoured half a loaf of bread.

"We should save the rest of this for tomorrow," I said.

Ella yawned, "Yeah. I'm tired. Let's clean up and go to bed."

We woke the next morning to a terrible, sulphurous smell.

"Ugh! What *is* that?" Ella wrinkled her nose.

"I don't know, but it smells like something crawled into the cave and died," I replied.

"Sorry, guys," said Rata. She was curled up on the floor. "It's my stomach." She moaned and ripped a loud fart. The smell was so strong I could practically taste it. I covered my nose with my sleeve.

"I told you not to eat that stuff," said Foggy Bottom.

"But it was so fluffy and delicious," said Rata mournfully. "I thought only you carnivorous dragons were gluten intolerant." Rata let out another fart and whimpered.

"Well, now you know."

"I'm sorry," said Ella. "We didn't know..."

185

"It's Rata's own fault. She's thirty-seven and should know better than to eat anything unnatural."

Rata moaned again, and then rushed out of the cave. "Excuse me!" she squeaked.

"Will she be okay?" asked Ella.

"Once all the bread is through her system—a couple of days I expect."

The day was wet, and the steady downpour meant we were confined to the cave all morning. With her upset stomach, Rata flew in and out of the cave all day like a demented bat.

"At least she's getting it out of her system," said Tui, when the little dragon had made another mad dash outdoors.

"I hope it's over soon," said Oliver. "Those farts are the worst!"

It was true. By lunchtime, the cave was stuffy and foul-smelling. A purple haze hung in the air. Everyone wanted to go to Haast and hang out in the Hard Antler for the afternoon, if only to get away from the farting dragon. We decided the only fair way to choose was to draw straws. Lacking straws, we put four one-dollar coins in a hat—whoever drew the two newest ones got to go to the village.

"Yes!" cheered Ella as she drew a shiny 2016 coin.

I drew the 2015 coin, so it was Ella and me sitting in the Hard Antler that afternoon with a pair of ginger beers and an order of chips. We had both taken our phones—to charge them and to take advantage of the Wi-Fi in the restaurant.

We had been sitting in the empty restaurant for an hour when, looking intently at her phone, Ella spoke up.

"Nathan. This is her. She's in the news."

"Huh?" I said. I'd been concentrating on a game of Hill Climb Racing.

"Ling Chang. This must be the Chang we're looking for." Ella leaned over the table, her eyes still on her phone. "There's an article in The Press about a guy who was caught at the Christchurch airport yesterday trying to smuggle a pair of jewelled geckoes out of New Zealand. Listen to this—*The man is suspected of being part of an international ring of criminals trading in wild animals. Among the man's recent contacts were found several texts to and from a wealthy businesswoman, Ling Chang. Ms. Chang was held briefly in China last year in connection to several cases of trafficking in endangered wildlife but was released without being charged. Ms. Chang owns several properties in New Zealand, and her company, LC Enterprises, has offices in Auckland and Christchurch.*"

"LC Enterprises," I repeated, typing the name into Google. "It's a livestock export business. Cattle, sheep, and goats."

"And dragons?" muttered Ella.

"It must be her," I said.

We both searched for information about Ling Chang and LC Enterprises, but our efforts yielded nothing useful. According to the company website, they'd exported ten thousand dairy cows, thirty thousand sheep, and a thousand goats to China last year, and were expanding their operations to Europe and North America in 2018. It didn't tell us much. Nowhere could we find any information about Ling Chang herself. She had no listing in the phone book, she wasn't named on the company website and, aside from her mention in the Press article, she didn't seem to exist anywhere on the Internet.

"There's a Ling-Ling Chang who's a politician in California," offered Ella.

"That can't be the same person," I replied. "Neither is Ling Chang the artist from New Jersey." I sighed. "Well, at least we have her first name now."

187

We saw no sign of the tall man in the hat that day, nor did Oliver and Tui the next day when it was their turn to go. On the third day, Ella and I went again. We were hopeful because it was Friday and there would likely be more people at the bar.

We weren't disappointed. By five o'clock, about a dozen men and women crowded the bar, and I spied the tall man in the hat among them. He was with two other men—one short and balding, with grey hair, the other young and brawny. After spending a few minutes at the bar, they moved to a table. Ella and I casually moved to one nearby where could overhear their conversation.

"So what's the plan for tomorrow?" asked the younger man.

"Mount Marks, if the weather's decent," replied the man in the hat. Ella and I exchanged worried glances.

"Didn't Geoff hit Mount Marks last month?" The short man picked up his bottle and took a swig.

"He did, but the weather packed in on him. Apparently he found tracks but wasn't able to follow them."

"D'ya think there's a lair up there? Seems unlikely."

"Unlikely, but there could be. If Geoff found tracks, it's worth a look. Hey, isn't that our number? Thirty-four?"

We waited while the men retrieved their meals from the kitchen's serving window. They ate in silence for a few minutes, then the short one spoke.

"Have you been to HQ since we took that last batch of eggs in?"

"I was there yesterday."

"Any luck with the dragon slayer?"

"None. He still refuses to talk."

My hands clenched, and it took all my self-control to stay quiet. These men had my father.

The young man laughed. "Never would have guessed they were real—the dragons or the dragon slayers. If Chang hadn't found me smuggling greenstone out of Jackson Bay, I'd never have been the wiser. Or the richer." He laughed again. "You can have your eggs, mate. I'll stick with the jade. No wonder it's so blimmin' hard to find—the dragons must be picking it all up."

"That and the gold," chuckled the man in the hat. "Chang says the eggs are worth more than their weight in gold, but gold doesn't grow up to be a deadly fire-breathing beast."

I couldn't sit still anymore and rose abruptly from my chair.

"Nathan," hissed Ella.

I ignored her and turned to the three men. My look must have been wild because the tall one raised an eyebrow.

"You okay, mate?" he asked.

I looked at the three men. Three grown men. If I said anything to them, they would know who I was. If I punched the tall man, like my hand was itching to do, it would barely hurt him. Three men against two kids; those odds weren't exactly in our favour. With an effort, I unclenched my fists.

"Just…not feeling well." I made my way to the door, and Ella followed.

"Nathan!" Ella had to jog to keep up as I hurried away from the restaurant.

I said nothing, my hands clenched again and my stomach churning.

Chapter 23
Dragon Catchers

The next morning dawned clear and sunny, and we prepared for the arrival of the dragon catchers. Tui erased as many of the dragon tracks as possible from around Foggy Bottom's lair. Then, we all walked around the lake, scrambled among the rocks, and generally made as many of our own tracks as possible. Tui and Oliver stayed outside the lair, hanging out by the lake. With luck, they could intercept the men when they arrived and prevent them from searching for Foggy Bottom's lair while, at the same time, learning more about where they were based.

I wanted to stay outdoors with them, but Ella cautioned against either one of us being seen.

"They saw us yesterday in the restaurant. They're going to think it's weird if they see us again up here. It'll just make them wary, and who knows what they'll do then."

So Ella and I paced in the cave with Foggy Bottom and Rata. We tried to get the dragons to flee for the day, but Foggy Bottom refused.

"This is my lair," she said, snorting fire. "I'll protect it with my life, even if I haven't got any eggs here at the moment."

"Besides," added Rata, "Storm Cloud assigned us to keep you safe. We can't do that if we're hiding in the forest somewhere."

The morning seemed to drag on forever. I kept peeking out the crack to check on Tui and Oliver. Not only did I want to confront the men who were holding my dad hostage, I also envied the others the chance to be outside in the sunshine and fresh air. Rata's stomach was still upset from the bread we had fed her, and she sat on my shoulder ripping purple farts all morning.

Finally, just before noon, I saw three men crest the rise above the lake. Tui and Oliver must have seen them too because they casually started drifting toward them.

"They're here," I whispered.

Ella pulled me back from the opening. "If they see you, they'll know where the cave is."

I chafed at the thought of not watching, but she was right. The cave needed to stay hidden. I strained to hear what was happening outside. The minutes ticked by. Then half an hour. I was dying to peek out. Then I heard Tui's voice close by.

"I wouldn't go up there, if I were you."

"We're experienced mountaineers. A little cliff-face is no trouble for us." I recognised the voice of the man with the hat.

"Yeah, but the top of this mountain is tapu."

"It's what?"

"It's tapu—sacred. You're not *allowed* to go there."

"Says who?"

"Says me." I could envision Tui standing with her arms crossed, glaring at the men.

A laugh. "And who do you think you are, girl?"

"I'm Tui Rahui, and I'm Ngāti Whātua, and this mountain is sacred to my people. You can't climb here."

The young man spoke up. "This here is Ngāi Tahu territory. Ngāti Whātua's got no claim on this mountain. And even if they did, what do you think you're going to do about it?"

"You can't climb here."

"And what makes this mountain so sacred?" asked the man with the hat.

"It's…it's got a tani—"

I cringed. *Don't say taniwha, Tui,* I thought as loudly as I could at her. It would be like telling them there was a dragon here.

"It's tapu. I…I don't know why. It just is."

It was lame, but at least she didn't tell them there was a taniwha on the mountain.

"Well, let's see for ourselves what it is that makes this mountain sacred, shall we?"

There was the sound of a scuffle. Shouts and a curse. A scream, cut off. Foggy Bottom knocked me over as she barrelled out of the cave from behind me. I had just gained my feet again, when Rata zipped past my head on her way out.

Ella and I could do little but watch from our perch in the crack above the lake. The three men had grabbed Oliver and Tui. Foggy Bottom circled menacingly around them, but couldn't strike with fire or claw without risking our friends. The men seemed to realise they could use Oliver and Tui as shields, so they dragged them along as they descended. Soon, they were out of sight down the mountain. Foggy Bottom still circled above, and then she disappeared too.

I ran to our packs and rummaged around for our climbing gear. I threw a harness to Ella, and we hastily prepared to lower ourselves out of the cave and follow the others.

We had barely reached the bottom of the cliff when Foggy Bottom came flapping back.

"Where have they gone? Why aren't you following? What's going on?"

"They've gone into the bush. I can't track them from above anymore. Rata is following."

"But—"

"She's following at a distance. She won't be caught. She'll come back and tell us where the men have taken them."

"That's brilliant," said Ella. I looked at her incredulously.

"Our friends have been kidnapped, and you think it's brilliant?"

"Yeah. If Rata finds out where they've gone, it'll lead us right to your dad, don't you think?"

"But what if they hurt Tui and Oliver?"

Ella's face fell. "Do you think we should call the police?"

"No," said Foggy Bottom. She sighed. "In all our plans with Archie, the most important thing we kept coming back to was that the revelation of dragons to humans has to be gradual and controlled. Official protections have to be in place before the public finds out about us, or there will be mayhem as every bloke who thinks he's a hero goes out to kill a dragon. If we call in the police, they'll find dragon eggs or maybe even dragons in addition to your friends. Then everything we've been working for will be lost."

"But we can't just sit here," I said.

"We have to. Rata is following them. For now, that's all we can do."

Rata didn't return until late that night. Ella, Foggy Bottom and I were keeping vigil in the cave, unable to sleep until we had news of our friends. When she zipped into the cave in a whir of wings, we all leapt to our feet.

"Martyr Homestead," panted Rata. Clearly, she'd flown her fastest all the way back. "On the…Martyr River…out past…Jackson Bay."

Ella and I sprang into action, packing our bags with things we thought we might need for a rescue mission— climbing gear, Swiss Army Knife, torches, and food and water in case it took longer than expected. As an

193

afterthought, I threw in the personal locator beacon—if all else failed, I was prepared to call in the authorities, and the PLB would do it nicely.

Rata, exhausted from her flight, curled up in the top of my backpack and fell asleep. I carefully zipped her in, so she wouldn't fall out on the way. Then we shouldered our packs and climbed onto Foggy Bottom's back.

It had clouded over, and the moon had not yet risen, so we could see nothing as Foggy Bottom sped through the black night. I shivered and pulled my hood up as it began to rain. Behind me, I heard Ella whine about the cold and wet, and I silently had to agree. It was going to be a miserable flight.

It was raining steadily by the time we spiralled down toward Martyr Homestead. Somewhere behind the clouds, the moon must have risen because I could pick out the wet roofs of a house and two sheds on the flat by the river. A patch of shrubby forest snaked up from the waterway to within a few metres of the house, and Foggy Bottom headed for this, bringing us down in a spot well-hidden by trees.

Leaving Foggy Bottom concealed, Ella and I picked our way through the brush toward the house. It was completely dark—not a light anywhere. The place looked deserted.

"Where do we start?" whispered Ella.

"The windows?" Not having ever rescued kidnapped friends before, I really had no idea where to begin. "Maybe we can see where they are from outside."

"Sure. It beats creeping around inside."

We approached from the back of the house, peeking into a bedroom first, where a lone form slept. The second window was also a bedroom. Two people lay inside.

We crouched below the window, whispering furtively.

"I can see people, but I can't tell who they are," I said.

"Well, they're not Tui or Oliver—they're too big," reasoned Ella. "Of course, we're assuming they've been kept together."

Ella's words stopped me cold. As I had played out permutations of our rescue mission in my head during our flight, Tui, Oliver, and Dad were *always* all together. Rescuing them would be a simple case of breaking in and bringing them out. We'd hop onto Foggy Bottom's back and be off. I didn't even want to consider the possibility that they weren't all in the same place.

"Let's finish looking in the windows—maybe it will be obvious once we've seen everything."

The next window revealed an open-plan kitchen and lounge area—dark, quiet, and empty of people. We rounded the corner of the building to the front entrance. Skirting the porch, we crept to the next window but, before we could reach it, a light flicked on.

Ella and I scrambled around the corner of the house into the dark and pressed ourselves against the wall. I held my breath and counted the seconds, waiting for the sound of a door opening and steps on the porch.

The light shone out across the empty yard, illuminating a pair of large trees and a cluster of startled sheep in a paddock next to the house. All remained silent. A minute later, the light turned off.

"Motion sensor," whispered Ella.

We both let out a sigh of relief and continued our circuit of the house. We found one more bedroom containing one other person.

"I don't think they're in the house." Only four people, and nothing about the house looked like it could hold someone determined to leave.

Without another word, we crept to the nearest shed, taking a wide arc around the gravel between the two buildings in the hope of avoiding more motion sensing lights.

The shed was windowless. We skirted the back, out of sight of the house, and slipped around to the side where the driveway came right up to the building. A large metal garage door took up most of the wall, and a small pedestrian door stood next to it.

"There's a window in the door," said Ella. I grabbed her wrist as she moved toward the door, stopping her.

"There's also probably a motion sensor there," I said.

We slid slowly toward the door, pressed against the building, hoping to avoid triggering any lights. When we finally reached our goal, we pressed our noses against the glass.

Skylights in the shed let in enough light to make out the layout of the interior. Ella's gasp mirrored my own. The shed was lined with large metal cages. Most of them were empty. Two contained small dragons. And two more contained people.

I should have waited. Ella and I should have made a plan. But at that moment the clouds parted, and moonlight streamed into the shed. I recognised my father's unkempt ginger hair. Dad was alive. And he was here.

"Dad!" I grabbed the knob and rattled the door. It was locked. "Dad!"

A light came on. Ella grabbed my arm and tried to pull me away, but I shook her off.

"Dad!" I pounded on the door. I could see that the people in the cages had awakened and were clambering to their feet. Oliver was in the same cage as Dad. Tui was in the other. I kicked at the door, but it wouldn't yield so, finally, I hurled my whole body against it.

The half-rotted wood of the door frame shattered around the lock and I burst into the shed. Ella followed me in, and we ran to the cages.

"Nathan!" Dad reached out with one arm and hugged me through the bars. Even in the dim light, I could see he was injured. His right arm was in a cast, and his right eye was purple and swollen. In my arms, he felt thin and insubstantial.

"We've come to rescue you," I said.

"I knew you would," said Dad. "But you and your friend have to get out while you can. This building is alarmed. They'll be in here in a minute."

"But we have to get you out," I said.

"And you will. The cages are locked, but there's a hack saw hanging on the wall over there." He pointed to the back of the shed. "Slip that to me, then get out of here. We'll cut our way out as soon as we can."

I ran to where he'd indicated, and snatched the saw off the nail where it hung. Before I could turn back to Dad, the lights snapped on and a voice rang out.

"Stop right there, kid." I turned to see the tall man from the Hard Antler. He was missing his hat and clad only in a T-shirt and shorts rumpled from sleep. He pointed a rifle at me. The young one, similarly attired, had Ella pinned on the floor.

"There'll be no one escaping tonight," said the tall man. "Put the saw down, and the pack." I dropped the saw to the floor and shrugged off my pack as the man advanced. He took me by the arm and shoved me into an empty cage, slamming and locking the door behind me. The young one locked Ella into the cage with Tui.

The third man—the short balding one—from the Hard Antler appeared at the door, followed by a middle-aged Asian woman. Both were dressed, though it had clearly been done in haste.

"Well, well, well. Who do we have here?" asked the woman, advancing to the cages. A curly-haired ginger?" She looked from me to my dad and back again, then laughed. "Archie McMannis' son. That's perfect."

A deep roar sounded from outside, and I smiled. Foggy Bottom would get us out. Our captors rushed from the shed. One set of footsteps ran back to the house and I thought I heard one of the men shout something about getting the other gun.

We could do nothing but listen as Foggy Bottom came closer. There was a gout of flame and a yelp. Then Foggy Bottom's voice boomed out.

"Release my friends, or I'll burn this place down and turn you to ashes." She spoke in Draconic. I wasn't sure our captors spoke the language, but I imagined they'd catch the meaning, regardless.

They must have, because the woman replied, "Breathe so much as a candle flame, and we'll kill all your friends, including the baby dragons and eggs."

"You won't have a chance to. You'll be barbecue before you turn around." Foggy Bottom had switched to English.

"It's not me who needs to turn around," replied the woman as a shot rang out. We all jumped at the sound, and Foggy Bottom roared. Another shot, and then a third sounded. Tui cried out and rattled the door to her cage.

The men shouted as we heard Foggy Bottom breathe fire. Flapping wings, another roar, more shouts—we held our breath, trying to understand what was happening outside. Foggy Bottom let out a moan, there was a great thud, then silence. I could see my own horror etched on the faces of my friends. The men had killed Foggy Bottom.

Chapter 24
Captivity

Half an hour later, the woman returned. She smiled as she approached the cages.

"Well, now, Archie. Had I known your presence here would be so profitable, I would have brought you here ages ago."

"There's no profit in killing a dragon," I yelled.

The woman turned to me. "Oh, the dragon's not dead. Just sleeping."

"But the shots we heard—"

"Distraction. Make lots of noise on one side, and shoot a few tranquiliser darts from the other. You're right—there's no profit in a dead dragon. But this one will make a fine start to my breeding stock. Now I just need to find a mate for it." She looked back at Dad. "Are there any male dragons likely to come and rescue you, Archie?" Then she laughed. "It hardly matters, does it? Now I have your son, you'll be telling me everything." She left the building, picking up Oliver's and my packs and flicking off the light as she went. The door banged shut after her, but bounced back open because of the broken latch. It hardly mattered. With no way out of the cages, the open door offered nothing but a tease.

"I'm sorry," I said, sinking to the floor and putting my head in my hands. "I totally messed up. Now we're all captured."

"Not all of us," said Oliver.

"Yeah, Rata's not here," said Tui.

I grimaced. "She was asleep in my pack."

"I assume that woman was Ling Chang," said Ella.

Dad confirmed that it was.

"I suppose we should be thankful it was Ling Chang and not Claus Drachenmorder who got us. Drachenmorder would have killed us all," I said.

"Where there's life, there's hope!" said Oliver.

"But not much," Ella muttered. "Don't forget, Drachenmorder's still after us too."

"Yeah, but he'll never find us way out here," said Oliver.

"No one will." Tui's voice was grim.

"No. That's why Chang brought me out here," said Dad. "That, and because she eventually realised she couldn't bribe me into working with her by wining and dining me at her Dunedin mansion."

Though we'd guessed enough to be able to find Dad, we didn't know the details of what had happened to him. Nor did he know our story. We spent the next hour relating our respective tales.

When Dad and Sir Bernie Dougherty, the head of the Royal Society of Dragon Slayers, arrived at James Peak to meet with Storm Cloud, Sir Christopher had shown up within a few minutes.

"Before I even knew he was there, Sir Bernie was dead." Dad sighed and continued. "I'm no slouch with a sword, but Sir Christopher is the best. When he drove me off the cliff, I thought I was done for."

"But you landed on a ledge. That's what Sir Leandro said."

Dad smiled. "He figured that out, huh? Excellent tracker, he is. Yes, I landed on a ledge. Broke my arm, but I was otherwise unharmed."

"What I don't understand," said Tui, "is how you escaped Sir Christopher."

200

Dad smiled. "Sir Christopher is a ruthless man. He *is* his sword—no conscience, just a killing machine. But he has one weakness. He's afraid of heights. I stayed silent, counting on him not to risk a peek over the edge, and I was right. He assumed I was dead and never checked."

"But weren't you scared, standing on a ledge above a cliff?" asked Ella. "You couldn't have climbed back up with a broken arm, could you?"

"I briefly thought about trying—but only briefly. I knew Storm Cloud would show up, and I figured he could give me a lift back up. I just hoped Sir Christopher would be gone by then."

"But Storm Cloud said you were gone by the time he got there."

"Dragons are notoriously late for meetings—dragon-time, we call it. I waited for an hour, and the weather was closing in. When two blokes showed up with a rope, I didn't question why they happened to be on James Peak—I accepted their help. My mistake."

"I expect they wouldn't have given you much choice anyway," said Ella.

"You're probably right."

"And the note?" I asked. "How did you know we would come looking for you there? And how did you manage to leave it?"

Dad smiled. "Well, my first thought was to set off my locator beacon, but the helpful gentlemen who pulled me off the cliff took my bag with the beacon in it."

"But you always carry a waterproof notebook and a pencil in your pocket," I said.

"In case I come across an interesting plant. Exactly. I asked to relieve myself, and while I had my back turned, I scribbled the note. I actually didn't expect you to find it. I thought Leandro might though."

"So where did they take you?" asked Tui.

"Well, I asked them to take me to the hospital in Queenstown to see about my arm. They said it could wait until Dunedin. I said I wasn't going to Dunedin, and they said, *you are now*. I tried to escape, but..." He shrugged. "What could I do with a broken arm? They bound my hands and feet and threw me into the boot for the remainder of the drive."

"Then what?"

"When we got to Dunedin, we pulled up at Ling Chang's place. Pretty flash, that one. Must be nice to have that kind of money. When I met Ms Chang, she apologised for my treatment—had a doctor come to the house to set my arm. She put me up in a swank bedroom with my own whirlpool bathtub. And my own guard at the door. Treated me like captive royalty, and then tried to get me to join her little dragon smuggling operation. When that didn't work, she threw me into the basement and tried to force information about dragon locations out of me."

"Force it out?"

"Don't worry. You don't need to know the details, but there's no permanent damage done. She's not a nice person, but she's not Drachenmorder. She's no murderer."

"So why are you here now?"

"Drachenmorder's thugs apparently started snooping around, looking for me."

"Must have been around the time Josh spilled the beans about our plans," said Tui. "About two weeks ago."

"That's about right. Anyway, I guess Chang still thought I'd talk, and she didn't want Drachenmorder to get her prize, so she flew me out here by helicopter in the dead of night."

Then we told Dad our story. At first, he seemed upset I'd gone to the School of Heroic Arts but, in the end, he admitted he couldn't have mounted a better rescue mission than I had.

"But all I did was get everyone captured."

"No," said Dad. "First off, you found me, which is more than Drachenmorder has been able to do. Also, in getting to me, you've alerted the dragons to the fact I've been kidnapped, and to the fact there is a dragon smuggler operating in New Zealand. And finally, you've befriended the dragons. Never underestimate what they can do."

"But what do we do now?" asked Oliver. We all looked expectantly at Dad.

"Nathan's the leader of this rescue operation," said Dad. "What do you say?"

I couldn't believe Dad was asking me what we should do. I nearly responded that he was the adult—he should tell us. Then I realised he trusted me to come up with a plan. He trusted me to rescue all of us. I wasn't about to let him down.

"Well," I began, "first, I think we all need to get some sleep. We can't escape until Foggy Bottom wakes up anyway—we can't leave her here, and she is our best hope for a quick getaway. In the morning, we'll see what the situation is. If we're taken out of these cages for any reason, it could be a possible chance to escape. We'll need to assess how to get any tools we need and how they're holding Foggy Bottom. It would also be good to find out about our captors' weaknesses—anything we can exploit to our benefit."

"A good plan," said Dad.

"Especially the part about getting some sleep," said Oliver, yawning.

Our cages were bare, aside from a bucket to pee in. There was nothing but the concrete floor to sleep on. None of us slept much. Next morning, everyone was awake, stretching out the kinks in their necks, when the young man from the Hard Antler came into the shed with Ling Chang on his heels.

"Ah, my little ducklings. How are you all this morning? Well rested?"

Nobody answered her, but Tui muttered, "Watch it, lady, or this little duckling will punch that smile right off your face." Oliver giggled, but one look at Tui, and I knew she was dead serious.

"Don't do anything stupid, Tui," I whispered.

Ling Chang appraised us for a moment, a false smile on her face.

"I think we'll start with the McMannis boy. Bring him to the office, will you, Colin?"

She turned and strode back out. Colin pulled a set of keys from his pocket. He fumbled around, trying to find the right one for my cage. Oliver, cheeky as usual, piped up.

"When does the cafeteria open for breakfast?"

Colin grunted. "When Ms Chang is done with you. And when we feel like bringing you food. Tell her what she wants to know, and you'll eat sooner." He found the right key, opened the door, and grabbed me by the upper arm.

I glanced wildly at Dad. He gave me a nod and a salute, but I could see the worry on his face. I let Colin pull me out of the cage.

Once I was free from the bars, the urge to shake Colin's hand off and run for the door was almost overwhelming. As if he'd heard my thoughts, Colin's grip tightened.

"Don't do anything stupid, mate. There are worse things than a cage."

Clouds hung heavily over the hills, threatening a downpour, as Colin led me across the yard to a long, low shed. We rounded the corner of the shed, heading for the door when I saw Foggy Bottom and let out a cry of dismay.

"What have you done to her?"

On the far side of the shed was a huge metal cage. Inside, lay the dragon, looking more dead than alive. Her scales were dull and grey, her eyes were shut, and her head lolled to one side.

"She'll wake up later today." Colin pushed me through the shed door into a room that felt like an oven. When I looked around, I understood why. Nestled in a crate filled with straw were four eggs. Dragon eggs. They were incubating them.

Colin didn't let me linger in the room. He pushed me through another door into a somewhat cooler empty room, and then through a third door into what was clearly the office. It was sparsely furnished—a wooden desk, a filing cabinet, and two office chairs was all it contained. Ling Chang stood at a window, looking out at the clouds.

"Thank you, Colin. Wait outside. Please sit down, Nathan." She gestured to one of the chairs.

When we were alone, Ms Chang sat down, elbows on the desk, her hands steepled in front of her chin. Her smile wouldn't have fooled anyone.

"Now, Nathan. You have a choice. Your stay here can be brief and not unduly unpleasant, or it can be long and nasty. The more useful you make yourself, the shorter and less painful your stay."

"And what about my friends and my dad?"

"Your father has been given ample opportunity and encouragement to make himself useful. He has chosen to be singularly unhelpful, and so he remains here. Your friends?" She shrugged. "I have yet to determine how useful they may be. But perhaps, I won't need them at all. If you were to provide me with the information I need…"

"What information do you need? And what makes you think I have it?"

205

"Let me tell you a little about my work, and then you'll understand what I need and why. I run a little trade in...exotic...pets."

"Illegal pets, you mean?"

Chang dismissed my question with a wave.

"As I'm sure you're aware, dragons are *the* most exotic of animals. The wealthy will pay ninety thousand U.S. Dollars for a mere Lear's macaw. They'll pay a hundred times that amount for a dragon."

"Nine *million* dollars?"

Chang smiled for real. "Yes. For one dragon. Half that for an egg. And because dragons don't officially exist, it's not officially illegal to sell them."

"But—"

Chang put up her hand. "I know what you're going to say—your father has bored me already with the arguments. But the truth is, I want the same thing you want—a healthy dragon population. I'm not a dragon slayer. I'm a businesswoman, and I can't have my stock slaughtered—it wouldn't be smart business practice. That's why I invited your father to work with me and help to develop a captive breeding programme for them. We would keep the species alive and provide a tidy profit for my business. A win-win situation for everyone."

"It's a win-win situation if the only other alternative is to slay them all, but it's not. Dragons aren't mindless lizards you can chuck in a cage and—"

"Enough," said Chang, raising her hand again. "Your father has obviously brainwashed you into thinking—"

"He did *not* brainwash me. In fact, until he disappeared, I had no idea he was even a dragon slayer. I didn't know dragons existed. It doesn't take brainwashing to realise that it's just not right to keep dragons in captivity, or to buy and sell them like cattle. Have you ever *met* a dragon?"

"I know what dragons are. But I also know a business opportunity when I see one." She leaned toward me over the desk. "That green dragon you brought here—as an adult female laying three eggs every two years, she is worth almost seven million dollars a year."

"As though she'll do what you want her to do."

"That's why I need you and your father. You understand dragons. You're dragon whisperers. You can show me where to find my breeding stock, and then keep them alive and happy in captivity so they'll churn out eggs. We'll all get rich into the bargain. I could work out a deal so you get a percentage of the profit."

I thought about our modest house in Lincoln. We weren't poor, but we weren't rich either. What would it be like to have a couple of million dollars a year? What would it be like to have a couple of million dollars gained by enslaving dragons?

"You'll get no help or information from me. I'm a dragon saver, not a dragon enslaver."

Chang frowned. "You're as stubborn as your father." Then, she smiled. "We'll see if he remains as stubborn now that I have you as *encouragement*."

She stood and opened the door, beckoning Colin in.

"Take him back. And rough him up a bit first. Something nice and visible."

I stood and backed away from Colin as Ling Chang strode out. He advanced toward me. I reached the window and fumbled with the latch behind my back, hoping vainly he wouldn't notice. He rushed at me.

Sir Christopher's combat training came back to me— *move in unexpected ways so the dragon strikes at empty air instead of at you.* Instead of moving away from Colin, I ducked under his arms and dove toward his feet. The move surprised and tripped him, but he still landed me a kick to the head.

I was closer to the door, though, and that had been my goal. I scrambled up and lurched toward it, only to be slammed from behind by Colin. I hit the floor hard, and my chin cracked loudly on the concrete. I was thankful my tongue hadn't been sticking out, or I would have bitten it off.

Colin pinned me down, grabbed my hair, lifted my head, and then smashed my face against the floor.

I cried out, and Colin rolled me onto my back to survey the damage.

"Quit whinging. It's just a bloody nose. It could have been worse." He pulled me to my feet and dragged me, clutching my nose, back to the cage.

"Nathan!" cried Dad as I collapsed on the floor. "What did they do to you? Are you okay?"

I sat up and grimaced. "It's all right. No permanent damage." My voice sounded thick and stuffy. I attempted a grin and wiped the blood from my face with my sleeve.

"I can't let them do this to you."

"Dad," I said. "They only gave me a bloody nose— 'something nice and visible' is what Chang asked Colin to do. They did it precisely to get at you. Don't give in to it." I swiped the back of my hand under my nose, wincing a little. "Look, it's already stopped bleeding."

At that moment, Colin returned and collected Dad. "Don't tell them anything," I mouthed to him.

When he'd gone, the others pounced on me for information.

"Did you see Foggy Bottom?" asked Tui. "How is she?"

I told them about Foggy Bottom in the cage, and about the eggs, and what Ling Chang had told me.

"What if Foggy Bottom doesn't wake up?" said Oliver.

"And how are we going to take the eggs with us?" asked Tui.

I smiled. Whatever mistakes I'd made, my choice of friends was perfect.

"Even more importantly," said Ella, "where's Rata?"

And it dawned on me—Ling Chang hadn't mentioned Rata at all. Surely, she would have said something about the little dragon—perfect for the pet trade and assumed extinct. If a big, dangerous dragon was worth nine million dollars as a pet, a sparkly little dragon that could perch on your shoulder must be worth twice that.

Chapter 25
A Deal

Colin marched each of us out to be questioned by Ling Chang, but nobody else came back with a bloody nose.

"She needs to work on her technique," said Oliver. "I mean, you know, in the movies they have all these clever torture techniques—machines that give electrical shocks, big guys with sticks, drugs that make you tell all."

"You *want* to be tortured?" asked Tui.

"Well, no, but all she did was try to convince me I could get rich." He scoffed. "Like that could be the only possible motivation in life."

"Maybe for her, it is," said Ella with a shrug.

"There's a sad thought," said Tui.

One of the other men—the older, balding one—came into the shed with a bucket of what looked like chopped possums. He tipped the bloody mess into troughs in the baby dragons' cages, and the animals pounced on the food.

He left and returned a few minutes later with a tray of toast with jam and glasses of milk. He pushed the food between the bars of our cages without a word. We thanked him, like good Kiwi kids but, afterwards, I wondered why we'd done that.

We were all famished, and two pieces of toast didn't go far to filling us up.

"So what have we learned?" I asked after polishing off my breakfast.

"Foggy Bottom is in no condition to fly us out of here at the moment, so escape is pointless," said Oliver.

"For now, yes. So we need to monitor her condition as best we can. Colin said she'd wake up later today."

"But who knows how long it will be before she can fly us out," said Tui.

"And there's the minor inconvenience of the cage she's in," said Oliver.

"And the ones we're in," added Ella.

"Yes, yes," I snapped. "We know the negatives. Let's look at the positives. Let's look at our assets. First, we've found Dad."

"No small feat," he said.

"Second, we've learned Ling Chang isn't completely ruthless. She's obviously a novice at torture, and she has no plans to murder us. That's hugely in our favour. It means we have time to work out a plan."

Tui, Oliver, and Dad nodded, but Ella rolled her eyes.

"Great. We can spend even more time being inexpertly tortured by these guys."

I raised my hand to cut her off and continued. "Third, we can be pretty confident they didn't find Rata."

"Oh!" cried Ella, her frown vanishing. "I forgot to tell you. When I was in Chang's office, the tall one with the hat came in carrying our packs. He tossed them on the floor and told Chang they hadn't found anything of interest, but they'd scored some nice climbing gear."

"So what happened to Rata?" asked Dad.

"Nathan had zipped her into the top pouch of his pack, so she wouldn't fall out when we were flying—she was exhausted after following Tui and Oliver here. She couldn't have unzipped it on her own, but I saw the top of the pack. There was a hole burnt into it."

"She escaped," cried Tui, pumping her fist in the air. "She'll get help for us, I'm sure."

Dad shook his head. "Don't count on it. I've known Rata for years. She's as ditzy as they come. It's surprising she managed to escape at all. It would be a miracle if she was able to focus on the job long enough to get help for us. If dragons can have ADHD, she's got it."

"Yeah, I kind of got that impression," I said.

"She did manage to follow when those men brought Oliver and me here," said Tui. "Give her credit for that."

"Okay. Let's not count on Rata coming to our rescue, but let's at least be ready to move if she does."

"Any other good news?" asked Ella.

"We know where the keys to our cells are."

"Yeah, in Colin's pocket. That's useful. Are you good at pickpocketing?"

"No. But the information is still useful. We can only get the keys if we know where they are first." I soldiered on because I knew Ella would next ask about my plan for getting the keys, and I didn't have one yet. "Another positive is that they've taken us out of the cells at least once. They might do it again. Especially, if we talk."

"Nathan, we can't tell them anything," said Tui.

"We can't tell them anything *true*."

"He has a point," said Dad. "I've refused to tell them anything so far, but Chang is clearly trying to use Nathan as a way to make me talk. If I were to indicate I'll talk to save my son, I'm sure Chang would jump at the chance to interrogate me."

"And can you invent a plausible lie about where she can find dragons?"

"She doesn't only want to know where to find dragons. She wants to know how to catch them, how to keep them alive in captivity, and how to breed them. There are all sorts of misleading things I could tell her."

Colin arrived at the shed door and began replacing the smashed door frame, putting a halt to our conversation. Having finished their meal, the baby

212

dragons began a high pitched chirping—like baby birds in a nest.

"Shut up!" called Colin from the door. "Ye've had your food."

The dragons kept up their chirping. Apparently, their breakfast had been as unsatisfying as ours had been.

"I said shut up!" Colin threw a chunk of four-by-two at the cages. It hit with a clang, and the baby dragons jumped back to cower silently in the corner.

Tui's fists clenched, and she muttered what I assumed were some choice insults at Colin.

"You're not going to make very good pets of them if you starve them, and then throw things at them," I said.

"As if I care," replied Colin, not bothering to look up from his work. "My job's to find them. What Chang does with them afterward is her business. Frankly, I think you'd have to be a friggin' idiot to keep one of those things as a pet."

I raised an eyebrow. Ella reached through the bars and tugged on my sleeve. I leaned close, and she whispered in my ear.

"He was the one who was smuggling greenstone, remember?"

I thought back to the conversation we'd overheard in the Hard Antler. At the time, I'd paid more attention to the fact the men had my father, but now I considered the rest of what they'd said. Colin was interested in the greenstone, and the man in the hat had indicated he was more interested in gold. These guys were just hired hands—they weren't really in on the smuggling scheme. I wondered if we could use that to our advantage.

213

We couldn't talk while Colin was in the shed. Tui paced, a scowl on her face. Ella sat on the floor, legs outstretched and eyes shut. Dad lay on his back looking tired. Oliver sat curled in a ball, with his arms wrapped around his legs. I stood leaning on the bars of the cage, trying to come up with a clever plan to get us out.

I looked at the baby dragons—southern blues. They couldn't be more than a week or two old—dog-sized, not dragon-sized yet, and without fire. We would have to rescue them too. Would we even be able to coax them out of their cages? They probably hatched in captivity and didn't even know they were imprisoned. They wouldn't be able to understand Draconic—might not have ever heard it. There would be no reasoning with them.

An angry roar and the sound of dragon flame startled me from my thoughts. Foggy Bottom was awake. Heads jerked up, and everyone smiled. Shouts rang out, and Colin dropped his tools and vanished.

I couldn't understand what the men were saying, but Foggy Bottom's words were clear. They consisted largely of Draconic curses and insults, some of which made us giggle when Dad translated them into English.

"You are bird droppings in your mother's left ear."

"Your father was a slime mould."

"You smell like a seaweed fart."

"Ha!" laughed Tui. "I should use that one on my brother."

Then we heard Foggy Bottom call out, "Nathan? Are you here?" She spoke in Draconic.

"Yes! We're in here," I called back, also in Draconic. "My dad, Oliver, Tui...we're all here."

I didn't think she'd hear me, but dragons must have excellent hearing, because she replied, "Are you well?"

"Yes, but we're in cages, like you. There are also baby dragons in here." I figured the more Foggy Bottom knew about our situation the better. "They have eggs in the other shed. Are you okay?"

"I have a splitting headache, and I'm dizzy. Hungry too. Whatever they used to put me to sleep was nasty."

"Chang wants to use you for breeding. We're working on a way to—"

Colin burst through the doorway and pointed a rifle at me.

"Shut up, you."

Chang might not be a murderer, but I didn't think it'd be wise to push Colin. I shut up. The commotion outside died down and, a minute later, Ling Chang entered the shed.

"You sure it was the McMannis boy?"

"Positive."

"Bring him." She turned and headed for the door.

As Colin wrenched me out of the cage, I wondered what sort of trouble I'd gotten myself into by talking to Foggy Bottom. Oliver gave me a thumbs-up, and I let myself be steered out of the shed.

I smiled as we rounded the corner, and I saw Foggy Bottom awake and angry, tail tip thrashing against the bars of her cage. Not that I was happy to see her behind bars, but it was so much better to see her up and alert than sprawled out like she had been that morning.

"Nathan." Foggy Bottom's voice shook the ground, and I felt Colin wince.

Foggy Bottom looked worried, and I realised I was still covered in blood from Colin's manhandling in the morning. I wanted to tell her Rata had escaped, but I still didn't know if our captors spoke Draconic, and I certainly didn't want anyone asking who Rata was. I opted for general assurances.

"We're going to get out of here. Be—"

Colin wrenched my arm nearly out of its socket. "Keep your mouth shut, kid."

He pushed me through the same doors as earlier, into the office where Ling Chang sat behind the desk. Colin shoved me into a chair, and she nodded to him. He left the room, shutting the door behind him.

"You speak the dragon's language."

"A little."

"Can you speak to all dragons?"

The wheels began to turn. It was clear Ling Chang didn't speak Draconic, and might not even know a common dragon language existed. How could I use that to our advantage? "As far as I know, yes."

Ling Chang's eyes widened. "Is that how you got that dragon to follow you here?"

A plan began to form in my head.

"Yes."

"Teach me this language." Chang leaned eagerly over the desk.

"I can't."

Chang's eyes narrowed. "Why not?"

"It's a skill only a few possess. Shows up in about one in a thousand people. No one else can make the right sounds."

"I'd like to test that." She wasn't buying my lie.

I raised my eyebrows. "Really? Dragon pronunciation is tricky. One poorly pronounced word, and you could be telling a dragon how good you taste with tomato sauce, instead of asking it to join your little menagerie here. And death by dragon is not fun—they like to toy with their prey." I shuddered dramatically. "Ever watch a cat with a mouse?"

Chang frowned and, sensing my advantage, I continued.

"Of course, I've been thinking about what you said this morning. Perhaps we can come to some sort of...arrangement. With my skills, I should think I would be worth a lot more per year than that dragon out there."

216

"How much do you want?"

"Nine million annually." I could hardly keep a straight face. Such a sum was so large, I couldn't even imagine it. That Chang took me seriously was a stark illustration of what Ella had hinted at—because money was the woman's only motivation in life, she assumed it was everyone else's too. I counted on that being true and hoped I could pull this off.

Chang scoffed. "That's ridiculous. I can't do nine million—I haven't got a single breeding pair yet."

"With me on board, you can have as many breeding pairs as you'd like. I can get you southern blues, New Zealand greens, Fiordland fringed, and scree dragons, just like that." I snapped my fingers.

"There are scree dragons?" she asked, leaning forward again.

This woman knew nothing about dragons. I was surprised she'd managed to find as many eggs as she had with so little knowledge.

"Nine million a year. I'll bring them in and train them—a trained dragon must be worth much more than a wild one."

"Nine million." Chang sighed. "Deal."

"Oh, and I'll need an advance. You can't blame me for not trusting you."

"Fine. You get your advance, but I keep you and your friends in custody. You can't blame me for not trusting you either." Her smile looked more akin to a grimace.

Chapter 26
Escape

My plan had only partly worked. I'd hoped to secure the release of everyone else with my deal, which it didn't do. But it achieved my other aim—to get Ling Chang out of the way. I demanded five million up front, in cash. She left the following morning to go collect it.

As I suspected, things changed as soon as Chang was gone. Within an hour, Colin showed up outside our cages.

"No more free ride, kids," he said, ignoring the fact my father was among us. "We're tired of cooking for you. You two"—he pointed at Tui and Ella—"you're gonna cook for all of us." He fumbled through his keys looking for the right one.

Tui puffed up with indignation. "Why you sexist—"

I reached through the bars between our cages and grabbed her arm to cut her off. I gave her a look that said, "This is an opportunity. Don't mess it up." She grimaced at me but kept her mouth shut.

After the shed door slammed shut behind Tui and Ella, Dad chuckled.

"You hit that spot-on, Nathan. I wouldn't have thought it, but getting Chang out of the picture was a stroke of genius."

Oliver's eyes lit up. "In the kitchen, they'll have access to knives and who knows what else!"

"You think they're going to let Tui and Ella leave with knives in their pockets?" Dad was not as optimistic.

"Even if they don't, they'll have opportunities to gather information about how we can get hold of the keys and any other tools we need. And they'll learn more about exactly who is here and their daily activities."

"It's a huge improvement," agreed Dad.

The quality of our meals improved too. Tui and Ella weren't fantastic cooks, but they made sure we got enough to eat and somehow managed to sneak us a bar of chocolate with dinner.

Within twenty-four hours, we knew there were five guns in the house—three dart guns and two ordinary rifles. They were kept in a locked gun cabinet, but the key to the cabinet was set right on top of it. The only men in the house were the three we'd already met, but a second dragon-catching crew was due to return later in the week. And Colin was really squeamish about blood and dirt.

"He made me cut up the possums for the dragon babies," said Tui. "Couldn't even look in the bucket without turning green. He washed his hands three times after he showed me where the possums were—he hadn't even touched them. The older guy—his name's Mark—he gave Colin a hard time about it."

We also knew that Colin shared a bedroom with the tall man with the hat.

"What is that guy's name anyway?" I asked.

"Who knows," said Ella. "They just call him Dude. That can't be his real name."

"Did you get a chance to see Foggy Bottom?" I asked.

"Yes," said Ella. "I fed her today. Those guys are terrified of her."

"Can you blame them?" Oliver laughed.

"I told her about Rata and about our plan to get us all out of here. She said she's feeling less dizzy now, and she's sure she's recovered enough to fly."

"What did she have to say about Rata?" asked Dad.

"Nothing good. She was glad Rata had gotten away but, like you, she didn't expect any help from her."

The only negative thing about getting enough to eat was the increased need to relieve ourselves. It was bad enough there was no privacy, but then we had to sit next to the buckets.

Tui and Ella noticed it most because they got away from it while they cooked. When Colin brought them back after breakfast on the second day of cooking, they wrinkled their noses.

"It smells like a sewer in here," said Ella.

"I wonder when Colin plans on cleaning our cages," said Oliver.

Ella snorted. "Colin? Never. The guy's obsessed with *dirt*. Washed his hands five times while Tui and I were making breakfast this morning."

Suddenly, I knew exactly how we were going to get the keys and escape.

"What are you smiling about?" asked Ella.

I told them my plan. At first, they thought I was nuts, but with a few refinements and contingencies, we were able to agree on it.

"So when are we going to do it?" asked Dad.

"As soon as possible. We don't know when Chang or this other team of dragon catchers will return. Better to do it when we only have three guys to worry about."

"We'll disable the guns when we're in the kitchen at lunchtime," said Tui.

"If we can," added Ella.

"It would be best to attack when Colin brings you back with our dinner. The others will be eating and might not notice he's gone," I said.

"That gives you lunch and dinner to disable the guns," said Dad.

"And it means that, if something goes wrong, night will be coming on. A little darkness might help," I said.

"What could possibly go wrong?" asked Oliver.

Tui smiled when she came back after lunch. "We super-glued the triggers and the bolts."

"Unfortunately, we ran out of glue, so there's still one dart gun functional," said Ella.

I looked at the others. "I think we need to just go with it. If we wait, they'll find the glued guns and the game will be up, don't you think?"

The others nodded.

We went over the plan once more, and I was far less confident in it now we'd reached the point of no return.

We tried to look nonchalant when Colin arrived to take Tui and Ella to the kitchen to make dinner. I nodded at the girls as he ushered them from the cage, and Tui fired me a salute behind Colin's back.

After they were gone, the rest of us took up our positions to wait for their return. It felt like forever before we heard a key in the shed door. I wiped my sweaty hands on my jeans, took a calming breath, and forced myself not to look as scared as I felt when Tui and Ella came back in, escorted by Colin.

As usual, the girls slipped dinner between the bars of our cages before Colin locked them back in their own. But the rest of us ignored the food. We drew forward, as if to collect it but, behind our backs, Oliver and I held our toilet buckets. Colin opened the door to Tui and Ella's cage. The girls stepped in and, as soon as they were clear of Colin, Oliver and I heaved the brimming buckets at him, dousing him in a foul slurry of our own waste. As Colin stood frozen in shock, blinking against the stinging urine in his eyes, I reached between the bars and snatched the keys out of his limp hand. Tui slipped out of the cage and gave Colin a shove forward. Ella assisted by tripping him and, before he even knew what had happened, Colin was lying on the floor of a locked cage. Taking the keys from me, Tui opened our cages. We didn't bother responding to Colin's incoherent shouts of rage and disgust. Instead, Tui unlocked the cages holding the baby dragons, and we tried to coax them out. They snapped at us and refused to budge.

"We should have brought food to entice them out," said Ella.

"Maybe Foggy Bottom can convince them to come out," said Tui. "We don't have time to waste."

"You're right, but we have to try." I took charge. "Tui, take the keys and release Foggy Bottom. Oliver and Dad, go get the eggs. Ella, see if you can find our packs— they were still in the office two days ago when I talked to Chang. I'll do what I can to get the babies out. If I haven't joined you by the time you've got the eggs and Foggy Bottom, come back, and we'll see whether Foggy Bottom can convince these guys to come with us."

The others left at a sprint, and I turned back to the dragons. Maybe, with only one of us, they wouldn't be so frightened. Of course, with Colin screaming in one of the cages, I wasn't so sure. I grabbed a couple of the burgers Tui and Ella had made for our dinner, narrowly dodging Colin's hand as he made a swipe at me through the bars.

As the dragons smelled the meat, their cries of fear turned to chirps of hunger.

"C'mon guys," I said, holding the burgers just out of reach. "C'mon."

They tottered forward faster than I'd expected. The first one snatched at a burger, grabbing my hand along with it.

"Ow!" I cried, jerking my hand and scaring the dragons back into their cages. They might be babies, but they were still big animals with sharp teeth. Blood welled up from four deep puncture wounds.

Choosing a less dangerous tactic, I broke the burgers into small pieces and laid them out in a trail leading from the cages to the door. I waited near the door, pressing my injured hand against my chest to try and stop the bleeding. The dragon that had bitten me was the first to investigate. It sniffed the air, then put its head down and made a beeline for the first chunk of burger. Sniffing along the floor, it ate the second and the third piece. The other dragon realised it was missing out and bounded out of the cage, barrelling into the first dragon as it reached the next piece of burger. Both of them went tumbling across the floor, snarling at each other.

"Oh brother! I'm never going to get these dragons out of here," I muttered.

Luckily, the tussle was short-lived, and soon the dragons were practically running at the door, hoovering up burgers in their race to beat each other to the next piece. I stepped backward through the doorway as they came on.

And backed straight into Sir Christopher.

Chapter 27
Disaster

Sir Christopher was ready for me, but not for the two hungry baby dragons that burst out the door after me. Before I could cry out in surprise, Sir Christopher clamped a hand over my mouth. But his grip failed when the baby dragons leapt on me, looking for more burgers. Their assault threw us both to the ground. I rolled away from Sir Christopher and the dragons and sprang to my feet, my combat training kicking in.

By the time I was on my feet, Sir Christopher had his sword out. I had no weapon at all. I remembered my dad saying that Sir Christopher was the best sword fighter. My heart sank. I reckoned my chances were slim to none against him. I took a deep breath and tried not to think about what it would feel like to be run through with a sword.

I don't know if the two baby dragons prevented my escape or saved my life. Oblivious to Sir Christopher and his sword, they mobbed me, licking my hands and nipping at my legs in the search for more food. As Sir Christopher advanced, I decided my only hope was escape. I turned to run but tripped over a dragon. Sir Christopher lunged at me, but the dragons were quicker. Instead of hitting me, his blow struck one of them. It howled in pain and turned on its assailant. It may have been only a baby, but it knew what teeth were for. It sank them into Sir Christopher's leg. Sir Christopher cursed and, with one deft stroke, sliced the dragon's head off. I winced and looked only long enough to note with grim pleasure that the dragon's mouth stayed firmly clamped on his leg, in spite of being detached from its body. Then I ran. The second dragon followed at my heels.

At that moment, I realised what else was going on around me. Sir Christopher wasn't alone—the two men he had met in the Alexandra cafe were struggling with Tui near Foggy Bottom's cage, and Drachenmorder himself had Oliver pinned to the wall of the smaller shed. Dad came running toward me with a length of metal pipe in his left hand. He was halfway across the yard, when I heard a *thwack*. A pink-feathered dart appeared in Dad's thigh. He stopped and looked dumbly at it for a moment as if he didn't understand what it was.

"Pull it out!" I yelled. He dropped the pipe and tugged the dart out. He took a step in my direction, then collapsed to the ground. In spite of the danger we were in, I nearly laughed. I knew the tranquiliser hadn't taken effect yet—Dad had fainted. He hated needles. Whenever we got our flu shots, he had to spend an extra half hour lying down before he could stand without feeling woozy.

I reached Dad and picked up the pipe he had been carrying. I turned back to face Sir Christopher. He was still trying to pry the dragon's head off his leg. The second baby dragon continued to shadow me, begging for food. It reared up onto its hind legs, planting its front feet on my shoulders. Its begging saved me. Dude's tranquiliser dart, fired from the porch, struck the dragon instead of me. The poor creature went wild from fear. It raced around and around, trying to reach the offending dart in its back. Then the tranquiliser kicked in, and it sank to the ground.

I didn't stick around to receive the third dart. I ran toward the melee taking place by the small shed. Dude and Mark clattered down the steps and ran across the yard behind me. Sir Christopher caught up with them, and we all joined the fray. Foggy Bottom, still caged, roared and slammed against the bars in frustration. Tui had worked herself clear of the others. She turned, so her attacker stood between her and Foggy Bottom, and then screamed the dragon's name. Foggy Bottom blasted the pair. I cried out, thinking Tui was toast. But the move was beautifully done. The man's clothes and hair were set alight, and he released Tui to race to the river and douse himself. Protected behind the man's larger form, Tui was unscathed. She raced to the door of Foggy Bottom's cage with the keys in her hand.

Whether the fight had two sides to it or three was hard to tell. Dude and Mark might have done better had they sided with Drachenmorder's band against us. Instead, they largely ignored us kids and focused on fighting the 'intruders'. We fought them all, as our carefully planned escape went horribly wrong.

Drachenmorder already had Oliver tied up—ankles and arms trussed with duct tape. As he turned from dealing with Oliver, Mark, wielding a rifle as a club, struck him on the shoulder. At some point, he must have discovered the rifle was glued. The two fell on each other, but I didn't have time to watch the proceedings. Dude had spied Tui trying to unlock Foggy Bottom's cage. As he took aim at Tui, I swung my pipe at him. The dart fired but struck Foggy Bottom instead. Tui turned just in time to duck Sir Christopher's sword. Then, I was engaged with Dude and didn't see what happened next.

Our combat training had focused on dragons, not people. We were good at dodging tails, claws and fire, but our technique didn't take into account things like weapons and grappling hands. Pleased by my first hit, I swung the pipe again for another. Dude promptly caught it and wrenched it from my grip.

At least now I was on familiar ground. I ducked and jumped as Dude slashed at me with the pipe. I backed toward the small shed where there was a stack of timber.

If I could arm myself again, I might have a chance. Mark called out, catching Dude's attention. Drachenmorder had Mark in a headlock. Dude broke away from me to go to his friend's aid. I took the opportunity to duck into the shed, where I came upon Ella rushing out.

"The key," she said breathlessly. "To Foggy Bottom's cage," she added in response to my confused look. "It wasn't on the key ring Colin carried." She pushed past me out the door. I spied my backpack—Oliver must have dropped it—and fell to my knees beside it. I had a pocket knife in there. If I could find it, I'd have a weapon, and I'd be able to release Oliver. I rummaged frantically in the bag. The knife wasn't there, but I did find the personal locator beacon. I pulled it out and considered the situation. It only took a moment to decide. I popped open the waterproof case and activated the device.

Rough hands grabbed me from behind and hauled me to my feet and out the door of the shed. In the minute I'd been inside, the fight had turned to custard. Ella lay next to Oliver in a similar state of taped immobility. Tui was struggling as Sir Christopher attempted to tape her. Foggy Bottom was still caged, her eyelids drooping with the effect of the tranquiliser. Dude and Mark both lay still on the ground. I didn't know whether they were dead or just unconscious. Drachenmorder's remaining thug, who had grabbed me, shoved me roughly to the ground. Soon, we were all laid out like firewood. It began to rain, and I blinked water out of my eyes as Drachenmorder and Sir Christopher looked down on us with satisfied smiles.

"How convenient, finding you all in one place," said Drachenmorder. "Saves us so much trouble."

"And they even made it easy on us by disabling their captors," said Sir Christopher, picking up the super-glued rifle Mark had dropped. "Whose idea was the glue? Very clever. Probably would have worked too, your little escape plan."

"I'm surprised to see you here, Professor Drachenmorder," I said. Our situation seemed hopeless at this point but, if I could keep Drachenmorder talking, maybe we could come up with another plan. "You don't usually do your own dirty work. I would have expected to see Professor Marshall here, not you."

"Marshall?" Drachenmorder scoffed. "What makes you say that?"

"Didn't you send him out to cut my climbing harness a few weeks ago?"

Sir Christopher laughed. "Marshall didn't touch your harness. He slept all day. I should have kicked him before I left."

"You?"

"Yes, me. Why do you think Marshall's never been knighted—he can't bring himself to kill a flea."

"But he makes us ride that evil horse, Flip!" exclaimed Oliver. "That horse is deadly!"

Sir Christopher laughed. "Flip was a circus horse. She's trained to throw her rider in just the right way to avoid injury. Marshall's good with horses, bad with kids."

"And worthless to me because he can't follow through on a kill," added Drachenmorder.

"I notice you haven't been knighted either," said Tui. "Did you get Sir Christopher to kill your dragons too?"

"I killed my own dragons," spat Drachenmorder. "But because I chose to use the best tools at my disposal, the Order refused to put me up for knighthood. All this mucking around with swords and horses—pah! It's medieval. We should be using rifles and helicopters against those vermin."

"Like your rich clients do," I said.

"My rich clients kill more dragons than all the dragon slayers in New Zealand combined. They do more to rid us of the beasts than the Fraternal Order of Dragon Slayers has ever done. If I happen to turn a tidy profit off it, that's my business."

"And what makes you think—"

Drachenmorder cut me off with a snarl. "I'm asking the questions here, not you. The only reason we didn't simply kill you all was to get information from you. Who is this Chang woman? What is she up to? Surely you all know."

"What's it worth to you?"

"The more important question is what it's worth to you. The more you tell us, the more of you will leave here alive."

Faced with Drachenmorder's brutality, I felt surprisingly protective of Chang, in spite of all she had done to us and to the dragons. Still, I couldn't imagine Chang and Drachenmorder working together, and the prospect of our enemies fighting each other was attractive. I figured it didn't matter what we told Drachenmorder about Chang.

"Ling Chang smuggles wildlife. She's collecting eggs and dragons, trying to develop a breeding programme, so she can maintain a steady supply of eggs and baby dragons to ship overseas for the pet trade."

His eyes widened. "She's *breeding* them? For *pets*?" I'd never seen Drachenmorder in shock before. If our situation hadn't been so dire, it would have been comical. Oliver stifled a giggle as Drachenmorder's eyes seemed to bug out of his face, and his neck grew red. Then the man collected himself, and his eyes narrowed.

"Where is she finding the dragons for her breeding programme?" I could see Drachenmorder's brain working—he could destroy Chang's business and increase his own if he knew where she had found the dragons. Even dragon slayers sometimes had trouble finding the elusive beasts.

229

From overhearing conversations between the men, we now knew a dozen places where Chang had found lairs. But I'd never tell Drachenmorder about them.

"I don't know."

"They do know." Sir Christopher kicked Tui. "This one shook her head at Nathan." He drew his sword and pressed it against Tui's throat.

"Where are the dragons?"

Chapter 28
Dragons and the D.S.S.R.

Tui's face went white with fear. A thin trickle of blood oozed from the scratch the blade had made on her neck.

"All right, we'll tell you."

Sir Christopher removed his sword from Tui's neck, only to point it at mine.

"Nathan, don't," said Ella. "He's going to kill us all anyway."

I trusted Ella's instincts when it came to people. And I believed Sir Christopher was capable of it.

Sir Christopher's grin made me shudder. "Tell you what. Nathan tells me where Chang has found dragons, and I let Tui, Ella, and Oliver go unharmed." The implication that my dad and I, and the dragons and eggs Chang had captured would be killed didn't escape any of us.

I didn't want to die. My palms grew clammy, and I began to shake with fear. I was thankful to be trussed and lying down because it made my terror less noticeable. If I'd been upright, I don't think my legs could have supported me.

I looked up at Sir Christopher. Dad was right. The man was his sword. No soul lived behind those eyes. All the respect I'd once had for him was gone, but his words about honour stuck with me. There was truth in those words, even if they had come from the mouth of this soulless man.

But killing was never honourable, whether it was killing dragons or people. The tools you used didn't matter. Honour was sticking up for what you knew was right. It was taking care of your friends and family. It was protecting those who couldn't protect themselves.

Either we would all die, or only some of us would. I didn't have to tell Sir Christopher and Drachenmorder the truth about the dragons Chang had found. I could protect those wild dragons, and I could save some of my friends. There was really only one thing to do.

"Release Tui, Ella, and Oliver. Once they are free, I'll tell you."

"You're in no position to make demands. Tell us first. If the information is worth the trouble, then we'll let your friends go."

He was going to kill us all, regardless.

I took a calming breath, like Sir Christopher had taught me. I considered whether I could, in my duct-taped state, land a kick. Could I roll fast enough to trip the man? Either move would probably end badly for me, but I couldn't lie here pretending I believed he'd let my friends go if only I told him what he wanted to know. I took another breath. I would try the kick.

Then the look on Sir Christopher's face stopped me. His nose wrinkled in disgust.

"What's that smell?"

When the stench hit me, I couldn't help but smile. I didn't dare take my eyes off Sir Christopher but I could feel the energy of my friends beside me change. They knew too.

It was the unmistakable smell of dragon farts.

Seconds later, a dozen small, sparkling forms swarmed around the side of the shed and mobbed Drachenmorder, Sir Christopher, and the remaining thug.

Cackling madly, Rata broke from the pack and flew down to land on my chest. "Nathan!"

232

"Rata! Can you get us free?"

"That's what we're here for, silly." She hopped to my bound wrists and took a deep breath.

"Not fire!" I yelled, realising what she was about to do. "Bite the tape off."

She nipped at the duct tape around my wrists. "Ugh! This is disgusting. It's sticky too."

"You only have to do the one. Once my hands are free, I can do the rest. I can get everyone else free as well."

"Good, 'cause"—Rata ripped a fart—"my stomach still hasn't settled down from that bread."

The gold fairy dragons might have distracted Drachenmorder and his men, but I knew they wouldn't be able to do much damage to them. Sir Christopher would make quick work of them with his sword.

As I pulled the tape from the others' wrists, I gave orders.

"There's a pile of timber around the side of the shed. Grab a piece and we'll attack the men together."

We selected our weapons and began a charge toward the men.

"Get down! Get down!" screamed Rata.

We dropped to the ground in the nick of time. A phalanx of southern blues swooped low over the shed and sent a burst of fire over the three men. The thug, clearly not a dragon slayer, broke and ran, his clothes smouldering. Drachenmorder and Sir Christopher dropped and rolled, as all dragon slayers are taught to do when caught in dragon fire. They were back on their feet in a moment.

The thug didn't get far. I was intent on Drachenmorder and Sir Christopher, making their way toward us, but out of the corner of my eye, I saw a large green shape drop from the sky. The thug made one terrified squeak before the talons of a New Zealand green silenced him.

"Drachenmorder!" Storm Cloud's angry voice shook the earth. As the dragon slayer stopped to look up, a torrent of fire enveloped him. I shut my eyes and covered my ears. When I dared open them again, Storm Cloud was climbing back into the sky, Drachenmorder dangling limply from his claws.

Sir Christopher dropped his sword and ran. He made it as far as Drachenmorder's SUV, parked a few hundred metres down the road. He opened the door and was about to scramble in when the ground underneath his feet shifted. What looked like gravel took the form of a scree dragon. It emerged in an explosion of stones, striking like a snake. Sir Christopher never made it into the car.

The southern blues came back for another pass, this time targeting the house with a concentrated burst of fire. The aging wood structure lit quickly and was soon engulfed in flames.

"They're going for the shed!" said Oliver.

"Colin's still in there," said Tui.

None of us liked our captors but, without discussing it, we knew we didn't want to be responsible for their deaths. We ran toward the shed, waving our arms. Ella and I called out in Draconic to try to stop them.

The dragons pulled up at the last minute.

"Thank you," we called. The dragons circled the homestead twice, then struck out toward the sea.

As we watched them leave, we saw Storm Cloud returning, his claws empty. He came in low, and landed awkwardly. Flat spaces didn't seem to suit him.

We ran to greet him.

"Well, now," he said. "I think the sharks will find Drachenmorder a tasty morsel."

"Oh, I didn't want to know that," said Ella, covering her ears.

Storm Cloud gave Ella a steely look. "He was a dragon slayer of the worst kind. All dragon slayers know if they live by the sword, they're likely to die by the claw." He laughed. "He's not the first dragon slayer I've dispatched."

We all looked uncomfortably at each other. Storm Cloud was helping us, but he was still a dragon. It occurred to me we needed to remember that, or we might end up fed to the sharks ourselves.

Storm Cloud's voice lightened. "Well, that was a good day's work. But where's young Archie? Rata said he was here too. And what's happened to Foggy Bottom?"

"They both got hit by tranquiliser darts," I said.

"Tranquiliser?"

"It puts you to sleep. That's how Ling Chang caught dragons. They should be fine. I think." Now that my own life wasn't in danger, I began to worry Dad might have gotten a lethal dose of tranquiliser. If there was enough in one of those darts to put a dragon to sleep, what would it do to a person?

"Come on, let's get your dad out of the rain, at least," said Ella.

"Yeah. Uh…" suddenly I felt drained. The immediate danger was over, and the shock of what had happened hit. There was a rushing in my ears.

Oliver's voice came to me as though down a long tunnel. "Sit down, Nathan."

Hands pushed me onto something smooth and warm.

"Head between your knees." I obeyed. I heard people moving about. Grunts and faltering steps. The sounds of someone moving my father indoors. I was ashamed I couldn't do it myself. In a few minutes, the hissing sound stopped and I felt blood returning to my face. I was sweaty and thirsty, but I felt well enough to raise my head.

"Sorry." I looked up to find my friends standing around me with worried looks on their faces. "I'm okay now." I realised I was sitting on Storm Cloud's tail.

"Look out!" Storm Cloud flicked his tail, throwing me off, and brought it down on Mark, who had raised himself up and was about to swing his rifle at Tui's head. Mark struggled frantically to extract himself from under the scaly appendage.

"Perhaps we should deal with these fellows first. I could use another snack."

"No," we all said.

"There's been enough killing," said Ella.

"And they weren't planning to kill us," said Oliver.

"More importantly, they may know where to find Ling Chang," I added.

Tui frowned. "They're still jerks."

"The cages?" suggested Ella.

We all remembered at once. "Colin."

Laughing, we explained to a curious Storm Cloud how we had planned our escape and how we'd left poor Colin, covered in excrement, in a cage in the shed. Storm Cloud picked up Mark, who screamed and cursed, and Dude, limp and unconscious but alive. We opened the large garage door, so Storm Cloud could get into the shed.

Colin was still frantically trying to clean himself, but when he saw Storm Cloud looming in the doorway, he squeaked, went white as a sheet, and fainted.

Storm Cloud chuckled. "I love it when they do that."

We put Dude and Mark into cages. As we were leaving the shed, we heard the growing sound of a helicopter. It took me a moment before I remembered.

"The PLB!" It seemed like a lifetime ago that, out of desperation, I'd activated the personal locator beacon.

The others looked at me curiously, and I explained what I'd done. It seemed foolish now. I had drawn Search and Rescue to us. They would see the dragons, and all the troubles we were trying to avoid by keeping dragons secret until they were legally protected would then come true.

Rata came zooming out of nowhere.

"Helicopter coming. Let's go!"

We decided it would be best if we all vanished. We clambered onto Storm Cloud and flew a short way, just to the edge of the forest, where we could conceal ourselves and watch.

The helicopter flew low and fast over the trees. When it reached the clearing around the homestead, it hovered for a minute, and then came down in the paddock between us and Foggy Bottom's cage.

"D.S.S.R.—what does that mean?" asked Oliver, reading the letters on the side of the helicopter.

"I don't know," I replied. No one else knew, either.

With the rotors still moving, two men jumped out of the helicopter. Even from a distance, there was no mistaking Sir Leandro's colourful hat and Professor West's prosthetics.

Whooping and hollering, we ran across the paddock toward them. Rata and Storm Cloud followed more cautiously.

We tumbled over each other, relating the events of the past three weeks. Both professors beamed at us, and Sir Leandro shook our hands, telling us he had been certain we could do it.

"Who are these people?" asked Storm Cloud.

"Excuse me, Your Majestic Greenness," said Sir Leandro in flawless Draconic. "I am Leandro Justo, Deputy Headmas—" He smiled as he corrected himself. "New Headmaster of the Alexandra School of Heroic Arts."

"He's the one who helped us to escape," I added, fearing Storm Cloud's temper might flare at the mention of the school.

"And I am Professor Daniel West. Pleased to meet you Your Majes—"

"Oh, enough with the fancy titles."

Oliver giggled, and the rest of us smiled, while Storm Cloud continued.

"I am Storm Cloud, head of the Draconic Council. I am pleased to meet any friends of young Archie. I am also pleased to meet the new headmaster of the School of Heroic Arts. We need to have a few words about the school." Storm Cloud's tone grew threatening, and I was about to say something to soothe his irritation, when Rata showed up and did it for me.

"Don't forget me." She laughed and zipped through the air, landing on my shoulder and peering at Sir Leandro and Professor West. "I'm Rata."

The dragon slayers' eyes went wide, and I knew what they were about to say.

"You're a gold fairy! But they're extinct."

Cackling hysterically, Rata tumbled off my shoulder, and then ripped a fart, which set us all laughing. When we recovered, I asked the question I'd been holding in since we recognised the men in the helicopter.

"But how did you find us?" I asked.

"The locator beacon, of course," said Sir Leandro.

"But I expected Search and Rescue to come."

"We did." He pointed at the letters on the helicopter. "Dragon Slayer Search and Rescue—D.S.S.R."

"There's a separate search and rescue just for dragon slayers?" asked Oliver.

"Of course. It wouldn't do for your ordinary mountain rescue crew to come after a dragon slayer— they'd either end up dead or they'd see something they shouldn't. And, of course, that locator beacon was mine. When you set it off, I knew exactly who was calling."

"But it looks like you didn't need us after all," said Professor West.

Chapter 29
A New Headmaster

Whether we technically needed Sir Leandro and Professor West or not, I was relieved they were there. Sir Leandro was a paramedic—he checked on Dad and doctored our many injuries. I told him I was fine. But when he raised his good eyebrow, I looked down at myself and saw all the blood. I had forgotten the dragon bite.

Ella unlocked Foggy Bottom's cage. The dragon still slept. Storm Cloud picked up the tranquilised baby dragon to take it to a local southern blue's lair.

"Bluebell will be able to tell who this one belongs to. I don't know all the southern blue family smells, but she will."

"And the eggs?" I asked.

"Eggs? I didn't know there were eggs too." Storm Cloud spat out a few Draconic curses directed at Ling Chang.

Oliver emptied his backpack, and he and Tui gently packed the four dragon eggs into it, surrounded by a cushion of straw. With eggs and baby safely clasped in his front feet, Storm Cloud lifted off into the gathering dusk.

"We forgot to thank him," I said as he faded from view.

"Something tells me we'll see him at school one of these days," said Tui.

School. Only an hour ago, I had been making peace with the certainty I would die. For the past three weeks,

I'd focused only on finding and rescuing my father. I hadn't considered what was to come afterward. My dad was alive. Did that mean I wouldn't be going back to the School of Heroic Arts? For that matter, with Sir Leandro in charge, would the school even continue? None of us might be going back. But what then?

There wasn't time to worry about the future right now. Night was falling, and we had much to do. The homestead was remote, but we knew it wouldn't be long before someone arrived, either to investigate the plume of smoke rising from the burning house or to attend to Ling Chang's business.

Dude was awake and rubbing his head when we entered the shed to question the men. The open garage door provided fresh air, but the place still smelled like a sewer.

"And you say my farts stink," said Rata.

We didn't get much information from the men. I don't think they kept anything from us—they simply didn't know much about Ling Chang's operation. As we had already worked out, Colin was a greenstone smuggler and Dude was pocketing dragon gold—he had overstayed his visa and couldn't get a regular job without risk of deportation. Neither of them cared at all about the dragon smuggling. They were only doing the work for Chang because it gave them access to dragon lairs. Mark, we discovered, was one of LC Enterprises' accountants. He was under investigation for tax evasion, and LC Enterprises had helped him quietly vanish, firing him from his position in the Auckland office (where he'd cooked the books for them), and spiriting him away to this remote outpost. He could tell us the market prices for dragon eggs, but he didn't know anything about where Chang herself was based or who she worked with in China.

Professor West sighed. "Well, at least we've got a clear course of action with these guys."

"And that would be?" I asked.

"Jail," offered Ella. "All three of them are criminals, even ignoring their kidnapping of five people."

"Can we punch them first?" asked Tui.

We installed ourselves in the small shed for the night. There was nothing we could do about the burning house, but a steady rain through the night kept the flames well under control and, by morning, the house was a smouldering ruin.

I was certain I wouldn't be able to sleep, with the events of the day threatening to replay themselves over and over in my head, but I was so exhausted that even the hard concrete floor of the shed couldn't keep me awake.

In the morning, we prepared to leave. It took some shouting and shaking, but we managed to wake Foggy Bottom. She was woozy and befuddled at first but, with a drink of water and a little time, her wits returned. We explained what had happened and sent her off home with Rata as an escort.

"Don't let her go back to sleep," I whispered to Rata before they left. "Not until all the tranquiliser is out of her system. I don't like that she's had two doses so close together."

"No problem. I'm good at irritating Foggy Bottom," Rata assured me.

As soon as Foggy Bottom had flapped heavily away, we put Dad on a stretcher and loaded him into the helicopter. He hadn't yet woken, but Sir Leandro was unconcerned.

"His colour is good. His breathing and heartbeat are regular. He'll be fine."

We piled into the helicopter, with Sir Leandro at the controls. It was my first helicopter ride, and it was great but, after riding dragons, it wasn't nearly as exciting as I'd imagined it would be.

We flew over tracts of lush rainforest and over the craggy peaks of the Southern Alps in a light rain. On the other side, the clouds cleared, and sun glinted off the glaciers below. I wondered how many unseen dragons we had passed. The landscape turned to the brown of tussocks as we entered Otago. I saw the school ahead of us and wondered what was happening there today, with four of the staff gone. I realised I didn't even know what day of the week it was.

We touched down gently on a flat above the school.

"Just in time for lunch," said Professor West. We piled out of the helicopter and stood together on the hill.

"What do we do now?" Ella's question mirrored my own.

"None of the students knows what has happened," said Sir Leandro. "I will be making an official announcement of the changes to school staffing later this afternoon. In the meantime, I suggest you all come with me."

"But what about lunch?" asked Oliver.

Sir Leandro smiled. "Professor West, do you think you could ask Miss Brumby to bring us something? And tell her to include extra cookies."

Carrying Dad's stretcher between us, we walked down the hill. I was surprised when Sir Leandro did not go to his chalet but, instead, walked up the steps to the Headmaster's office. He strode in the door, holding it open for the rest of us to enter. As we carried Dad in, Sir Magnus looked up from his desk in surprise.

"What's this? Nathan? Archie?"

"Magnus. Drachenmorder has met his last dragon," said Sir Leandro. It was a dragon slayer's euphemism for 'he's dead'. Sir Magnus gasped, and Sir Leandro continued. "Sir Christopher is similarly…gone. As former Deputy Headmaster, I am now Headmaster until a new appointment is made."

"But, what's happened?"

Sir Leandro held up his hand. "I have certain matters to discuss with the present company, and then I will relate the situation to you, and we will review the school's accounts together. In the meantime, please go to the Lodge and help Professor West bring our lunch over."

Sir Magnus scurried out the door, casting curious and worried glances at us all.

"Let's go to the kitchen, shall we? Those dragon heads in the office give me the creeps."

We followed Sir Leandro in and set Dad down on the floor. The change must have roused him—he scratched his face, and then his eyes flew open.

"Dad!" I leaned over him with a smile but jumped back a moment later when he rolled over and vomited all over the floor.

Someone called for water, and Tui pressed a glass into Dad's hand. He sipped gingerly at it, before vomiting again. Sir Leandro appeared with a tea towel and threw it over the mess.

"That's better." Dad sat up and looked around in confusion.

We filled him in quickly on events, and then Sir Leandro got down to business.

"The Alexandra School of Heroic Arts will be undergoing some dramatic changes in the next few weeks. With the death of Claus Drachenmorder, I propose to change the nature of the school to bring it in line with Sir Archibald's work on dragon conservation."

Dad laughed. "That won't go over well with the Royal Society of Dragon Slayers."

"No, it won't. But with Sir Archibald McMannis as our headmaster..."

Dad looked up sharply. "No. I'm not an administrator, Leandro. You know that. Besides, it has to be approved by the board."

Sir Leandro waved his hand dismissively. "You're Patriarch of the Fraternal Order of Dragon Slayers International—the board couldn't possibly turn you down for the position. Let's face it—you can't be worse than Drachenmorder."

Dad smiled.

"Think of it as an interim position—to help the school through the transition from dragon slaying to dragon saving. You're the best person for that job. You know better than anyone else what's needed to preserve dragons."

"C'mon, Sir Archibald," said Oliver. "Dad always said you were a great leader."

"Did he?" Dad looked genuinely surprised. "I never was certain what your father thought of me."

The others joined in, encouraging Dad to become our new headmaster. I grew silent. I wanted Dad to say yes, but what would that mean for me?

Finally, he gave in and agreed to a three year term.

Then Sir Leandro turned to me.

"Now, we have the issue of Nathan. Dragon slaying is a hereditary position. New dragon slayers are not trained until their parents are deceased." I slumped in my seat. The thought of going back to my old life—to a life without dragons—was depressing. Sir Leandro continued. "I think the time has come to abandon that tradition. Dragon conservation is a more comprehensive sort of career and will require different skills and training. In fact"—he swept his gaze over all of us—"we're going to need all of your help to make the transition. We'll face resistance, not just from the dragon slaying organisations, but also from many of the students here at the school."

"Yeah, like Hunter Godfry," said Tui.

"Exactly. Many believe in the romance and mystique of dragon slaying. We'll need strong student leaders to work with the student body and ease them into a new way of thinking about dragons. I'm counting on you to be those leaders."

We all sat a little straighter, and Tui gave me a thumbs-up.

"Do we get extra cookies for that?" asked Oliver with a grin.

"Cookies?" said Professor West as he bustled in the door with an armload of food. "I think Miss Brumby has you covered."

Appendix
Dragons of New Zealand

New Zealand Green Dragon

These are the largest of the Southern Hemisphere dragons, reaching a length of thirty metres. They are endemic to New Zealand, but are closely related to the southern green dragon, which is found in the Andes mountains in South America. New Zealand greens once ranged throughout the Southern Alps. Before human colonisation of the country, they preyed primarily upon moa. As moa were driven to extinction, the dragon population plummeted. In desperation, they turned to hunting a wide mix of prey, including kiwi, takahe, seals, and the odd human. Scientists believe that, until European colonists introduced deer, goats, and sheep, the small remaining population of New Zealand green dragons survived by spending a large part of each year in hibernation, conserving the little food they could find.

Today, the New Zealand green dragon remains critically endangered. Only small populations survive in higher elevations. The exact location of these populations is kept secret to prevent poaching.

Southern Blue Dragon

The southern blue dragon inhabits coastal regions throughout the Southern Hemisphere. The primary prey of this twenty-metre-long dragon are seals, and its numbers in New Zealand have increased with the protection of seals in recent decades. Southern blues are shy and solitary creatures for most of the year, living in coastal caves in remote areas and foraging primarily at night. Some nest on the mainland, but it is thought that many breed communally on offshore islands. However, no breeding grounds have ever been located.

Fiordland Fringed Dragon

These secretive forest dwellers probably once ranged throughout the forested areas of New Zealand but are now restricted to remote areas of Fiordland. At fifteen metres long, they are more adept at moving through the forest than the larger New Zealand green and tend to prefer dense bush. Their name comes from the distinctive orange neck fringe the males use as a mating display. To attract females, male Fiordland fringed dragons gather in groups of about a dozen individuals during the mating season for communal displays. They originally probably fed on kiwi and small moa, but today the Fiordland fringed dragon subsists largely on introduced pigs and deer. Its vestigial wings are used for steadying itself in the treetops.

South Island Scree Dragon

These dragons are so well camouflaged, they weren't formally identified until 2001, and it is unclear how many of them exist. They spend most of their time buried in the rocks on scree slopes, with only their eyes and nose sticking above the surface. The few sightings of these dragons indicate that they are ten to fifteen metres long, with rather short wings. Their scales are dull grey, with lichen-like green and orange markings. Nothing is known of their feeding and mating habits.

North Island Fire Lizard

This small (five metres from nose to tail) primitive dragon has no wings but is capable of fire production. Once, it could be found in nearly every hot spring on the

North Island, but it is now restricted to a small area around Rotorua. It is semi-aquatic and spends the winter months hibernating at the bottom of hot pools. It preys primarily on wading birds such as weka and pukeko, which it ambushes from underwater, relying on its superb camouflage to avoid detection.

Gold Fairy Dragon

Thought to be extinct, the last confirmed sighting of a gold fairy dragon was in 1938. This highly iridescent dragon was the smallest dragon ever to have lived. It reached a maximum size of only fifteen centimetres from nose to tail, with a wingspan of twenty to twenty-five centimetres. Despite its name, its colour ranged from green to blue to copper, and individuals might sport multiple colours. It was an omnivore, eating insects, fruit, and mushrooms. It was highly sought after for the pet trade, but its agile flight made it difficult to catch. It was most likely driven to extinction by introduced rats and stoats, who feasted on the dragon's eggs.

Tuatara

Though not technically a dragon, the tuatara is thought to be the ancestor of all Southern Hemisphere dragons. This primitive reptile is endemic to New Zealand. It was once found throughout the country, but survives today only on predator-free offshore islands and mainland sanctuaries.

#####

About the Author

Over the course of my career, I have been pleased to call myself an educator, entomologist, heritage interpreter, and an agroforestry extension agent, among other things. Through it all, I have written stories and poetry for my own pleasure. I published my first writing as a child in the 1970s, and used to confound my science teachers with poetry, scribbled at the end of essay  questions. Now, after completing several novels, I'm pleased to be able to call myself an author.

My first love was the natural world, and it plays a large part in most of my stories. I currently live in New Zealand and enjoy spending time in the mountains.

Have I encountered dragons there?

You'll just have to visit and discover for yourself.

Discover more of my stories by visiting my website at
https://robinneweiss.wordpress.com/

Acknowledgements

Thank you to all those who reviewed The Dragon Slayer's Son in its early stages: Ian, Liadan, Lochlan, Nan, Rachael, and Seph. And thank you to Jackie for a helpful late-stage review, and to Lorna for her thorough copy-editing.

Extra special thanks must go to Ian, who spawned the entire Dragon Slayer series (there will be more) by leaving a letter from Sir Magnus MacDiermont on the dining room table one morning. You are the greatest source of writing prompts ever.

Made in United States
North Haven, CT
16 November 2022

26830247R00143